Radiant

About the Author

Judy Sapphire is an attorney and writer who makes her home up and down the New England seacoast. She has worked as a corporate and a public interest lawyer, in state government, and on political campaigns. She is an avid reader and art lover with a penchant for public sculpture. *Radiant* is her first book.

Radiant

JUDY SAPPHIRE

BELLA
BOOKS
2022

Bella Books, Inc.
P.O. Box 10543
Tallahassee, FL 32302

Printed in the United States of America on acid-free paper.

First Edition - 2022

Editor: Medora MacDougall
Cover Designer: Kayla Mancuso

ISBN: 978-1-64247-393-3

PUBLISHER'S NOTE

Acknowledgments

First, thank you to my wonderful editor Medora MacDougall and the terrific, hardworking team at Bella for their good humor and insights.

Thank you to my family of origin and in-laws, notably the descendants of Edward Doty and their spouses and children. I am also blessed to have the love and support of clever and compassionate friends. Special thanks to Lindy R. Greek, Becky Runstin, and Vanessa Ephanistaine for your steady stream of text messages and for cheering me on. Thanks to Kassie J. Slica, Kyle Volemice, and Jonah Sheann for your enduring friendship and encouragement. My gratitude also goes out to the guidance and good counsel of two brilliant writers and teachers: Sandie L. Sirens and Theo P. Airplane.

Most importantly, thank you to my wife and son for being my home wherever we are.

Finally, thanks to you, the reader! I hope this book brings you some modicum of joy.

CHAPTER ONE

Jenny hit *Send* and looked out the window at Boylston Street below. Boston was usually sleepy, but it was oppressively quiet a few minutes past midnight. She had been in the office since 8:37 Sunday morning, thirteen minutes after the special, high-pitched *ping* she had designated for emails from her boss, Michael, had woken her. *Call me now*, the email said. She put him on speaker so she could listen to him bloviate about the upcoming settlement discussions while she quickly braided her hair, threw an oxford and a blazer over the pair of yoga pants she'd slept in, and topped off the outfit with her black, shin-length down coat. She walked the ten blocks from her South End condo to the office with her hood pulled tightly around her face, trying to gird herself against the sharp winter wind. Michael wanted her to run all the settlement numbers again. Each and every contingency. The economic experts had already been through it—three times—but Michael didn't care. It would be tedious, and it would take at least twelve hours. Maybe sixteen.

Jenny hadn't planned an exciting weekend anyway, but there was something especially depressing about beginning and ending her week in the same exact spot, thirty stories above the street, drinking the same stale plastic pod coffee from the office kitchen and eating the same turkey sandwich from the deli in the lobby as she did almost every day.

She counted the billable hours up in her head: 14.4 hours for Sunday, 0.1 for Monday. Maybe all her work would get her a begrudging "thanks." She wondered what Michael had done during the day. Probably played a round of golf in Tampa. She never knew where he was, but she was expected to be tethered to her phone and mere minutes from the office at all times. Only two more years to go until she paid off her law school loans. What next? It didn't even matter. Anything but this. At least she knew that tonight, she'd get herself home, warm up, take a shower, turn on something on Netflix, and fall asleep in front of the TV before another high-pitched ping from Michael snapped her back into reality when the sun came up.

As she was throwing her phone into her bag, she heard an alert—the low guitar strum for her best friend from college, Davis. *You up?* the text message read.

Yup, all ok? Jenny typed back quickly.

Where are you?

Office. Going home.

The phone rang. "Michael is such a bastard," Davis said by way of greeting.

"He is that," Jenny responded, grateful that Davis was always on her side, without even knowing what had happened.

"Okay, so I know your day has sucked, but I need a favor. I'm at work right now, too. Can you meet me?"

Jenny sighed. The plan for her last few waking hours really sounded good. She had planned on opening a bottle of wine, too. But Davis hardly ever needed a favor. He had even stopped haranguing her about how little they got to hang out. They had lived together when she was in law school, and he was getting a PhD in art history. Now he was an assistant curator at the Albus Booker Museum, located only a few blocks from Jenny's office.

"I'll be right there," Jenny said, wishing she'd worn long johns and warmer socks. The T wasn't running, and it was a cold walk.

Davis was waiting for her at the service entrance, holding an armful of folders. His normally gelled hair was a floppy, pancaked mess on the top of his head, his contacts had apparently dried up so he was wearing glasses that were too small and wiry to be fashionable, and his normal uniform, a black T-shirt and slightly tight black pants, looked stretched and wrinkled. When Jenny remembered what she was wearing and where she'd been for the last several hours, Davis confirmed what she feared.

"You look like hell," he said. She twisted her braid into a knot at the top of her head and straightened her cashmere scarf.

"You too," she said, following him inside.

He stopped in the stairwell and slumped against the railing. "She's upstairs so we have to whisper."

"Who?"

Davis's eyes got wide. He leaned toward Jenny and whispered, "Blake Harrison."

Jenny looked back at him, not knowing the name or why she should. In response to her silence, Davis said it again, a little more slowly. "Blake Harrison."

"Sorry, I—"

"The star of this year's Whitney Biennial. She did those huge towers made of hair."

Jenny wanted to laugh but could tell that Davis would have been hurt if she had. This was why she didn't like contemporary art. She had some Monet posters on her wall at work. That was about as far as she'd go. She had no interest in towers made of hair. That's why she usually liked the Albus Booker Museum, which Bostonians just referred to as the Albie. It was small, but it was focused on the classics. Its founder was some Frick-like baron who collected stodgy western art—all unquestionably Jenny's taste. They had some Greek amphoras, a few Rembrandt drawings, one of the world's few Vermeers, Degas watercolors, and a few Rodins. Just what she liked. It was one thing she and her boss Michael had in common.

"Well, Blake is upstairs where we're installing her show, and she's freaking out and threatening to walk, and I need a lawyer."

A lawyer. When Davis started working at the Albie, he invited Jenny to events and tried to fix her up with his friends. After about a year of Jenny standing him up because she had to fly with Michael to interview a witness, or Michael needed her to rewrite a brief, or Michael needed her to go to D.C. immediately because a settlement had fallen through, Davis got creative. The museum needed occasional pro bono legal help with its art lending contracts, and Davis recommended Jenny. Michael let Jenny do it, because he liked bragging that the firm was a "sponsor" of their more high-profile shows. Jenny, in exchange, got to spend a few hours every month at the museum with Davis, reviewing and drawing up new contracts. It was her favorite thing about her job, and it wasn't even supposed to be part of it.

Jenny sat on the stair next to Davis and patted his hand. "Start from the beginning."

"Blake's show opens Friday. We don't usually do contemporary, but this new installation of hers is in conversation with the masters, so the director went out on a limb, said I could book it. So it's on me."

Jenny nodded. "Okay, congrats. What happened?"

"I mean, before the Biennial it wouldn't have been a big deal, but now here she is, and we're already getting press."

Davis's knee started bouncing frantically. Jenny squeezed his thigh, gently, trying to root him in the moment. "And?" she said.

"She's refusing to work because we transposed two of her measurements. For one of the rooms there is an 18-foot-long wall with a door, and a 14-foot wall without a door, and we put the door on the wrong wall, and now she says she refuses to install the exhibit, and she's going back to New York." Davis's voice was speeding up in a kind of panic.

"So, you want me to—" Jenny searched Davis's face. His brows were knit.

"I'd call the General Counsel, but she's in Rome dealing with that Greek amphora thing and didn't answer my email, and frankly, I want to be able to handle this myself, I mean, handle it with your help. I just don't know what to do. She won't even talk to me now."

Jenny sighed. This Blake character sounded like far too many of Davis's artist friends. An irrational, arrogant bully. "So, she's refusing to work because one wall is the wrong length?"

"Two walls, actually, but yes."

"What's going in the walls?"

"Nothing. Nothing at all. I mean. Lights. It's nothing but light. She's recreating paintings, but just the light. To give the feeling of being in the painting, but with…uh, well, without the painting."

Jenny suppressed an eye roll. "You have the contract?"

Davis handed her the stack of paper. Jenny thumbed through the folder and checked the key provisions as he looked at her expectantly, knee still bouncing. She hadn't drafted the contract, but whoever had had done a decent job. The museum was well protected.

She gave Davis a smile. "This looks good. So. What do you want me to do?"

"Jenny, she's a little scary. Like, she's just sitting there refusing to work because of the walls. If she goes—I'm gonna lose my job—"

"You want me to tell her she's legally obligated to stay?"

"Just make sure we open on Friday, okay? It's going to be an amazing show. She's brilliant. I mean—"

"She sounds like a fucking diva," Jenny said. As the words came out of her mouth, the door at the top of the stairwell swung open with a clunk and light flooded in.

A woman was standing in the doorway, backlit so her thin silhouette was well-defined, but her features were still visible and bathed in a kind of dim golden light. Her chin was turned up a little, but Jenny could see a slight smile and heart-shaped lips. Her eyelids were dark and heavy, which made her light brown eyes seem especially alive. Her hair was short, like a few months ago it had all been shaved off, and the tidy strands looked like if a palm ran over them, they'd shoot sparks. She was wearing an oversized silk button-down shirt and leggings. Her feet were bare. She had only appeared at the top of the stairs for a moment, but Jenny felt like she'd been taking her in for hours.

Finally, the woman spoke. "That's not a very nice thing to say about someone you've never met."

Jenny's face flooded with heat, and she looked plaintively at Davis, who leapt to his feet and looked back and forth at both of them for a few beats until he swallowed audibly and said, "Um, hi, Blake. We were just—"

"And you are?" Blake said, looking down at Jenny, still with a slight upturn on her lips.

"Jennifer O'Toole, the museum's attorney," Jenny said, in a loud, low voice she didn't know she had.

CHAPTER TWO

Blake had been sitting down on the floor of the museum, telling herself to control her breath. She had lashed out at the curator. What was his name? Daniel? Douglas? Davis. *Davis.* He seemed nice enough, and terrified of her. She had threatened to leave. *Breathe in, breathe out.* She shut her eyes to the gallery, trying to envision how it would look in five days. The lights in, the walls up, the paint on, every surface shimmering exactly as she had imagined.

Boston was a strange little city, and this conservative jewel of a museum had taken a chance on her art, even before all her success at the Biennial. The Albie, everyone called it. She should stay and make it work.

But they had built the walls wrong, and when they did, all Blake could see was everything she'd drafted so precisely failing to fit together. So she had raised her voice and threatened to leave, and Davis had scampered out of the gallery. She took a few more deep breaths. She knew the reputation she was getting. Blake Harrison was difficult to work with. *A bitch.*

She knew she had to be careful. Stave off rumors, be polite. But trying to rein herself in made her angry, too. This was her job, and she took it seriously. As if Richard Serra hadn't ever yelled at a curator. As if it were out of line for her to want—no, *need*—everything to be according to her specifications.

But she knew she couldn't alienate the Albie, no matter how justified her anger. She crossed her legs, put her palms facedown on her knees, breathing in the smell of sawdust and thick white primer paint in the gallery. She took another deep breath. Finally, slowly, a solution materialized. She would ask Davis if they could move the door instead of restructuring the walls. That would mean the flow of the people through the gallery would change, but the room would have the right dimensions. The mistake was fixable. She simply wanted it to be taken seriously.

When she approached the staircase to fetch Davis, she heard two voices, Davis's, and another woman's. Had he called in reinforcements? Another curator to try to talk her down? She smoothed the front of her shirt and tried to make her best combination of an "I'll be nice" and a "Don't fuck with me" face. Then she heard it—the woman—*who the hell was she?*—saying, "She sounds like a fucking diva." She was clearly talking about Blake. Anger and hurt ignited in Blake's body so quickly that before thinking what she was doing, she twisted open the loud metal latch, the door clanged open, and she looked down at them.

Her breath caught in her throat. Her callous accuser was, quite simply, the most beautiful woman she'd ever seen. She was wearing a starched white oxford and a blazer with, strangely, yoga pants and Reeboks. But it was her accuser's slight open-mouthed gaze back at her that made Blake fear she might tumble down the stairs. Her eyes were a bright, dazzling light brown, and her chestnut hair was piled on the top of her head in half a braid. Blake realized that, though it had not been for very long, she was staring.

Blake straightened her spine, broke eye contact, and said, "That's not a very nice thing to say about someone you've never met."

Her accuser didn't seem to flinch, but Davis set about in a panic, looking around the stairwell as if there might be a secret door that would lead him out to oblivion or as if he'd lost a puppy.

Was Blake supposed to be scared of Davis and this lawyer? Blake had planned on apologizing, but now she wouldn't dare. She had every right to be upset about her standards not being met. This Jennifer character, looking up at her so intently, was surely the type to attack every poor paralegal who missed a deadline or mucked up the number of spaces after a period. This was Blake's gallery, for the next few weeks, anyway, and she wasn't about to cower in fear.

"Well, Jenny—can I call you Jenny?" Blake said. Jenny nodded. Blake nodded back. "Please come in."

Blake pushed her body against the door to hold it open while Jenny walked slowly up the stairs. Jenny was wearing a down coat that looked like a big black marshmallow, so they barely touched when she walked through the threshold, but Blake took in a quick breath when they were close. She smelled of vanilla tea. Her posture was perfect. Some of the cold air from the stairwell followed her in, and Blake got goose bumps on her arms. Jenny's eyes, blazing in front of a small gathering of fine crow's feet, were even more beautiful up close.

Stop, Blake told herself. *Focus.*

Davis slunk by, and Blake let the door close with a loud clap. The three of them stood looking at one other in the middle of the gallery, stark against the fresh, sticky, white walls.

"Well, what seems to be the problem?" Blake said.

Jenny, still unflappable, still with a very tightly controlled low voice, said, "If you leave, you're in violation of your contract."

Blake turned to Davis. "This is how you wanna play this?"

Davis looked down.

Blake sucked in a breath, and her voice came out steely. "I told Davis that the gallery rooms haven't been built to my specifications. We have five days and the installation can't possibly be finished in time if you can't get the builders back to restructure two entire walls."

Jenny responded immediately, clipped. "My understanding is that two walls were transposed. So your claim is that it's a material breach of the contract?"

"Your legalese is meant to intimidate me?"

"I'm trying to understand your position."

"My position is that if the museum can't build the walls the way I need them built, then I can't do the show." Blake took a step back. Stating her case so plainly had been satisfying, but still, she was scared. It wasn't so much that Davis had proven himself incompetent. Mistakes were mistakes. It was that neither of them seemed to understand how much the mistake mattered. Blake put her hands on her hips and tried to remember to breathe, oscillating between her desire to storm out and her desire to make things work.

Jenny's eyes were holding her gaze a little too tightly. They were hard, angry eyes, belying their light, inviting color. Moments before, she had called Blake a "fucking diva." Blake replayed the words in her head. Well, if that's what Jenny already thought, then that's what Blake would be.

"I'm leaving," Blake said, and she turned around, making a loud show of throwing her notebooks and laptop into her bag.

"Blake." Davis's voice. "Please."

Blake struggled with this part of the job. Only a few months ago, she spent weeks upon weeks doing one of three things— eating, sleeping, or working in her studio. Well, four things. New York had no dearth of beautiful women. But now, she was expected to negotiate with galleries, sign contracts, explain the construction to carpenters and curators. The press had even been calling. She was exhausted, and she didn't know how to act. She was supposed to be an artist. This was a whole new world.

Blake looked over at Jenny. She was taking a step closer, her arms by her side, head tilted slightly, as if she could sense Blake's softening but was still on the attack herself.

"Look, if you go," Jenny said, "we're going to sue you for breach of contract. We'll argue back-and-forth about whether the museum breached first by building the walls the way they did. Even if there was a breach, though, it's a basic tenet of contract law that you have to try to mitigate losses. You can't answer a mistake with a full breach. Think about Davis here, whose job is on the line, and frankly, you should think about me, who clients pay seven hundred and fifty dollars an hour to argue their cases. I won't let this one go. The press won't look good either, when, hot off the heels of your Biennial triumph, you decide to snub one of Boston's premier—but financially struggling—museums. Especially after they took a chance on you and booked this show before you made a name for yourself with a hairball?"

Blake was stung by the words, but part of her wasn't sure why. She usually relished the kind of disdain people had for her more far-out pieces. That was the whole point, to create visceral reactions. Strangely, though, she cared what Jenny thought of her—and about the "hairball." Blake set down her bag, signaling that she wasn't leaving yet—but not because she'd been beaten. Because she had more to say.

"You don't need your work to be perfect?" Blake asked, staring Jenny down.

"Excuse me?"

"You're a lawyer, so I bet when you're drawing up a contract like that one you proof it a thousand times and if God forbid it gets screwed up, you have to redo it, and you bill your clients to redo it, because you won't let it out if it's not perfect, right?"

"Look—"

"Right?" Blake said it forcefully, but as if part of her was conspiring with Jenny. Jenny's face softened just a smidgen, but a smidgen nonetheless, and she nodded, her eyes settled. Seeing an opening, Blake took a deep breath. "This is the same thing. The La Tour painting is 50 by 37 inches, portrait. I'm recreating the light as if you're standing inside the painting. All the light sources have been carefully calculated to have the viewers enter the installation from the bottom of the piece so it gets brighter as they move closer to where the candle would be. If the door is on the other side, then the experience of the light is completely different."

Davis sighed in apparent admiration, but Jenny was inscrutable. She seemed to be yielding, but Blake couldn't be sure. Then Jenny looked at Blake and said, with the lightest tone she'd used all night, "Do we have to move walls or can we recut and reframe the door? Have you hung the lights yet?"

Blake smiled, just a little. Jenny's solution was exactly what Blake had been ready to suggest before they met. Maybe something had gotten through. Blake would have let herself grin, happy for a resolution, but Jenny had rearranged her features into a hard stare, cutting off Blake's smile so it came out as a smirk.

"Yes, I suppose we can do that, if we can get it done before my team gets here with the lights tomorrow afternoon," Blake said, letting Jenny have credit for the idea.

Jenny turned to Davis, all business. "Is that possible?"

He nodded and pulled out his cell phone. "I'm just gonna call—"

"Great," Blake said, cutting him off, finding herself flustered by Jenny's ping-ponging tone. She had to get back to work. That's where she was most comfortable. That's where she needed to be. "So we're done here," Blake said. "Jenny, pleased to make your acquaintance, and if you don't mind, it's very late and I still have work to do."

The phone in Jenny's pocket made a high-pitched ping. Blake watched Jenny's face drop its chiseled veneer for a moment into a real look of sadness. Jenny pulled out her phone and looked at it, then back at Blake.

"Me too."

CHAPTER THREE

Michael was in Jenny's office when she arrived Monday morning. His feet were up on her desk, his blue shirt stretching across his chest, his tie flopped to one side of his stomach.

"Good morning!" Jenny said as brightly as she could, thinking, as she often did when presented with Michael's physical form, *Fuck you, fuck you, fuck you.*

He took his feet off her desk, in a gesture that could have been polite, but was done so slowly, it was anything but.

"I've been waiting for you," he said.

Jenny flushed, but told herself not to appear weak. Michael hated weakness. And she had come to hate it in herself. She swallowed the nearly automatic "I'm sorry" and said instead, "Thanks for your patience."

He smiled. A little one, but there it was, a rare sight.

"I have a voice mail from the president of the Board of Directors of the Albus Booker Museum," he said, "expressing his great appreciation for your efforts enforcing their contractual rights." He folded his hands over his stomach and looked at her, daring her to speak.

"I'm glad," was all she said.

"Yes. The gratitude of Sheldon Stackhouse is always a good thing. He's the son of the president of Grant Bank. Did you know that?"

Jenny shook her head. She hadn't. Grant Bank was one of the firm's biggest clients. All the men and their connections. How did Michael keep track?

Michael got up to leave but stopped in Jenny's door. "I need you to go over the damages figures for the hearing next week, but that shouldn't take you more than seven or eight hours, should it?"

Jenny shook her head, wondering what other monstrosity of work he was about to pile on her desk. Instead, he said as he disappeared through her doorway, "If you are inclined to go home after that, I don't anticipate needing you until our conference call at nine thirty tomorrow morning."

Jenny flopped in her chair, surprised. It was extremely rare for her to have an hour on a Monday evening, let alone a few. She wondered how Stackhouse had learned of her help and whether it had been Davis who called him to praise her.

Jenny popped her head into the office next door. Lydia was an associate who had started on the same day as Jenny, but, through some stroke of constitution or luck, loved her job at the firm. "I think Michael just gave me the night off," Jenny said.

"Oooh!" Lydia spun around in her chair and clicked off her bill timer. "What happened?"

"Davis called me—my friend from college—he was at the museum and needed me to talk this artist down. She makes these rooms—"

Lydia's eyes got huge. "Blake Harrison?" She said the name in a whisper, almost reverently, just as Davis had.

"Yes," Jenny said, studying her friend. Was this really that big a deal?

"She's amazing, Jenny. You've heard of her, right?"

Jenny shook her head. "But apparently the Albie people are happy, and that makes Michael happy."

"Plus, you did an amazing job redoing the damages estimates all weekend. So, what's the plan?" Lydia asked.

"Well, I still have a bunch of things to do before I leave. It's not even nine, and he needs me to go through a whole host of other economic models—"

Lydia almost spit out her coffee she laughed so quickly. "I meant tonight. What are you going to do?"

"I have some laundry to do, and I wanted to watch that documentary about the North Korean gymnasts."

"God, no wonder we can't find you a girlfriend. What would you talk about on a first date?"

Jenny laughed, but it stung a little. It's not like that hadn't occurred to her before, how narrow her life had gotten, how transactional, how boring. It was part of the reason she and Melinda had broken up. Jenny was always at work, focusing on that, instead of their relationship. But why was she always at work? Wouldn't she have focused on Melinda if she loved her more? As the relationship started to crumble, Jenny found refuge in her work. She let everything else fade.

"I still can't believe you met her," Lydia said in Jenny's silence.

"Blake?"

"Yes!"

Jenny's mind went back to the night before. Their interaction had been brief, but it had lodged itself in her mind. The way Blake stood so defiantly at the top of the stairs, petite but somehow statuesque. Her perfectionism. The urgency with which she spoke about her work.

"Well, I've never heard of her and everyone's so excited. And she was…" She trailed off.

"She was what?"

"I called her a diva, and I meant it." Jenny swallowed, remembering their exchange, feeling embarrassed and a little guilty that Blake had apparently heard the expletive-laden insult. "I did not like her," she said, with a little more conviction in her voice.

"Well, then I feel for Davis, having to deal with her."

"Me too," Jenny said, deciding to visit Davis on her night off. She needed to thank him if he had called Stackhouse. And she needed to make sure that everything was underway now that she knew Michael cared about it at all.

Later that night, Jenny stood outside the service entrance of the museum, texting Davis. She held the phone in her hand, waiting for him to write back. She put her ear to the heavy, steel "staff only" door, but she couldn't hear anyone inside. She walked along the gate to the front marble steps. A banner, the same size as the one that had been there for months advertising the Goya show, was new, in bright red: *Legendary Light: The Rooms of Blake Harrison.* No wonder Davis was nervous; it was getting top billing on the front steps. Jenny pulled her down hood tighter around her face. A few flakes were starting to fall— the onslaught of the winter. It was the kind of quiet night that promised snow. The city would look beautiful in the morning.

Jenny checked her phone again. Nothing from Davis. She walked back around to the service entrance and tried banging on the door. Still nothing. Then, just as she was turning away, she heard the door click open and Blake's voice. "Hello."

Jenny spun around to look at her. Blake was wearing a white tank top with carpenter pants. There was a hammer hanging in the belt loop of the pants, the first time Jenny had probably ever seen them used properly.

Jenny, on the other hand, was wearing a three-season wool suit from Brooks Brothers with the signature slip in the front. Navy pinstriped. Topped off with her down parka with shearling around the hood and a goose icon on the shoulder. She wondered how she looked to Blake and then felt embarrassed when she caught herself wondering. What did it matter? Why should she care what Blake thought of her? She was here to see Davis. That's all that mattered.

"Is Davis here?" Jenny asked, a deliberate distance in her voice.

"No. Meeting with the Albie Board. You two have more legal threats you want to throw at me?" Blake crossed her arms across her chest, a gesture of defiance. Jenny let the door slam behind her and looked at Blake. Her eyes were dark, hard, intent. She kept her forearms spread across her breasts, looking at Jenny.

"Thanks for letting me in," Jenny said, deciding to let Blake's comment go.

"You can wait in Davis's office for him if you'd like," Blake replied. Neither one of them moved for a moment, until Blake turned out of the silence, rather abruptly, and started walking up the stairs. Jenny followed her, not being able to avoid enjoying the view of Blake and embarrassed to realize that she was. Who wouldn't, though? The low-slung pants, long waist, hips that were somehow straight and sensual at the same time. Jenny shut her eyes for a moment, trying to shake herself out of staring. She didn't like Blake's art, let alone her personality. That damned tower of hair. She'd Googled images of it last night; even a picture made her want to gag. "Hairball" was right. Walking up the stairs behind her had proven to be a different visual altogether, however. *Get a hold of yourself, Jenny*, she thought. *Not your type, not your type, not your type.*

The museum was much more alive with activity than it had been the night before. Power tools were buzzing, and Blake's gaggle of lithe assistants were painting the walls. She smelled fresh sawdust and paint. Jenny wiped her brow. Even though she'd been out in the cold, she was sweating at the temples all of a sudden.

The walls had been painted saturated colors, deep blood red in one of the rooms. Jenny felt herself walking through the gallery. She had hardly been telling her limbs to move, but even in its unfinished state, the installation was magnetic. She felt pulled to the color, the light. She felt Blake following her. "That's the Vermeer," Blake said, the flat tone of her voice indicating she didn't want to be playing tour guide. Jenny kept walking anyway, peeking into the next room to her right, painted a bright cold blue. "That's the Hockney," Blake said, hanging in the doorway, tapping a screwdriver lightly against her palm.

Jenny nodded and saw three men carrying a wall frame toward her. She stepped back, almost tripping on an errant two-by-four and bumping into a sawhorse. Sawdust clung to her coat. Blake looked at her almost sourly, lips pursed, as if bracing for her to complain or scold her. Somehow, though, even though she disliked Blake, she didn't want Blake to think of her as a stuffed shirt. She took off her coat and said, "Can I help while I wait for Davis?"

"Yes, I suppose," Blake said, as if she were the one doing Jenny a favor.

CHAPTER FOUR

Blake hadn't expected the lawyer to show up. Definitely not. She had shown such contempt for Blake last night, called her a "fucking diva," hated the very idea of her art, and threatened her with a lawsuit—all in the span of about three minutes. And then there she was, standing outside the service entrance, her chestnut hair in a tight bun at the back of her head, her body covered up in a thick down coat, but somehow still sexy, as if her body was so extraordinary every curve could still be seen through the coat. The cool blast of air should have made Blake cold, but she stood there, sweating. Well, she'd been working hard, helping the carpenters rebuild the wall. That must be why. The gallery was warm with all the activity. Yes, she decided, that was it, as the lawyer, her face still seeming full of contempt, walked by her and up the stairs.

Even more surprising than her being there in the first place, was that she offered to help. Blake wasn't sure how this would go. Jenny was wearing a suit from work, a starched oxford, and pearls, for God's sake. What help could she offer? Plus, Blake was pretty sure that Jenny had never held a hammer or nail, let alone a radial saw. But, shocking Blake again, Jenny pulled off her heels, put on a pair of ballet flats she was carrying in her briefcase, and went right up to the biggest, burliest of the carpenters and walked away from the conversation with a pair of safety goggles on and a drill in her hand.

Blake tried not to stare at Jenny, who, across the room, looked wholly incongruous in her perfectly tailored suit as she helped put up the frame of the new wall. Yes, she was gorgeous, her bun coming undone a bit. She took off her suit jacket and rolled up the sleeves of her shirt, showing her toned arms, with a few freckles on the forearm. No ring, she noticed. *Probably living with some other lawyer*, she thought. A prick who wears cashmere sweaters and shoes with tassels and is planning the perfect proposal on Valentine's Day at the top of the Eiffel Tower or something.

Blake hammered the nails for the light fixtures into her two-by-fours, swinging wildly, strangely angry at the thought of Jenny wearing some preppy guy's ring on her finger. Jenny, wearing his button-down in the morning. What was wrong with her? Why was she thinking about Jenny at all? It was abundantly clear she was straight. For one thing, she hadn't let a single glance linger on Blake, which was unusual. It was simply a fact that she had a reliable effect on a certain type of woman. And Jenny clearly wasn't the type.

She had to focus. She was out of her element, directing the installation of her whole gallery. She recognized this in herself, how she fixated on women when things got tough. She'd get blocked, bored, read a bad review, and have someone look at a piece and decide not to buy it, and end up tussling in bed with someone beautiful. For the distraction, and to remind herself she was good at something.

This tendency of hers had spawned a tradition, suggested initially by Steve, her manager, that she be monastic in the week before a show. He knew her better than she did herself, sometimes, and that's why he got a cut. He said a few years ago, "Let's just see how it goes. No women." Blake agreed and had made it a tradition ever since. She eschewed alcohol, too. Everything that took her focus away from her work.

She was in that week. For her own sanity, she needed to comply, including inside her head. This show meant more to her than most of the others. Sure, it was small-time compared to the Biennial, but she had to ride that wave of publicity. This show was the one she'd been dreaming about for years, configuring and reconfiguring. She became an apprentice to an off-Broadway lighting designer just for this, volunteering in small black box theaters to understand filters and spotlights and diffusers. This was the show that would caress its viewers, bring them in, make them feel the warmth and the light of paint the way she always did.

Blake, ever since she was a kid, had relished, almost more than anything, wandering through the Met and getting lost in it. She felt like paintings gave her a portal. After her dad died and her mom carted her around to a series of new boyfriends' apartments, she'd take the train up to the Met, sometimes not telling her mother where she was going, because she knew she wouldn't understand. Sure, Blake agreed with the Guerrilla Girls about the excruciating sexism of the establishment. But those concerns always faded away when she was face-to-face with one of the greats. A Vermeer that beckoned her into a room. A Bruegel that made debauchery seem like it was all about sunlight, spanning across centuries. And of course, the Joan of Arc staring, melodramatic, upward through the trees, the dappled light across her face seeming to radiate out of the painting and into the gallery where it hung. She remembered when the Ellsworth Kellys were installed. They were made to stand in front of; they were made to subsume the eyes with color and with feeling.

The paintings were the one constant in her life, her mooring whenever the waves of grief or loneliness threatened to capsize her. This exhibit was her love letter to that. It was going to be perfect.

And now, strangely, Jenny was helping to install the show. They worked for an hour, on opposite sides of the room. Blake found herself looking over at Jenny more often than seemed polite, letting her eyes linger as she watched her carry the wall frame over to the windows, affix the braces, pull the tape to measure where the hinge brackets should go. Jenny worked with a focused intensity, measuring, remeasuring, making sure that everything was perfect. She probably was a very good lawyer, Blake thought. As she worked, some of the polished veneer couldn't help but soften a bit. A few wisps of hair had fallen into her face. She had taken off her heavy-looking watch. Beads of sweat were on her temples. She didn't seem to mind that sawdust was clinging to her suit. She seemed to be fully embodied in herself, lost in her work, but still, she was cold to Blake, distant, not looking in her direction. Blake kept thinking she might catch her eye, even if she didn't know what she'd do when she finally did, but Jenny never looked at her. It seemed deliberate.

Davis appeared beside Blake, interrupting her momentary staring.

"How is it going?"

"Very well." Blake took a deep breath and threw her shoulders back, trying to capture the stance of a perfectly confident, in-control professional. "My team has painted several of the rooms already and we are working on starting the light fixture boards. Jenny and the carpenters have put up the frame of the auxiliary wall already. I think we are on schedule."

"Jenny's here?" Davis asked, unable to suppress a smug little smile. He erased it quickly, though, and turned to Blake, his earnestness returned.

"Waiting for you," she said, with more of an edge than she intended.

Davis seemed to want to scamper away again. Something in her tone seemed to scare him. Her diva reputation in full force? She'd done nothing last night to help that, sitting in the gallery, telling him she'd leave.

"Davis?" He turned, startled, seeming again like he'd been scolded. "I'm sorry about last night. I was on edge. I should not have threatened to leave."

His mouth went a little slack in surprise, but he managed to gather himself in a quick moment to respond. "Please don't apologize. I should not have threatened to sue you."

"You didn't." Blake gestured across the galley at Jenny, who was running a piece of Masonite through a table saw. "She did."

"Well, I apologize on Jenny's behalf."

"I don't think she'd want you to," Blake said, just as Jenny looked over at Blake and Davis. A scowl came across her face when she saw them both looking at her.

Davis waved, but Jenny didn't respond. She just turned back to the table saw, blowing sawdust off the blade. *Beautiful*, Blake couldn't help but notice again, as Jenny leaned over to take out the pin holding the blade in place. *She hates me, and she's beautiful.*

CHAPTER FIVE

A few hours later, Jenny and Davis were sitting next to one another at the bar of the Parrish Cafe. Davis was drinking IPA out of a stein with his name etched on it, and Jenny was having chardonnay.

"It's so weird you drink wine at Parrish," Davis said, with a mock scowl.

"It's weird you drank the equivalent of four kegs of beer in a month to earn that mug, so we are even."

He smiled. "That makes me smart, not weird. Discount for life!"

He held up his stein with a whoop and was joined by two women at the end of the bar who held up theirs. The bartender grabbed it from Davis and filled it to the top again.

Jenny shook her head but couldn't help smiling. "I don't get it."

"What I don't get is that I've seen you more in the last twenty-four hours than in the last six months. Everything okay?"

"You asked for my help the other night, Davis, not the other way around."

"Yes, but you showed up again tonight. When have I ever seen you on a weekday?"

"I'm not sure. Things have been weird. Michael basically gave me the night off," Jenny said, feeling the wine slosh around in her head. "Thank you for putting in a good word with Stackhouse, Davis. That was great."

"You are welcome. But you shouldn't be so excited about a night off. I get nights off all the time. Normal people don't work Monday nights. Even people at your firm don't work Monday nights."

"Like Lydia?"

"Yes, like Lydia. But I'm talking about you. Do you ever think…" Jenny could see Davis starting to blush a little.

"Just say it."

"Well, you work a lot. That's all I mean."

"I have loans to pay off, Davis." What right did Davis have to criticize her? She was doing well. Tons of people would be thrilled to have her job. She wasn't one of them. But that didn't change its necessity.

"I know, Jen, I wonder if it's time to shake things up a bit? It's been a few years, right? I know I vowed to stop giving you crap about working for Michael, but now he's made you grateful for a Monday. Maybe it's gotten out of hand."

Davis was right. She thought she'd go to the firm for a year. Maybe two. And then go on and do what she wanted. The problem was, she didn't know what that was. It's not like she'd gone to law school with some heady sense of idealism. It was simply what she always expected that she'd do. Straight-A student, law school, job at a firm, make her parents proud. Sure, she was ambitious. She wanted to work at the best firm, in the most demanding department, with the most high-profile clients. Lately, though, she wasn't sure why. The truth of her aimlessness was so plain, she wanted to recoil from it. She wasn't like her friends who wanted to be doctors. Or environmental lawyers. Or even the few wannabe actors she'd known in high school. She had wanted a good, stable job. And then, there she was, an overworked lawyer right out of central casting.

Jenny looked down into her glass and back up at Davis, wanting to change the subject. "Look, I thought this would be fun. I'm trying to have fun on—"

"Your night off. I know. And really, thanks for coming over. Last night and tonight. I'm happy to see you." She smiled, wanting to move on from thinking about her boss. Wanting to drink a little more wine. Or maybe a lot.

Davis seemed eager to settle in, too. His face stretched into a mischievous grin. "So," he said, looking at Jenny intently. "Blake was staring at you."

Jenny's neck became hot. She pulled at her collar. "Was not."

"Was too."

"Was not."

"What are you, five? She was staring at you, while you were bent over a table saw, manipulating power tools."

Jenny's whole face was red, she could feel it, the splotches that inevitably appeared when she felt the least bit vulnerable. At work she'd become adept at wearing the right makeup and even suppressing it. It used to be that whenever Michael asked her to do anything she'd turn pink. She was sure that he noticed, knew it was her tell, and exploited it. Over the years she'd learned how to dial it back. A series of swallows, self-coaching. But after Davis mentioned Blake, there was nothing she could do. The blush came on fast and furious. The chardonnay was gleefully egging it on. Davis didn't bother pointing out the obvious. He smiled at Jenny, smug.

"So what if she was staring at me?" Jenny said. "I'm sure she hates me, after what I said."

"And you care?"

"No," Jenny said quickly, gulping her wine, knowing even as she said so that it wasn't true. She cared what Blake thought of her. She had to. That's why she'd helped build the wall earlier. But she wasn't about to admit that to him. "I came to thank you. See how everything was going. That's all."

"Okay," he said, smile still not fading. He clinked his half-drunk stein with her empty glass. "To friends helping friends." Then, to the bartender, "Another round!"

"Are you trying to get me drunk?"

"You're doing it all on your own," he said.

She was. Trying to obliterate something and maybe succeeding. She wasn't sure what. Loneliness? It wasn't that, exactly. She didn't feel lonely day-to-day. She had Lydia and Davis and brunch with her parents every once in a while. She didn't miss Melinda. Not really. Right?

"I saw Melinda," Davis said, as if on cue.

Jenny felt her body collapse a little at the bar. Another swig of wine. Another pita chip. Another olive. "Oh?"

"She seemed really happy. She still has that annoying way of laughing, though, remember the honk?"

"I didn't know you thought it was annoying."

"Well, I know you thought it was annoying."

"Was she with anyone?"

"Yeah, a somewhat cute girl with very, very straight bangs, but it was unclear if it was a girlfriend."

"Isn't that annoying?"

"What?"

"Not being able to tell."

"You should talk!"

"What is that supposed to mean?"

"Jenny, no one knows you're gay. Like, at all."

She felt her insides tighten again. Maybe her singular focus had cost her some kind of outward authenticity. Maybe. She was only hurting herself. "I'm not dating anyone, so it doesn't really come up," she said finally.

Davis seemed to sense the wave of hurt passing through her, so he softened his approach. But he wasn't letting it go. "If you want to date someone they kind of have to know who you're into, don't they? Melinda wasn't right, but you want someone, right?"

Jenny nodded and said what was scaring her. "Maybe Melinda was right. And I let her go."

"If she was it, you wouldn't have let her go." Davis took Jenny's hand and squeezed it. She felt herself breathe deeply in gratitude.

"How are your someones, anyway?"

Davis, mercifully, let her change the subject. "Well, I have Jacob from grad school, off and on, and Gary from Grindr. I'm thinking Gary will come to the opening. He's very chic. And unlike some other people I know, he knows who Blake Harrison is and is totally impressed about the show."

"I'm impressed too."

"So you do like her!"

"No. I don't. But I'm happy for you."

"Thanks, Esquire."

"You're welcome. Next round is on me."

"Another round?"

"I don't get the night off very often. Might as well go to work tomorrow with a well-earned hangover."

"I'll drink to that," Davis said.

The next morning, she indeed had the hangover. Whether it was well-earned or whether she was just out of practice, she couldn't tell. She opened her dry mouth and it felt like it was stuffed with cotton. Reaching for the water bottle she'd apparently had the forethought to put beside her bedside table, she knocked over her alarm clock, which went off with a screech as it hit the floor, making her temples pound.

Idiot, idiot, she thought, pulling her legs, with great effort, to the side of the bed so she could stand. Her foot crunched on something on the rug, beside the neat pile of her clothes from the night before.

"Fuck!" she screeched, as if there were anyone to complain to or blame but herself. Her tired, drunk self. She knelt on the rug, feeling for the object. Her fingers touched cool metal. A drill bit.

She palmed it and leaned back on the bed to examine the bottom of her foot. No blood. Good. The last thing she needed today was to have to explain to Michael that she needed the morning off for a tetanus shot.

She would have to go back to the museum later and return the drill bit. And thank Davis for putting her in an Uber home and making sure the guy had a five-star rating and wasn't going to drive her to Revere and back just to jack up the charges for a drunk girl. That's what she would have to do. She must have slid the bit into her suit pocket when she had finished the wall.

Blake hadn't even said thank you. She'd said nothing. In fact, when Jenny left, she didn't even nod in her direction. Now Davis was telling her that Blake was staring at her? It didn't make any sense.

She turned on her coffee maker. She'd managed to set it up the night before. The grounds were in, waiting. Her fastidious habits died hard.

The coffee mug warmed her fingers, and the first sip woke her from the inside out. She sat at her kitchen table, laptop on, and typed in Blake's name. There were series of articles about the Biennial success, more pictures of that godforsaken tower of hair. She found a *New York Times* article covering the Biennial with a picture of Blake in all black, her head closely shaven, standing in front of a graffitied wall that was identified as the side of one of the buildings she grew up in. "I would agree my art is sensual," Blake said in the interview. "Installation is my medium of choice because I can regulate, or at least attempt to influence, all of the viewer's senses, not just sight."

The *Bitch Magazine* article from a few months back had a picture of Blake gleefully holding up a paper-mache vagina, and the caption, "Queen of the Art World: Blake Harrison Can't Be Reigned In." Oh goodness, the puns. "Art is supposed to be fun," Blake was quoted as saying. "It's messy, it's sometimes uncomfortable, it's awkward, and sometimes, it can be transcendent. It's like sex. It should never be boring."

It was the kind of thing Jenny would have normally rolled her eyes at, but she found herself reading the words a few times. What had happened to her that she was personally acquainted with such a character? Likening her art to sex? Paper-mache vaginas. *Please.*

So, Blake was apparently a diva and a sex fiend. Good to know. Jenny couldn't stop. She went back to the search bar, typed in "Blake Harrison" again, and clicked on images. The first few pages were of the repulsive hair, culled from Instagram, but then came more official news photos and press releases. One was of Blake in a tuxedo with purple sequins, posing with a tall woman in a red dress with wild black curls piled on her head at an art opening for someone Jenny had never heard of. Another was of Blake, staring into the camera for a kind of head shot, almost completely bald, connected to her webpage. Then, a few more of Blake and various women of all shapes and sizes, all beautiful, next to her at fundraisers and museum openings. One of the last was from the Costume Institute gala that summer. Blake wearing a long-sleeve jumpsuit with a plunging back, next to a woman who looked like a young Angelica Houston in a bright orange mini dress. Jenny was used to dismissing such outfits—such events—as irrelevant. Silly. Resolutely not her world. But somehow, looking at the photo of Blake, she wasn't feeling indignant. It was a different emotion altogether—but one she couldn't quite believe kept announcing itself. Jealousy. Why did Blake want to be draped with those women when somehow she couldn't even give Jenny the time of day? Unless Davis was telling the truth? Why did Jenny care?

Jenny turned the drill bit over and over in her hand. She was such an idiot for having taken it. She was such an idiot for getting drunk with Davis last night. She was such an idiot for looking at pictures of Blake Harrison on the Internet. And now she was late for work.

CHAPTER SIX

Somehow, for the third day in a row, Blake found herself at the top of the stairwell looking down at the lawyer. She was dressed much as she had been the day before, a skirt suit with pleats, but there was something more relaxed about her. Her hair was again in a bun, but her whole comportment had a new air of softness.

Jenny looked up at her from the bottom of the stairs. Blake almost told her that Davis would be back in a few minutes, but stopped herself, allowing herself to wonder, just for a moment, if maybe Jenny was actually standing at the bottom of the stairs for her and no one else.

"I brought you something," Jenny said. Blake's heart started beating faster. She felt her cheeks flush. She stayed steady at the top of the stairs, wondering. She clenched her fists together, willing herself to remain calm. She needed what she had said to Steve—that she was monastic the week before a show—to be true. Even though Jenny wasn't interested—couldn't possibly be—Blake had to remain monastic in thought, too. She couldn't let anyone get to her. Not Liza, Steve's assistant, who was scampering around the museum in sheer shirts and leggings. Not Jenny, not even a thought. Nothing.

But Jenny had brought her something. "What is it?" she asked, trying to sound only mildly curious. Jenny started walking up the stairs and stopped a few short of Blake. She dug her hand into her pocket and showed Blake a drill bit, flat on her palm.

"I seem to have taken that home with me last night."

Blake smiled and shrugged, afraid the drill bit was just a drill bit. Or could it possibly be pretense for her visit? She couldn't fathom. Maybe there was no uptight banker boyfriend after all. Her head felt cloudy. "Thanks," she squeaked out, again berating herself for how much she was feeling, how much she was fixating, totally unbidden, on this strangely impenetrable woman in front of her.

Jenny turned and set off down the stairs. Blake wanted to call back to her, but she had enough self-control to resist. She turned and let the heavy door begin to close behind her. Before it did, Jenny's voice, sounding a little tentative, came through. "How did it go today?"

Blake snapped herself back and opened the door. Jenny's hands were in her pockets; her full lips were pursed a bit. She seemed nervous, and somehow confident, too, staring up at Blake. Bold.

"Let me show you," Blake said, and without thinking, put out her hand, reaching toward Jenny, who was standing a few stairs below. Jenny walked quickly, and reaching Blake, took off her gloves, shoved them in her coat pocket, and gave her right hand to her.

Blake almost gasped when their fingers touched. Jenny's hands were warm and smooth and there was something electric in their fingers together. Her whole body tingled. Every bit of her felt like it could feel Jenny's fingers, from the tip of her nose to her kneecaps. She wanted to glance back to see if she felt it too but was afraid her own face would reveal too much. So she kept her hand touching Jenny's as they walked up the stairs, not gripping too hard, but not letting her hand go limp, either, until they were both through the doorway into the gallery and the heavy door shut behind them. Jenny pulled her hand back, rather abruptly, and shoved it back into her coat pocket. Blake could still feel the heat of her fingers on her palm. She wanted to rub the spot, but she didn't. She just looked straight ahead into the gallery. A few of the lights in the Hockney room were on, a cool blue.

"What's that?" Jenny said, seemingly oblivious to what had happened and how much of an effect the simple, quick touch of her fingers had had on Blake's whole body.

"I'll show you," Blake said. Jenny took off her coat and left it on a stool in the corner of the gallery. Blake had to look away when she did it, suddenly aware that everything Jenny did was making her body ache. The oxford she had on was split alluringly at the neck. Blake noticed the thin gold chain glistening against her clavicle. A few freckles on her décolletage.

"This is the Hockney room," she said, trying to steady her voice. She went to an electrical panel at the side of the wall and turned on all the lights. What had just been a blue glow became almost blinding, drenching Blake and Jenny in hot light. The walls were painted a glossy, cool white that made the whole room glow, making it feel like they were being warmed, not just lit. Blake felt her body spread open on cue. There was no other way to react—the light made everyone feel loose. She had imagined this room, designed it, and tested it, and still, she was amazed at how well it worked. How well she worked. She glanced at Jenny, who was doing exactly what she hoped any visitor would. She was tilting her head toward the brightest corner of the room, outstretching her arms, in a way that appeared to be thoughtless, soaking it in.

Jenny looked at her, as if startled by her gaze.

"Hockney. The painter. I remember seeing something—a poster I think—but I think I know the image. Very…scrubby."

Blake laughed and then saw Jenny's face fall a little.

"You're right!" she reassured her. "His paint. The way he paints is scrubby." Jenny's face relaxed, but not completely. Blake was surprised that she was a capable of any embarrassment around her.

"I think that's a really accurate word to describe the paint. What I'm doing here is the light," Blake said.

"Overall? Or specific to one painting?" Jenny smoothed her skirt and tried to appear to be academically taking it in, but still, her face was pointing upward.

"Specifically. Did you happen to come across the one of the pool and the diving board?"

Jenny nodded. "Yes, it's at the Met, right? It's blue."

"Well, this light is meant to feel like if you were standing inside of that painting."

Jenny said nothing but breathed. Blake tried not to watch her, but she couldn't look away. She tried not to ask herself why Jenny was there, why she'd gone from calling Blake a "fucking diva" and referring to her Biennial piece with disdain to standing willingly in the room, soaking herself in the light.

"What does the light feel like to you?" she asked, wanting to stand closer to Jenny, but holding still.

Jenny held her eyes closed as she answered. "Like the sun is too bright, and there's white marble everywhere, and it's still pretty early in the afternoon but I've already had a few cocktails and that plus the sun is making my skin feel very red."

"What can you smell?" Blake asked, daring to push open the door to Jenny a little more.

Jenny began intoning. "I can smell chlorine and sunblock. The cocoa butter kind, sweet, mixed with salt, too, and squeezes of lemon to make your hair lighter. There are people, limbs warmed by the sun."

"What can you hear?"

"Not much. No words, it's low chatter, a few giggles, the light kick of the beach ball. I feel like I can hear the sun moving across the sky, slowly. Like it makes a sound. And it's so hot out, but it's not humid. It's dry, comfortable sun, and it's shifting across me, warming my skin."

Blake wanted to dance in gratitude. Jenny understood. She understood on a level beyond her head, beyond her eyes. She understood somewhere deep inside her body. She had built the room and Jenny was fully inside of it. It was the greatest affirmation anyone could have ever given to Blake, and somehow, it was coming from Jenny. She smiled, not being able to suppress a grin. She had done it. The rooms were a success.

Then, as if Jenny could feel Blake staring, she opened her eyes.

"That's beautiful," Blake said. "What you said—That's exactly what I'm going for."

Jenny walked quickly out of the room, as if trying to shake something off. Blake followed her, shutting off the blue lights and turning back on the gallery overheads, wanting to remember everything Jenny said, but following her out, trying to hold onto the moment.

"The others?" Jenny asked, twisting her face back into professional composure and pursed lips as if she had not been reveling in David Hockney's pool.

Blake hoped Jenny couldn't sense how off-balance she felt. This was it. This was why she had so stay strong, push aside all thoughts besides the art. There was still work to do.

She tried to control her voice, appear casual. But she started talking nervously. "Well, Vermeer. La Tour with candlelight. The Hockney is the most modern. I stay away from Monet because that light is so diffuse it's actually not that interesting. I have Manet's bullfighter, the one at the Gardener. And in the corner it's a Bruegel, the dancing sun-drenched one with the light filtering through bushy trees with all the zaftig people eating."

"Zaftig?"

"Yes. What? It means—"

"I know what it means," Jenny said.

"You're surprised I use it?"

"It's a really good diner in Brookline, that's all," Jenny said, "but I haven't been there in ages."

"Zaftig? A diner?"

"Yeah." Jenny looked down, as if she'd said too much. Some wave of sadness seemed to pass over her. A memory of some kind. Blake found herself wanting to know what it was—to sit there and watch the reels with her—to tell her it was going to be okay. She fought the impulse, so strong, to say, "Want to go? Tomorrow morning?" She imagined what Jenny would look like out of her suit, in something comfy, eating a stack of pancakes. But no. She probably had grapefruit for breakfast. Something cold and acidic.

Blake realized she'd paused and Jenny hadn't picked up the thread of the conversation, so they were standing in silence. She smiled at her, and she felt warm doing so, like by smiling at her she was saying something. *Come with me. I like you. You're beautiful.* In a short, very short, too short second, Jenny seemed to be smiling a similarly loaded smile back, something full and knowing. It was starting out at the corners of her lips, but Blake wasn't imagining it, was she?

Then a voice interrupted the delicate silence. Before Blake realized what was happening—that whatever moment they'd shared was being obliterated—Liza, the bouncy assistant, was walking across the floor to Blake and Jenny was stepping back.

"I think I've heard of that place," Liza said, sidling up to Blake and looking at Jenny. "In Coolidge Corner, right?" Jenny nodded, her eyes seeming to dart back between Liza and Blake, not knowing where to rest.

Liza gave a little wave. "I'm Liza. Installation assistant, Blake's manager's gopher, whatever you want to call me, I am at your service." She stood even closer to Blake—proprietarily close. Too close. Blake wanted to step back, but she didn't trust herself to move.

"Why haven't you left yet?" Blake asked Liza. She wanted it to sound cold, and it seemed to. Liza either didn't notice or didn't care, because she waved her arm and said, "Finishing up." Then she leaned in closer to Blake and said loudly so that Jenny could hear, "Let's go to Zaftigs tomorrow morning."

Exactly what Blake had wanted to say to Jenny but hadn't. Because it was a crazy thing to say.

"Order the latkes," Jenny said. Blake couldn't figure out her tone. Somewhere between bemused and resigned. Nothing like what she had been saying in the Hockney room. Nothing that easy, nothing that raw. Jenny walked over to her coat and pulled it from the stool, almost yanking it. Blake watched her go, mouth too dry to say goodbye, until Jenny was about to open the heavy door.

"Thanks for the drill bit," she managed to squeak out, already hating herself for not putting in more effort to rescue the moment.

While she stared at the closed door, Liza's hand found the small of Blake's back. The cacophony in Blake's head calmed a bit. She would be lying to herself if she didn't admit that she had craved the touch, just a little. A distraction from the stress. Her familiar pattern. She didn't move and looked over at Liza. There she was, all light and willing, still in her sheer shirt and purple lace bra, bright red lipstick painted on like an invitation. "You've had a long day," Liza said, starting to circle her palm on Blake's back. "Where are you staying tonight?"

She was not subtle, Blake had to give her that.

"Liza, I'm not taking you back to my Airbnb."

Liza gave a fake little pout and turned Blake around so they were squarely facing one another, resting her hands on Blake's hips.

"You sure?"

Blake nodded yes, but even as she did, felt her resolve weaken. Liza was sexy, absolutely, full lips and gorgeous breasts. Creamy skin. They'd slept together before, a few months ago back in New York, when Steve had hired her to cart equipment back and forth from Blake's studio. Disaster. A fun disaster. Liza dug her thumbs into Blake's hips, gently, but a little insistent. Blake's breathing quickened. Liza even smelled good—something coconut, probably in her wave of perfect, bouncing, spherical curls that would be lovely to pull on while her face was buried beneath—

"Really," Blake said, jolting herself awake and jumping back from Liza's grip, "I'm monastic the week before a show." But again, even as she said it, she started to waver.

"Monastic? Really?" Liza said, reaching her lips up to Blake's neck.

Blake moved her jaw back, avoiding Liza, and cracked her knuckles and looked down at her feet, trying to stop the flames in her cheeks. She would not sleep with Liza. She should not sleep with Liza.

"The way you were looking at that lawyer didn't seem too monastic to me," Liza said.

"What the hell do you mean?" she said quickly, before she could temper the automatic intensity of her voice.

"Hey there," Liza said, smiling a little. "I'm teasing. She's very cute."

"I didn't notice," Blake said, deliberately more softly, to bring Liza's focus back on Blake and away from Jenny.

"Not as cute as you," Liza said. Blake was relieved they were back in their pattern, not sure how to account for her panic when Liza mentioned Jenny, but knowing she wanted to keep something secret, even if she wasn't sure what it was.

When Liza leaned in to kiss her, Blake complied. She tasted of mint and bubblegum over a clove cigarette, and her tongue was aggressive. Soft, but too muscular for Blake. Blake tried to soften it, push back, find the rhythm, but instead, Liza went full throttle and bit her lower lip—*hard*.

Blake's body went cold and stiff without her needing to tell it to. Liza didn't notice, though. She started squeezing Blake's ass as they stood. Blake pulled back even more and, still getting no response, finally said, "Hey!" With Liza's tongue still in her mouth.

Liza pulled back, grabbing her tongue—had Blake bitten it by accident, in response?—and looked at her, wide-eyed.

"Sorry," Blake said. "I gotta go."

Liza managed to smile. She blew Blake a kiss, even though she was a few inches away.

"Your loss," she said.

Blake smiled, wanting to be kind. "I know."

But she didn't feel like she knew anything. All she knew was that Liza wasn't Jenny. If that had been Jenny's hands on her hips and Jenny's tongue in her mouth, she wouldn't give a second thought to the gallery opening or her need to focus. She wanted Jenny. However strange, illogical, or impossible as that was.

CHAPTER SEVEN

Jenny hurried down the stairs, not stopping to look at her watch. She didn't know how late it was or how long she'd been mooning about the gallery like an idiot with Blake. What had she been thinking? She needed to get back to work. She had meant to stop by and return the drill bit. Get some fresh air. See the art, like Lydia had suggested. That was all. That was supposed to be all. Instead, she'd taken off her jacket and started telling Blake that the light made her smell skin and sunscreen and hear the fucking *sun*. What the hell was wrong with her?

The cold hit her sharply when she pushed on the heavy door out of the stairwell. The night lights were glowing up at the museum's columns. The facade was small but stately. The Albie was a jewel. She didn't understand the tourists who ran through, the ones who had read about the museum in a guidebook and checked it off, doing the MFA and the Garner and the Albie all in one day, not savoring anything.

But how dare she criticize anyone for not savoring, when she had forgotten how to do anything but work? She hadn't savored anything in years. Sure, late at night, sipping another decaf coffee, she sometimes found some sort of equilibrium. She alone could figure out how the opposing counsel's expert, a renowned PhD in economics, was wrong about damages incurred seven years ago, down to the point-100th percentage point. Yes, she was sure it seemed strange and stale to most people, but she was good at it. That's when she was happiest, sitting in her dark office, building a case, digit by digit.

That was work. Did that count? Shouldn't there be something else?

The snow had turned to slush. Her boots stamped it down, harder and harder, until she felt like she was marching. She wanted to get back to the office, back to the familiar, the industrial carpet that smelled of ink and soap, the hum of the HVAC of the building at night, and yes, the yellow flickering florescent lights overhead, not that blinding blue that made her cheeks hot and made her talk too much. None of that.

"Jenny? Is that you?" She whipped her head around at the voice, the slightly nasal, chipper tone, so achingly familiar to her somewhere deep inside, but also distant. Because it had been a while. Two years.

Melinda. She smiled, toothy. She looked happy. Unselfconscious. With Jenny, she had tiptoed, wanting so badly—too badly—to be liked, to be loved, to be doted on, always asking for reassurance Jenny couldn't give. But now— Jenny could see it in an instant—Melinda had a new confidence. Her hair was unwieldy still, but peeking cutely out from her knitted cap. Her wide cheeks were rosy, glad.

They hugged. The cold night and the puffy coats helped, because they didn't have to negotiate touching. "Heading home already? Not working late so much anymore?" Melinda asked.

Well, she hadn't wasted any time. As if Jenny had been missing her complaints about her late nights.

"You look great," Jenny deflected.

"Well," Melinda said, "smiling for two!" She stuck her stomach out in Jenny's direction. Jenny looked down at her and thought that, yes, the down coat was puffy, but not that puffy. Melinda had a belly. A baby. Jenny tried to smile, but her eyes twitched a little, so she said what her face wouldn't show. "Congratulations, Melinda. That's great."

"It is! We're so excited. My fiancée—Stephanie—she's a lawyer like you—well, not like you at all—she, like, works, like, normal human hours, she does housing law, like, real estate, she's given so many of our friends great advice, but you were always like, well, are you doing a stock split as a bank with C-class shares? And if so, I can help you! Anyway, we're getting married in June and I guess we'll carry the baby down the aisle. Because we said, well, let's try, because we heard that it can take a while, but everything fell into place on the first try!"

Jenny nodded again and said, "Yes, yes, congratulations," because that's what she was supposed to say. She felt relief, most of all, that it wasn't her baby in Melinda's belly. God help her. She had done the right thing. Still, a sadness nagged at her. She wanted to run away. "That's great," Jenny repeated, not knowing how to move things along. "I'm so glad you are happy."

"I am!" Melinda grinned. "So, are you headed to the condo or—" She started prying.

"Oh, just out for a walk." Jenny smiled, tight-lipped. She wanted to end the conversation, but she couldn't tell Melinda she was going back to the office. She had some pride left.

Melinda gestured at Newbury Street. "I'm meeting Stephanie at Stephanie's. Ha! She loves it there. And we figure, better go out while we can, right?"

"Good thinking," Jenny said, looking up at the Prudential. "I'm, um, going to the Top of the Hub."

Melinda smiled. "Law firm thing?"

"No, a date," Jenny lied, improbably. Stupidly. "I got here early so I was out for a stroll."

"On this lovely night?" Melinda tilted her head. Jenny wondered for an instant if she was about to call her on the nervous fib.

"Well. You don't want to leave Stephanie waiting at Stephanie's," Jenny said, afraid if she stood there any longer she would start sprinting in the other direction.

Melinda smiled, as if the mere thought of her fiancée brought her joy. Well, it did, it seemed. The smile was real. Melinda was still Melinda, but her happiness was new, and it was clearly present. So was her bedrock kindness. Jenny always knew it was there, beneath layers of insecurity and passive aggression.

"You want to come with me and meet her? Before your date?"

"No, thanks." Jenny tried to say it kindly, as if she would ever consider doing so.

Melinda reached for Jenny's hand for a moment. Jenny complied but kept her body back so they wouldn't get too close. She remembered the brief touch of Blake's hand at the top of the stairs. How different that had been. Skin to skin. How she had missed it when it was over.

"It was so good to see you." Melinda smiled, taking her hand back and clapping her mittens together. "I'd been meaning to call with the news."

"Congratulations, really."

Melinda giggled again, gave Jenny a perfunctory wave, and turned, trudging off in her boots. Strangely, she looked more pregnant from behind, like the shift in her center of gravity was more noticeable when Jenny saw her walking away.

Jenny walked to the Prudential Center, figuring she'd make half of her lie true. Her ears popped in the elevator as it passed the office on its way to Top of The Hub, and the bar was so empty they offered her a seat right over the view of a snow-covered Fenway Park. It was hard to make out much at night, but she could see the diamond clearly. The last time she'd been to Fenway was with Melinda, who sat on a stick of gum and spent the whole game scowling and picking at the back of her jeans. Jenny had even offered to buy her new track pants at the gift shop, but she frowned at that, too.

Jenny picked at a cheese plate and a gin and tonic and pulled out her phone. She didn't know Stephanie's last name, but a search for *Melinda Stephanie Boston Wedding* brought up their wedding photographer's website. Their engagement pictures, each in matching jeans and black T-shirts, posing in the arboretum. Nice, artsy shots of them, framed in a canopy of fall leaves. Davis had remembered Stephanie's severe bangs, and there they were, framing her face like the brim of a hat. Jenny read the photographer's note underneath the blog post. "You know when you meet a couple and you're sure they're meant for each other? That's Melinda and Steph. When they are in each other's company, the whole world seems to fade away. Their love is palpable! What a joy to photograph! Can't wait for the wedding!!!"

Jenny sat back in the chair, suppressing an eye roll at the multiple exclamation points. So they were happy. Good for them. She rested her legs on the rungs of the table beneath her. She let her eyes search the glass below, looking down at the view of the city she loved, even on its coldest days. She was home here. But like the cold front that always seemed to be trailing in from the seaport, the thought came back to her, the same one she'd been having the last few days. The unbidden, chilling thought. *I should be happier.*

Melinda had done it, somehow. She had found the right person. Jenny had been right to let her go. She had known that. Still, something gnawed.

Jenny thought of Blake. At first she was a diva, a bitch. Not the kind of person Jenny would ever look at twice. Then she seemed to Jenny to be exacting, in a way she recognized. And tonight, she had seemed passionate and mellow at the same time. A nice combination. Blake had every reason to be happy. The show, the burgeoning fame, and the arm candy, in an apparent never-ending rotation. Who had interrupted them? *Liza.* They were probably on the floor of the museum right now, in some state of undress.

She gulped at her drink, tense at the thought. She had noticed, sure, that Blake was attractive. In that overconfident way Jenny never really liked. She was the kind of woman Jenny would stand as far away from at the bar as possible during a mixer. What did it matter? As if Blake would ever look twice at her anyway.

It was just as well. Her little run-in with the art world was over. Back to real life. She looked out at the inky black view, letting her eyes blur and the shapes change. *I should be happier*, came the thought again, and then, the next question, *What would it take?*

CHAPTER EIGHT

Blake called an Uber to get back to the apartment Steve had found for her. Neither Steve nor Blake knew Boston very well, but he knew her well enough to put her in a small one-bedroom in Inman Square. Someone must have tipped him off that it would have enough of a mix of bars and used bookstores to get Blake through her stay. It felt a little like Brooklyn—in a small town, self-conscious, adolescent way—but still, she was grateful to be in some semblance of home.

That night, however, her little furnished apartment felt like a prison. She wanted to get out, but she didn't know where to go. She wasn't looking for company, and God knows where she'd find any if she was. Liza must have known this was a dry town in more ways than one. *No*, Blake needed something different than a retro cocktail in a dark, purposefully hard-to-find bar. The show was coming along, but the pressure was mounting. She couldn't be distracted by anything, especially not by the thoughts of Jenny that were clouding her mind. The way she had gazed up at the light in the Hockney room. The way she had placed her coat on the stool. The brief touch of her fingers. She needed to do what she always did to recenter herself.

She fumbled in her duffel bag and pulled out the plain, unlined notebook covered in brown paper and six pencils, bound together in the piece of fabric that she'd ripped from the arm of her father's favorite green chair when they had cleaned out his apartment.

She kept on her coat, switched her mittens for fingerless gloves, and walked down the stairs to the street. She thought she'd seen a bus stop a few blocks from her apartment, but she couldn't remember where. No matter. She'd walk until she found one. Sure enough, a huddle of cold people, their breath making a collective little cloud into the street, stood a few blocks down, outside an Indian restaurant. She waited with them, her fingers itching, hoping that wherever it took her, at least the bus was on a long route.

Inside, the windows steamed. She got a seat in a side-facing seat by the door. Perfect. She opened her book, locked her eyes on the profile of the man in front of her, to the right, an angular-looking man with an unkempt head of straggly hair and a waxed mustache. Complicated, serpentine lines of the fabric and his skin. Rich textures. Almost immediately, she felt herself relax. The blood rushed to her fingers so that she was all fingers and eyes—no head, no brain, no body, no heart—just eyes and fingers, as if she could melt into the bus completely and in splendid anonymity ride and look and look and ride. After a few moments it wasn't even her eyes that were doing the seeing; it was her fingertips instead. They had eyes on them, not a concrete kind, not like there were pupils on the tips of her fingers, but like her skin itself could see.

The man with the mustache. The woman holding a dog in a carrier. The three teenage boys, with languid bodies draping over the seats, laughing. Everyone bundled up, but then sweating on the bus. She drew the thick air, she drew the smells, the sharp burning rubber when the bus put on its brakes. She drew the yellow light coming in from outside and the white light from inside and the blue glow of people's smartphones on their faces, reflecting in their glasses.

Everyone got off the bus in Porter, so she did too, riding down the long escalator into the cavern below, the slush on the stairs sparkling a little. Fewer people on the subway than the bus, but just as alive.

Blake went to Braintree and back again. She switched at Downtown Crossing into the Green Line as everyone seemed to be doing and rode the screeching trolley until it popped out from underground. It was snowing again, and Blake drew that, too, the fogged-up trolley car with the bleak lights of the city trying to peek through. The way the cloud cover seemed to keep the light inside the dome of the city, so everything was a little brighter. She liked that. She liked that she could sense the sky.

She kept drawing. Across from her were sitting two women, a couple, it seemed. The one with the slightly tangled hair was pregnant, conspicuously cupping her belly, as if she wanted everyone on the train to comment on it. Blake sketched the shapes their bodies made, the semicircles where their arms were woven together, the fake fur collar of the pregnant one's jacket, the rectangle made by the harsh bangs of her partner, and the long earrings falling to her shoulders, cutting the space. "She seemed so sad," the pregnant one was saying.

Blake drew. She caught the bridges of their noses, the slightly close together eyes. Every bit of them both.

They got off the train at Mass Ave, and Blake kept riding, flipping to the next page of her book as they departed, hearing the familiar buzz in her head, the one that meant she was safe, home within herself, and it didn't matter where she was or what anyone thought of her.

CHAPTER NINE

For the rest of the week, Jenny's life went back to normal. Michael made her recalculate damages in all of the expert reports again. One of the reports, by a hack named Chris Van Croughton, was nonsense, the assumptions insupportable. Any academic with integrity wouldn't have stood by them. Jenny had said as much to Michael, gently, but he and Van Croughton were old friends from UPenn, and Michael didn't seem to care if he was a hack. Jenny had to correct the calculations and somehow cobble together an argument as to why the methods were sound. The memory of Blake and the bright artificial sunlight hitting her face would have to wait.

Lydia found her in the office on Thursday morning. Lydia was barefoot, as usual. She was so comfortable at work, so goddamned happy, that she took off her shoes as if she were in her living room. "Please tell me you went home last night."

Jenny nodded. "For a little while."

"You're not even prepping for trial. You're in discovery. What is his deal?"

"He has me basically rewriting all the expert analyses."

"Why?"

"Well, he's got a point. Our expert had to make some pretty out-there assumptions about how much the share prices actually would have gone up without the—um—incident—"

"Fraud. I get it. So?"

Jenny turned her screen around to face Lydia, the Excel spreadsheet was already in column "TJ." "See," Jenny said, "I've been running new macros all morning—"

Lydia put her fingers in her ears. "La-la-la. I don't know what you are talking about." She leaned into the computer screen. "This is why you do securities fraud, and I do trademark disputes. I cannot handle this math. Nice spreadsheet. Really impressive. Some might even say sexy."

Jenny laughed, feeling unaccountably relaxed. It had been an odd week, starting with the phone call from Davis. She was glad things were back to normal.

Michael showed up to upend them again, darkening the doorway to her office. Lydia smiled and smacked her gum. "Hi, Mike," she said, allowed such nonchalance because they were not in the same department and would never work together. She slinked by him and out Jenny's door, but stayed behind Michael in the hallway, so when Jenny looked at him, she could see Lydia behind him, making crude gestures with her hands.

Michael stuck his thumbs in his belt loops and leaned on the doorjamb. Lydia blew air into one cheek and rolled her eyes.

"I need you to come to the opening reception at the Albie tomorrow night," Michael said, as if he wasn't inviting her to a party, but instead telling her she had to fly to Newark and take two depositions first thing tomorrow.

"Excuse me?" Jenny tried not to look too surprised, but it was tough.

"The museum is having a gala in connection with opening the Blake Harrison show. The director sent me tickets. There will be clients there. I cannot have an empty table. I need you to come."

Jenny jumped a little at the mention of Blake's name. She had the quick, strange thought that Michael shouldn't be able to say it. Not the whole thing. It sounded wrong, somehow, coming from him.

Behind Michael, Lydia made a huge surprise face and started gyrating while miming sniffing and tasting wine pretentiously. Jenny wanted to laugh but stopped herself.

She did not want to give Michael the satisfaction of knowing that he was inviting her to an event she wanted to attend. She couldn't quite account for it. It wasn't like her to be gallivanting about on weeknights. She didn't relish the idea of having to sit with Michael the length of some benefit meal. On the upside, she could be there to support Davis. Something else was nagging at her too. She could barely admit it to herself, but she wanted to see the finished show. She wanted to see Blake. See Blake and her art.

So, she said, "I would be happy to attend." Behind him, Lydia started jumping up and down, continuing her gyrations.

"I need you to prepare to meet with both McLaughlin and Beavers next Wednesday afternoon at four," he said. "Which means you have an extremely busy week ahead." He turned to leave, hoisting his chinos up a bit higher on his hips, unattractively unselfconscious, as always. Lydia was right behind him, pretending to be fascinated by the paper clip jar on the secretary's desk.

She swung back into Jenny's office. "This is intense. It's black-tie. What are you going to wear?"

"I don't know. Are you serious? Black-tie?"

"Yes, those things always are. Let's go shopping."

"I can't. You heard him. I have so much to do."

"You work too much."

"You do too."

"Not like you. Call me when you are done with the reports. I don't care how late. We're buying you a dress tonight."

Neiman Marcus was still open at ten. Lydia had been texting Jenny pictures of dresses for the last half hour, each with a varying degree of formality.

Jenny just wrote back *Y, N, Y, N, N.* The "Y"s were sitting in a dressing room when she got there. They looked stranger in person. She wasn't used to dresses. She wore suits. Skirt suits, sure, but there was nothing that made her feel more powerful and more safe than a crisply laundered oxford. None of these dresses looked remotely like an oxford. They were candy-colored and flowing with straps of different sizes. They were much, much brighter in person. They would not do.

"Can't I wear a suit?"

"No!" Lydia said as if she had suggested wearing pajamas.

"I'm a lawyer. I read once, when you're at a party of fashionable people, don't try to dress fashionably. Just wear black."

"You can wear a black dress, just not any black dress. Here. Try one of these."

Lydia opened up the dressing room door next to the one they'd been looking at, revealing a rack of a dozen black floor-length gowns. "One of these will work," she said. Jenny let her hands flip through the fabric of each. She took a deep breath, determined to try them all on, if only to thank her friend for being so thoughtful. The candy-colored gowns had been a ruse. "You were never going to make me try on the orange ones?"

"No," Lydia said, guiding her into the room.

They had tried on three, each of which Jenny deemed too revealing. "I cannot sit next to Michael and eat dinner with my cleavage showing. That's an absolute no."

Lydia handed her the next candidate, a dress with a high collar that was shiny, but not too shiny. It looked like a tuxedo version of a gown.

Lydia stood outside the door as Jenny unzipped the dress to step into it. "So, Blake herself will be in attendance, I take it?"

Jenny swallowed, hard. She was relieved that Lydia couldn't see her. In the dressing room mirror, she could see her cheeks had gotten pink.

"I guess," was her lame reply.

"I wonder if she'll bring a date." Jenny's cheeks were still red. The dress was on, but she didn't want Lydia to see her face and the strange reaction she was having to even the most casual mention of Blake. She didn't reply. Lydia continued, her voice a little softer from outside the door, "Did you know she's gay?"

"Um," was all Jenny said, reeling. Yes, she knew. She knew it the first moment she saw her, sure, and she'd Googled it, for God's sake.

"You did! You can tell? God, I didn't know. Anyway, she's a huge player. My friend goes to RISD and critiques art and has some insider art world stuff, it's like *Life & Style*, but pretentious, and she kind of alluded to it, but the subtext was clear. Okay now, come on, let me see."

Before Jenny could let her body react to the idea of Blake as a player—which, again, she could tell, couldn't she, watching Liza and Blake all over each other, hearing Blake's husky voice—Lydia had stepped into the dressing room to assess Jenny's outfit.

"Oh my God," Lydia said, her voice much quieter, serious. She stood behind Jenny, zipped it up, and stepped back as Jenny adjusted the fabric.

"Perfect," Lydia said. Jenny didn't bother saying "You think so?" or anything remotely self-deprecating. Because it was perfect. Modest, with long sleeves, but with a deep V-neck flanked by a tuxedo collar. The gown was form fitting, but the fabric was thick and structured, so there was nothing out of place. She looked smooth and feminine and young, but exquisitely powerful. She could feel it. The glimpse of herself in the mirror made her shoulders shoot back, improving her posture, darting her breasts out in front, making her chin reach up, so it looked like she was ready to make a speech.

"Incredible, yeah," she said, feeling like she was looking at someone else in the mirror. Or not someone else, really, but the best version of herself. "Thanks, Lydia."

"You are welcome. I'm jealous, actually. You're going to see the whole show before anyone."

"I already saw the Hockney room," Jenny said.

"When?" Lydia's question came out like a squeal. Jenny felt happy. A few days ago, Lydia was accusing her of never getting out of the house or the office. How quickly she'd turned things around.

"The other day when I went to return the drill bit."

"And?"

"And Blake turned on the lights and showed me the Hockney room."

"What was it like?"

"Sunshine."

"Wow, what a nuanced review."

"Don't tease. You asked me. It's the right word. The light feels almost hot, but it's blue and cold and intense, like marble. At the same time, it felt like bright, midday sunshine on your face. It was actually..." Jenny trailed off and sighed. Might as well tell the truth. "Amazing."

"So you showed up and she gave you a tour?"

"Kind of." Jenny's heart was beating fast. She felt like she wanted to prove something to Lydia, that she was moving out of her comfort zone. That she wasn't the bore Lydia had accused her of being. And she liked talking about Blake. God, she liked thinking about Blake. It was hard to admit it, but once she did, all she wanted to do was talk about her. Tell Lydia everything. Even though there was nothing to tell.

"Still think she's a diva?"

"Maybe," said Jenny. "Or maybe she's simply exacting."

"Sounds like someone else I know," Lydia said, looking at Jenny through her reflection in the mirror, still standing side by side. She smiled, something clear and mischievous. She let her eyes rake over Jenny's curves and laughed.

"Whatever you are getting at, let it go. She's got some girlfriend from New York," Jenny said into the mirror.

"That girlfriend won't be in this dress tomorrow night, will she?"

"I'm not going after Blake Harrison," Jenny said.

"That's fine," Lydia said, arranging Jenny's hair in gentle waves down her shoulders. "She'll come after you."

CHAPTER TEN

Blake sat in the handicapped stall of the Albie's basement bathroom, trying to breathe deeply. It was opening night. She was wearing a white silk shift, vintage, with straps made of hair. A nod to her Biennial victory. But she didn't feel like she could savor anything. She was nervous; the nervousness felt like a whole other person living inside of her. This was supposed to be another grand night. The room exhibit, her secret pride and passion for years, finally coming to fruition. More notoriety meant more money. More money meant more freedom. More freedom meant more art. She was on the cusp of real success, and it was even more than the cusp; she was entering into a very elite, lucky world where institutions wanted to pay her to make art. Individuals wanted to collect her art. Her art was making money. It was the pipe dream of every artist, and it was real.

But she was hiding in the bathroom. Nights like this did not come easy. She knew how to do lots of things—or at least, a few very important things. She knew how to work alone in her studio all hours of the night, thinking, reframing, creating, living and breathing her art. When that got to be too much, she knew how to flirt with women. She also knew how to make delicious oat pancakes. A perfect cup of coffee. What else? There must be something else.

She did not know how to schmooze with donors. Some of her buyers were here tonight, along with some former grad school classmates. The head of the Boston Arts Commission. And a lot of rich people.

So many rich people.

She looked in her bag, took out her bright red lipstick, and, without looking, put it on expertly. She had thought about dying her hair blue, to stand out, to say, "See, kids, I'm still a punk rocker inside," but she didn't. She kept her buzz cut its natural brown color, the dark, almost black shade she inherited from her mother. Mama would laugh and say, half dismissively and half admiringly, "my little chameleon" whenever she did something new to her hair, including the wigs she sported for years. Blake was used to pretending. She could pass for straight, though she didn't have much interest in that anymore. Oh, and she could pass for a man. It had been a while, but she'd done it. Bound breasts and a baseball cap. What fun. Could she pass for unflappable?

She heard a dull knock on the stall door. "Blake, honey?" Steve's voice. "You ready? It's still cocktail hour, but they want to do the director's welcome, and you've got to stand and smile. You know the drill."

"Yep," Blake said, trying to sound upbeat. "Gotcha. Then what happens?"

"Then they go upstairs to the installation, and when they come back, dinner."

"Do I have to talk in the gallery?"

"No."

Blake sighed, relief coursing through her. Steve would have warned her earlier if he'd expected her to speak, but still the confirmation was appreciated. She could meet and greet and listen to the patrons comment on the art and go home unscathed. She could do this. She'd be a good sport.

She pushed open the stall, and when Steve saw her he audibly gasped. "Amazing dress," was all he choked out as he rubbed his slow-growing reddish beard in seeming introspection. Blake savored the effect she was having on him for a moment. Catching herself in the bathroom mirror behind him, she had to agree. The white silk had a shine to it, and it picked up and reflected the light, even dazzling under the tinny basement fluorescents. She'd had it tailored so even though it was a relatively simple sheath, it fit her perfectly, giving the dress the structure of her own subtle curves. Even though it was winter, her nose and cheeks were adorned with freckles, and her skin looked bright against the fabric. The straps, which were woven like rope, made her look like a Greek statue come alive.

She turned away from the mirror. The most important thing, she reminded herself, was that the show was finished and people would like it. She linked her arm with Steve's. He muttered as they walked up the marble steps into the main gallery, "Really exquisite."

The small but stately atrium of the museum was decorated mainly with light. Blake had suggested this, and Davis had run with it, to great effect. The marble walls looked like they were adorned with curtains, but it was the rich shine of spotlights Davis had installed in the ceiling. The colors were changing very slowly, but Blake could sense the changes, without even looking, as the tone of the whole room shifted depending on what color filter was being rotated in. The red made everyone more talkative, and then slowly, very slowly, they were enveloped in a quieter blue. Instead of flowers on the tables, there were LED lights attached to wires, sitting in metal vases, illuminating the space around them with what looked like little bubbles. It looked like the chairs were floating off the ground, because there were warm white lights attached to the bottom of the seats.

Steve grabbed two champagne flutes from a passing tray and handed one to Blake.

"Monastic, remember?" she said, putting the glass down at the nearest table and signaling for water instead.

"Excellent," he said, and Blake wondered if it had been a test. But he seemed disappointed to have to toast alone, holding his lone drink up to Blake, quietly saying, "Cheers."

"Indeed!" a voice behind them piped in. "Ms. Harrison, I trust everything is to your liking?" It was Davis, shaking slightly, as usual a little nervous in her presence.

"It looks magnificent, Davis, yes."

"Magnificent?" His eyes grew wide. "Wow, thank you."

"Truly," she said.

Blake's heels were making her tower over Davis, so she was looking down at him a bit. Davis looked up at her, all starstruck nerves. Then he seemed to notice his eye contact was boring too deep a hole in her face, so he looked down and mumbled, "Great dress."

She thumbed one of the shoulder straps of the dress and whispered, "This is some of the hair from the Biennial piece." Davis looked up at her and then at the strap. She could tell he wanted to touch it, but she didn't offer. He took a deep breath, seeming to collect himself. "Well, that's just genius. Playful and irreverent but also pulled off in a classy way. Not self-conscious, but self-referential. Wow!"

"Thank you," Blake said, pleased that she was able to let Davis in on a little secret, and even a little flattered by his approval. She hadn't quite expected what an artist he'd turn out to be, transforming the space so completely. She noticed that another spotlight had begun rotating on the ceiling, making the innards of the dome look like they were a thick green velvet curtain.

Steve tugged on her forearm. "Come on. There are people you need to meet."

Forcing herself to be satisfied with seltzer and lime, Blake made the rounds. First up was the director of the museum, Walter Smith. He was known for favoring the art of dead white men and acting nearly like one himself. She was surprised that he had welcomed her show at all. Now he was gazing at her warmly. His thick brown mustache made her think of some of her friends' fathers from childhood.

"I took a peek at the show. Congratulations. You've done us proud." Blake smiled. A woman appeared at Walter's side and grabbed Blake's hand before he could introduce her.

"I've been telling Walter how excited I am to meet you. I don't always come to these openings, Christ Almighty, they can be so bloody boring. But I said, I have to support this artist because she makes phalluses out of HAIR."

Walter smiled, a bit sheepishly, but with clear adoration. "This is my wife, Amy," he said, and Amy gave a small curtsey. She was short, with a massive head of graying curls. Her accent was British and bouncy. She inhabited her body like she would rather be dancing.

She kept shaking Blake's hand, and Walter stepped back, apparently used to being upstaged. "When I saw it at the Whitney, I stood there looking at it and my throat just contracted in horror. Literally. I wanted to throw up. I gagged," Amy said.

Blake laughed, loving the frankness and the irreverence.

"Now this," Amy said, "this reverent, beautiful show. It's just gorgeous. I went upstairs earlier. You go from gags to beauty."

"I've been criticized for that, you know," Blake said, relieved that she felt like she was talking to a friend and not one of the uptight glitterati.

"That's, if you don't mind my saying so, utter shit. What, they want the same thing from you over and over? It's all visceral. It's all part of this delivery of the senses. Oh, if I have to look at one more sodding Rembrandt—"

"He can be visceral too," Blake said.

"Oh yes, I like the paint. The problem is that it's all a little square. Like Walter, bless him, but you see what I mean. We've moved on. I keep telling him this. Why confine ourselves to little squares? Isn't that what all these art movements have been for? That's the revolution! In with the new, new, new!" She opened her mouth wide and laughed loudly, it was almost a cackle, and then, swallowing the sound quickly, cocked her head and asked, "So, who else do you need to meet besides my husband and me? I know most everyone here."

It was Amy who escorted Blake around the room. Blake tried to cloak herself in Amy's confidence, meeting the deputy mayor, the heads of two area colleges, and a few art professors. Amy took her over to a table of collectors. Blake took a deep breath, telling herself that her art spoke for itself. All they wanted was a face with the name. She didn't have to say or do anything she didn't believe.

When she walked up to the table, she noticed a couple she knew from New York and felt slightly more comfortable. But the rest were new to her and looked rich in a different way than New Yorkers. In New York, the men, even if they were on the other side of sixty, were still in tight pants and soft cashmere sweaters, sometimes with chains from pocket watches, and with bright pink argyle socks. The women were in tight pants, cage wedges, and tunics, all black and elegant lines. Here, the men were in tuxedos and they wore their money on their wrists and on their feet, not ostentatiously but not hiding anything either. The women here were similarly anachronistic, it seemed to Blake—one in a yellow Chanel suit, matching pumps, matching manicure.

"Truly remarkable," Yellow Chanel Suit said. "We're thrilled to be here to witness the debut."

"Tonight is about supporting the museum, of course," said a man next to her in a gray Armani, "but it's also about supporting you. I know you have representation, but I want you to know if you ever need anything, call me personally." He slid a card across the table. Blake held it, not sure where to put it. She fumbled for a moment, realizing she was without pockets, without a clutch, and she wasn't about to stick the man's card in her bra.

"I'll take that," said Amy, and Blake smiled, feeling rescued by her new apparent friend.

"Do you have a personal favorite?" Yellow Chanel asked. It was a question Blake usually didn't answer, but for some reason she was starting to feel more comfortable and more talkative than she usually did. Something about the lights or something about Amy next to her. "I like what the Hockney room does to people," she said. "I was in there—I saw—a person who claims not to understand art at all—she had to take her jacket off because of the light." The collectors were looking at her. Blake felt herself choking on her words a little, growing flustered again, her mind on Jenny. "I mean—"

"It certainly affects people. I'm partial to the Vermeer room, myself," said Armani. "There is a reverent quality to it. Chapel-like. The light is silence."

The table nodded, and silence overtook the whole rotunda for a moment. Everyone paused, not realizing how loud the music had been. Walter's baritone came through the speaker system. "Please join us upstairs in the gallery." The cacophonous sound of scraping chairs and setting down of glasses overtook the room, and a wave of bodies then overtook the main stairs to the rooms.

Blake stepped aside, nodding for Amy to go ahead, wanting to be last one into the gallery so that she could sneak in just in time for her introduction. Her stomach flipped in abject terror. As well as she knew the rooms had turned out, she could not overcome the nerves from bearing witness to so many people experiencing them. She had been heartened when Jenny had basked in the light of the blue room, but this was different. There would be so many people at once, people who would be making decisions about whether or not to invest in her in the future. Someone from the MacArthur Foundation was reportedly at the gala, too. Blake took a deep breath, trying to compose herself. *They'll like it*, she told herself. *They'll reach out for the walls, the air, just like Jenny. They'll feel the light. They'll push their faces toward the light.* She let herself remember, a few days ago, standing with Jenny in the gallery before Liza interrupted them. She was afraid to dissect it too much, afraid to find out what it was, but something had passed between them. Something sudden and slight. The thought of it made her feel buoyed, just a little. Catching herself in the memory, she admonished herself for her lack of focus. Tonight was about the rooms. Not memories of a certain woman inside of them.

Hearing the last of the rush of feet up the marble staircase, she opened her eyes. There, walking quickly up the stairs of the rotunda toward the installation, the reverse direction of Cinderella, was Jenny herself. It was as if Blake had conjured her up. She was wearing a gorgeous, hip-hugging black gown. Blake couldn't see her face, but she knew her figure somehow from behind, amazed that in just a few meetings Jenny's gait, her comportment, had become so familiar. She let herself look, for a moment, at the gorgeous hourglass figure ascending the stairs. Those Brooks Brothers suits had nothing on this dress. Jenny looked like a queen.

Clunky footsteps sounded from across the rotunda, and Blake slid herself behind a pillar, not wanting to be caught watching even more than she didn't want to catch herself thinking. A voice yelled, "Jenny!" and Jenny turned quickly around. Her hair swung, softly landing in perfect waves around her shoulders. The dress hugged her front curves just as well as her back. Her chest was set off with a gorgeous tuxedo collar and the lines of the dress somehow seemed to travel up her body to her bright face and intelligent, glowing eyes. Blake almost sighed, daring to wonder for a moment that maybe what had passed between them was real interest, as she'd hoped. But any daydream was interrupted by a loud, low, but almost screeching male voice. "Jenny!" the voice said again, and a man with a mop of blond hair and a perfectly fitted black suit was galloping toward Jenny. Blake watched as he held up to Jenny a shiny black clutch and said, "Here you are" with a grin. The blond touched Jenny's palm with the tip of his fingers as he handed her the clutch. Taking the stairs, too, but a few steps behind her, the man, undetected, let his eyes travel up her body, apparently savoring the back view of Jenny just as Blake had done. Oh goodness, had she ogled her so monstrously, too?

Then he did something that made Blake's skin go cold. He placed his hand on the small of Jenny's back and let his palm rest there, somewhere between jealous and tender.

So that was him. The banker Blake had imagined when they first met. The asshole who she imagined would propose on Valentine's Day and who checked his stock portfolio on his phone after sex.

Blake wanted to hit something, and she wasn't even sure exactly why. Had she really been so off? Why did she care? Jenny didn't even like her. Why was this making her so upset? She told herself to breathe. In and out. There was no need to be fixated on some uptight straight girl. She had work to do. How dare she let her mind wander so thoroughly. She made her way to the staircase, poised to make her own entrance. Jenny could have her blond stud. Blake had her art.

CHAPTER ELEVEN

Jenny had arrived at the gala feeling hopeful, glad she had gone shopping with Lydia for the dress, excited for what the night would bring. It was true. She didn't get out much. This was another step in the right direction. But oh, how quickly promise could turn to disaster.

First, she caught Michael in the crowd, wearing an ill-fitting tux. He was standing next to his wife, engaged in a different conversation with a group standing off to the side. Jenny had met the wife, Mia, once, long ago, at a long, boring firm dinner at a mediocre restaurant with very heavy utensils, and Mia had seemed suspicious of her, like she wanted to know who was going on so many business trips with her husband. If only she knew that Jenny had pleaded with her secretary to always book their airplane seats several rows apart.

Mia was wearing a long purple sack of a dress that hung on her as if she were an under-stuffed scarecrow. Her eyebrows were drawn so thick they looked like bolded punctuation marks. She looked like she was pouting about something, but Jenny remembered that she wore the same expression the last time she met, so it seemed to be her default. Mia waved at her, saying not, "Hello," but, "Wait here." Turning back, she said as an accusation, rather than a compliment, "You look pretty." Jenny watched as Mia went to the line for the bar and started talking to a preternaturally handsome man, about Jenny's age, with a head of blond hair that looked like a plastic Lego cap. Mia and the man looked over at Jenny at the same time, the man smiled, and the two of them walked toward her. The blond handed her a glass of wine. They shook hands. His hands were slimy from the condensation of the drinks. "And you are?" Jenny said.

Mia laughed overenthusiastically, and said, "Oh, Jenny, don't be coy. I know Michael prepared you. This is my dear nephew Brandon. We are so excited for you to get to know one another tonight."

Brandon smiled. His teeth, predictably, were blindingly white. Jenny had several concurrent thoughts. The overarching one was, "God help me. Get me out of here." Then she thought of Lydia and Davis, who had both recently told Jenny that she was acting like a closet case. Jenny had scoffed, but they were apparently right. Next, she felt angry. The presumption! The impropriety! The sheer inconsiderate blindsightedness of Michael! What boss in his right mind thinks it in any way appropriate to set a subordinate up with his nephew? My goodness, if she ever told HR at the firm…well, what? They'd laugh. No harm done, they'd think. Then, she had the strange, unbidden feeling of being flattered. She thought Michael hated her, but he apparently thought she was good enough for this "dear" nephew. Or was Mia, silly, sour Mia, so threatened by Jenny that she had arranged this? The final thought was, as much as she wanted to push it away, of Blake. Blake wouldn't be sitting at her table. She would be otherwise engaged. This was her big gala. But somehow, in the back of her mind, to have to be talking to this Brandon character, instead of Blake, was an especially crushing disappointment.

Jenny took a deep breath, trying to tame all the thoughts in her head, all the anger. "Pleased to meet you," was all she said. No recrimination for Michael, who was standing a few feet away from her and who had still not said hello. Three hours. She could give it three hours.

"Have you been to this museum before?" Brandon asked.

Jenny tried not to let her face look as annoyed as she felt. "Yes, hundreds of times. I do pro bono work for them, too. I take it you haven't been?"

"Nope."

"New to Boston?"

"Been here about ten years. Just very busy. Art's not really my thing."

"So you're here…" Jenny tried to contain her rage.

"Same reason you are. Uncle Mike asks you to do something, you do it, right?" Brandon smiled, as if this was fine, fun, enjoyable. She felt a roiling in her stomach. She didn't say yes or nod, but she couldn't deny it, either. She did do whatever he said. The thought made her sick.

Jenny swigged the wine. At least the wine was good. She fought the urge to check her watch. Cocktail hour, salad, main, dessert, done. She could do this.

Michael appeared behind them, clasping each of their shoulders. "Jenny, Brandon is an excellent golfer!"

"Oh, you play?" asked Brandon, looking relieved to have some common ground.

"No," Jenny answered.

"She's got a head for numbers, though," said Michael, as if the two were related.

Another swig of wine. "That I do," Jenny said, wanting to roll her eyes, but knowing no one would be there to catch them.

They engaged in an interminable session of "do you know?" from college and graduate school until, finally, the director of the museum called them all upstairs to the gallery. Jenny sped off rather quickly, wanting to separate from Brandon at least for a little while. She ended up in the back of the crowd, trudged up the stairs, and turned when she heard Brandon coming. Her clutch. In her hurry to escape him, she'd forgotten her clutch. He handed it up to her. And as they walked up the stairs, he put his hand on the small of her back. *Get that fucking hand off my back*, she thought, still walking up the stairs but wanting to run in the opposite direction. It was too much. She breathed in, involuntarily girding herself against his touch. It wasn't threatening, but it was proprietary and uninvited, which was enough to make her mad. But she had to keep that smile plastered on, because Michael was waiting for them. Just a few more hours, and she could go home, rip off this stupid dress, and sit, as she should have been doing, in front of her laptop watching YouTube videos with a glass of red wine.

She would get through the gallery talk and the salad course, to smooth things over with Michael, and that was it. She'd excuse herself before the mains, before dessert, before any more mingling. She would go home and make it very clear to Brandon—somehow, politely—that she never intended to see him again. She shifted over on the stairs, and his hand didn't follow. Well, that was something. They filed into the back of the gallery. Davis was already talking.

"Blake Harrison is quickly establishing herself as one of the most promising artists of her generation. Her pieces are in conversation with the masters, but wholly her own. She combines immense technical skill with a sensitivity to emotion. Her oeuvre to date—"

Brandon leaned in and whispered in Jenny's ear, "What technical skill?"

Jenny ground her teeth and said nothing, straining to hear the rest of Davis's talk.

Michael appeared on her other side, so she was flanked by the two of them, nephew and uncle. She clamped her arms across her chest. Michael had apparently heard Brandon's whisper. "I agree. I don't see how hanging a few lights is technical skill. It used to be that art was a real vocation. Look at Michelangelo. He didn't have a crew or a team. He didn't have machines. This, I don't even know what to call it. It's just blank walls and we're supposed to be impressed."

Jenny recognized the sentiment. She had it herself, hadn't she? She revered the old masters and thought Blake's tower of hair was distasteful and a waste. Before she met her, before she saw the rooms, she had dismissed Blake as a diva. The rooms were something different, though. They were thoughtful, sensitive, alive. And the effect they produced—Jenny could still feel Hockney's sunshine—came from real technical skill, of course. How else could Blake manage to bring that dream to fruition? She had made a whole series of new worlds.

Jenny didn't have it in her to say that to Michael and Brandon, though. She couldn't get into a debate about Blake's art standing there in the gallery. It didn't matter anyway. She just needed to get this night over with. So she stood, frozen between them.

"It's true," said Brandon. His voice was getting a bit louder. Jenny shifted uncomfortably, wanting to escape them, but the gallery was crowded. They were packed in. "Art is now all about concept. Not skill. You have this girl—"

Suddenly, something caught on the bottom of Jenny's dress, making her lose her balance a little. Brandon steadied her with his hand on an elbow, and Jenny twisted around to see what had happened. When she turned around, she saw Blake, who was trying frantically to extract her stiletto heel from the hem of Jenny's dress while at the same time turning to exit the gallery. Blake looked up at her, yanked her shoe, which ripped Jenny's dress at the hem, and something passed between them in an instant. Blake's eyes looked dark and angry, and Jenny realized that Blake had heard what Michael and Brandon had said. Jenny opened her mouth—to say what exactly?—but Blake was already turned and walking through the doorway, limping a little, like Cinderella, with her shoe in hand.

Jenny slumped, wanting to lean on something, feeling the muscles in her legs weaken. Brandon stood by limply, oblivious to what had happened, besides registering somehow that someone—he apparently didn't realize it had been Blake— had bumped into her. "Your dress okay?" he asked. Jenny just nodded. As if that mattered.

A few moments later, Jenny could hear, despite the loud thrumming of embarrassment in her ears, Davis say, "Please, everyone give Blake Harrison a hand," and Blake appeared beside him, coming through the door at the front of the gallery, standing in front of everyone in her white silk, looking radiant, with a well-considered, closed-mouth smile on her face. She looked proud and strong and fierce and, above all, supremely intelligent, surveying the crowd, saying nothing, as if to affirm that art would speak for itself. But Jenny could see that the confidence was a veneer. Masking something. Nervousness? Could it be that behind that expression the indomitable Blake Harrison was scared of the crowd? They were basking in her promise, her newfound fame. But Jenny thought back to when they had first met—when Jenny had called her, carelessly, thoughtlessly, a diva, and Blake towered over her at the top of the stairwell, arms crossed. There was something that looked like it might crack beneath the surface. A bit of hurt right underneath the fearlessness. Jenny, stupid Jenny, had done it again. She let the commentary of the buffoons flanking her go unchallenged. She hurt Blake.

When the talk was over, Jenny peeled quickly away from the crowd, wanting to run away, looking for the back staircase down. She was too embarrassed to bump into Blake again—too ashamed to apologize. As if Blake would care if she apologized. She was just a lawyer who hadn't understood, and now here she was, having agreed to come with Michael to the opening, caught again in his agenda, his needs, his time.

She resolved to go back to the table, feign some kind of stomach illness in short order, and escape. But on the second landing, she noticed the door to the gallery with the Vermeer was slightly ajar. She had visited that gallery so many times during law school. Whenever she felt the stress bubbling up, she'd come to the museum, sit on the wide bench, and stare at the open door and the orange light streaming through the narrow gap. It made her feel calm, like she was welcome just to be warmed by the light and eventually she could walk through the door of the painting. She needed that sense of calm now. She pushed through to the gallery, relieved that no alarms sounded. She'd never been in the rest of the museum after hours. Some of the lights were still on and the exit signs, but it was very dark. The green rug felt plush beneath her heels. Her dress was swooping a bit behind her as she walked. She gathered it up and sat on the bench in front of the Vermeer, breathing deeply, feeling not like herself. She wondered how in the course of a few days she had begun to feel so off-kilter. Sure, she had a job she hated, no love life to speak of, and no plans to change anything. That had been the case for a long time. Now, she was uncharacteristically unmoored. She concentrated on the slit of light hitting the back of the chair in the painting, the side of the woman's face, her red shawl. She concentrated on her own breath.

Jenny heard quiet footsteps behind her and turned, expecting a security guard to usher her out. Instead, it was Blake, standing with her arms across her chest, a very unwelcome expression on her face. It was almost a smirk, but there was no mirth in it. Blake sat down on the other side of the bench in silence, her back to Jenny. "I find I prefer the Manet in the next room," she said.

Jenny swallowed, hard, not being able to find words. She could feel the heat of Blake's back on her back, somehow, like her body had a force field around it that touched Jenny even when there was space between them. "Blake, I—"

"There you are!" Brandon came bounding into the gallery. "Michael and I have been looking for you. He said you both have to go, the client, um, called some meeting?"

Jenny whipped around, disappointed to see Brandon but glad to be rescued from the conversation she was apparently incapable of having.

"BlueCoast?"

"Sounds right," Brandon said. He put out a hand to her to help her up from the bench. She stood up on her own. He shrugged. Only then did he notice Blake sitting there, looking at them both, with the same pained eyes as before. "Congratulations," he said, having apparently realized who she was, and then, to Jenny, "I didn't know you two knew each other."

"We don't," Blake said, and before Jenny could say anything to contradict her—they did, a little bit, didn't they?—she walked out of the gallery.

Jenny didn't watch her go. Instead, feeling a mix of self-hatred and relief, she turned to Brandon and said, "I have to change first. Tell Michael I'll see him at the office."

CHAPTER TWELVE

What the hell had just happened?

Blake didn't know where to go. She watched Jenny run out of the gallery, as if she were allergic to Blake, into the arms of her dull baboon of a boyfriend, back to work. At this ungodly hour. Jenny was a workaholic robot. Worse, a straight, workaholic robot, in love with the rude Ken doll who called Blake a "girl" and said she had no technical skill.

Blake felt fury rise up in her chest. At first, it was directed at Jenny and then at Jenny's boyfriend with the bathmat hair and then at herself. She should get back down to the gala, back down to the people who cared about her art. She had more work to do tonight, and this was supposed to be her triumph.

Instead, she was glowering in a dark gallery, fixating on Jenny. Something had passed between them in the Hockney room, hadn't it? And on very bench where she was sitting, the silence between them felt heavier, more leaden than it had any cause to. Jenny in that dress—Blake tried to shake the image out of her mind. It was no use. *Think about the donors,* she admonished herself. *The MacArthur. The art, for God's sake.* She had to focus.

Blake tore out of the gallery, trying to gather some of her practiced grace. The upturned chin, slightly narrowed eyes, shoulders back. It worked. When she wandered back into the rotunda, it was like everyone wanted to touch her. The crowd parted, but not enough, so she still had to brush by, greet everyone. She tried to soak in the praise. "Perfect execution." "Visionary." "Just delightful!" Amy found her again, linked their arms, and pulled her out of the crowd. "Let's get you hydrated."

Blake smiled, grateful for the rescue, feeling like she was already on her way out. Not just out of the gala, but out of the city. Back home, away from the cold and the austerity. Back to her studio, her friends, her usual haunts, and her next project. Back to creating.

"Journalists next? We'll get you done so you can at least get dinner," Amy said, guiding her to a small set of tables and cameras that had been set up by the ticket counter. Blake nodded, trying to channel the confidence she knew she needed to project.

"I've got to get back to my husband," said Amy. "I'll find you later. Darren Rosenfeld is over there. Next to him is Amanda somebody who has, apparently, nearly one million Twitter followers. I'd talk to them both, for sure. Need anything after I introduce you?"

Blake shook her head, trying to seem nonchalant, but the nerves were creeping in, making her jittery. She hadn't thought she'd have to do interviews tonight, on top of everything. Her eyes were darting around the room, searching for Steve. Davis. A friendly face. Anyone. She thought, for a moment, that what she needed was connection. She felt so unmoored, she didn't know where to go.

"Just say hi," Amy said. "It's not an interview. You're doing great." She turned to the small press table and said brightly, "Ladies and gentlemen, this is the indomitable Blake Harrison, my new best friend." Blake curtseyed, just as Amy had done earlier. Darren and Amanda laughed and sidled up to her. *Calm,* Blake told herself, as the flames started in her cheeks.

"It's stunning," Darren said, grinning. "How did you come up with the idea?" He was being casual, and it didn't feel like an interview. Maybe Amy was right. Blake told herself to relax. It wasn't a hard question.

"Spencer Finch had a show at the MassMoca years ago," she said, giving Finch credit, as she always did when she told anyone about the rooms. "He made a whole room of candlelight. I loved the idea of using light as its own subject, I studied painting, and I have a reverence for the medium." Darren was looking at her with bright eyes; he seemed entranced. "So, you know how when you see a really truly wonderful painting, you just want to go inside?" she said. Darren nodded enthusiastically. "This is my fulfillment of that fantasy."

He grinned, and Blake relaxed a little. She could do this, even without Steve standing beside her. "Listen," Darren said, "do you want to come on my show later this week? I'll have the network call you. It's local, just a fifteen-minute spot on New England News, but people watch it. Okay?"

Blake's stomach churned at the thought of having to discuss her work on television. But he seemed kind. An appreciator, not a critic. It sounded like public access or something. "Sure," Blake said, trying to head off the feeling of dread.

Amanda introduced herself next. She had a platinum undercut, bleached eyebrows, and a nose ring. "I'm going to post the interview as a helluva long Twitter thread, all right, and then I might put the audio up on my SoundCloud, okay? Boston arts scene, etcetera." Her voice was low. Maybe she was a smoker. She fiddled with the microphone attachment to her cell while Blake waited, leaning against one of the columns near the press area. She became nervous all over again, terror seeping through the veneer of confidence and elation at the show. Why did she have to talk about her art at all? Couldn't people just see it? Be in it?

She noticed an errant thread coming off near the waist of her dress. She picked at it with her short nails, but only made it worse. The thread was like Jenny. The more she saw her, the more she thought about her curves, her collarbone, the more she imagined her fingers gripping her thick hair, the more distracted she got. She was not supposed to be thinking of any of those things. She was supposed to be thinking about what Amanda would ask. The table of directors. The patrons and the educators. *Focus*, she admonished herself.

"Okay, I'm gonna start," Amanda said, holding her iPhone up near Blake's mouth. "So much is about identity now," Amanda said, "that I wonder how you react when someone sees you as a queer artist."

Blake took a deep breath and gave one of her smiles, the kind that she had actually practiced in front of the mirror for occasions like this one. "Well, Amanda, thanks for the opportunity to answer that. I think it would be naive of me to say that my identity doesn't figure into my art. Of course it does. My identity affects how I perceive the world and how people perceive me in it. Sure. At the same time, some of my art is abjectly about identity, and some isn't, and some can go either way."

"Your Biennial piece?"

Blake took another deep breath, thinking about the catalog copy Steve had written for her and the interview answers he'd jotted down for *ArtForum*. She could remember some of the sentences verbatim. "A lot of people saw the tower of hair as being somehow about lesbianism. I understand that. But if a cisgendered heterosexual man had made it, I don't think they would have said so. It might still have been perceived as being about sex, but not queer sex, I'm fairly certain. What I care about is the reaction to my art. That immediate spark. If that is informed by what people know about me—a picture they've seen, something they've read—then so be it. I can't control that. All I can control is what I put out there."

"You've developed a reputation for being quite persnickety."

"Show me an artist who isn't exacting and demanding about their execution and I'll show you an artist who has no hope of success." Blake made a note to thank Steve later for how well he'd worked to prepare her before they left New York.

Amanda tapped the screen of the iPhone and smiled at Blake, signaling the end. She let her shoulders relax a bit. Amanda had gotten her soundbite, and Blake had worked to seem accessible but above the fray at the same time. She would not deign to interpret her art for anyone. That part was a little bit easier, because it was genuinely what she loved about her job. The ability to commune without words. Presenting the art and then just letting the experience happen. It was a privilege, she reminded herself, to be so utterly lacking in control.

Amanda leaned on the narrow column next to Blake. "You want to grab a drink?" she said, in that same low voice, but it was more of a whisper. "I heard the champagne is excellent. Off the record?"

Blake looked her over. She was younger than Blake by several years. She had the kind of grunge look Blake had sported at that age—the early twenties bravado, the very deliberate lack of polish. Amanda smiled, one eyebrow arching up, black eyeliner coming with it.

Blake looked back at her, wondering for a moment what it would feel like to say yes. Sure, she had made her pre-show monastic rule, but tonight it was technically open. So not even her own self-imposed celibacy was stopping her. Nothing was. It would be so easy, and so typical, of her to smile back. Watch the typical effect she had on women take shape. Blake would nod and snake one warm arm around the small of her back, kiss her lightly on the nape of her neck, whisper something like, "I have some beers back at my place," and that would be that. They'd be in some state of undress in Blake's little apartment in no time, and the pressure of the show, the nervousness of the interviews, the wondering what everyone was thinking as they walked through the rooms—it would all be gone.

Amanda was packing up her bag, apparently trying to appear nonchalant waiting for Blake's answer as she coiled up her charger cable. Blake flashed on the memory of Jenny helping build the walls with her sleeves rolled up, and then she fell deeper into memory, reveling in the image of Jenny ascending the stairs and the feeling of heat they had generated when sitting back-to-back.

Maybe she did need a distraction this evening. She looked back over at Amanda, wondering if being tempted—even just a little—by a cocky tweeter signaled the rightful end to her night or just the beginning. Amanda's eyes caught Blake's for a moment, and Blake went on autopilot. She couldn't help it. She blinked, smiled, and ran her hand through her close-cropped hair, glanced away, and she knew Amanda was hers.

Davis interrupted her then, seemingly buoyed by a newfound confidence that the success of the night had brought. "What can I get you?

"Nothing," Blake said, shocked for a moment out of her staring at Amanda.

He nodded, and they stood in companionable silence for a moment. Blake wanted desperately to ask him why Jenny seemed to hate her so much. But she needed to hold it together. Maintain the cool, professional exterior. "Thank you very much for this evening. Can you tell Steve I left?"

Davis looked over at Amanda and back at Blake. "Alone?" he asked.

CHAPTER THIRTEEN

Jenny arrived at the office in her basic black pantsuit and carrying two cans of Red Bull. This would be an all-nighter. The judge had issued a special order scheduling the Daubert hearings for the next week. BlueCoast hadn't seemed concerned, but the CEO was apparently going to visit the office in person tomorrow, and despite all of Jenny's work, they were behind on the outline. They had to finish it tonight. Jenny had had a few glasses of wine. Three? Was it three?

Michael looked her up and down over the top of his bifocals when she walked into the conference room he'd had the night secretaries set up. "That was fast," he said. "Sit down." Jenny opened her laptop. It was only ten. "We'll go through the data, then the outline, and you can do a mock examination of me. The client is going to be here at eight a.m. That's ten hours. Sufficient?"

Jenny nodded. Sure, terrific. Overnight in a conference room with the man who had tried to set her up with his nephew.

She opened up one of the cans of Red Bull and slid it across the table to him. Might as well share.

"Thanks," he said, taking a swig and suppressing a burp. "I hope you didn't have as much wine as I did."

"I may have," she said.

"Sorry to cut your date short."

Jenny grunted, not wanting to engage. Now was not the time. She had been castigating herself over and over on the cab ride home and back to the office. Even Brandon had become one of her victims. If he liked her, she'd hurt him through lies of omission, too. When had she become so silent, so unwilling to stand up for herself? No matter. Now was the time to prepare for the motions. After that, she'd wave the pride flag in Michael's face, tell him it was wrong to set her up like that, and then what? How had she made such a mess of everything so quickly?

Michael cracked his knuckles, sending shivers of disgust down Jenny's spine. "Walk me through the numbers, champ."

"Champ." That was a new one. Must be the wine. She hooked her laptop up to the video screen in the room and called up the spreadsheet.

"Holy mother of God," he said as the Excel spreadsheet columns cascaded across the screen into view.

"It's not as complicated as it looks." Jenny explained it all, trade by trade, stock drop by stock drop. She fetched them Keurig coffee twice, and Michael got up to get the third cup, in an uncharacteristic show of equality, chivalry, or wanting to move his legs. The Red Bull and the coffee had made her jittery, but she still felt sleepy. Jenny yawned, too big to stifle, and Michael laughed. "Well, this is shit, isn't it?"

"No, the calculations are correct—" Jenny said, sitting up straight, ready to lunge at him.

"No, I mean the fact that it's three in the morning and we're here. Look, I need to sleep. I'll see you in four hours. Go home."

Instead of going home, Jenny went back into her office with her laptop, ate a stale granola bar pilfered from Lydia's desk drawer, and stared out the blank, black window. The exhaustion was making her delirious. Why hadn't she challenged Brandon when he'd said Blake had no skill? Called her a girl? What did it matter if Blake could draw in perfect Archimedean perspective? What did it matter if she could render the human figure like Degas? She knew how to make people feel.

Jenny recalled the Hockney room again, the sun soaking her skin. Blake knew how to make her feel. Jenny's head fell back in her office chair, and she sunk into an anxious sleep, staying only right beneath the surface of waking, dreaming that Blake was shouting at her, calling her a coward, and kissing her. Jenny woke up with wet lips and a feeling of profound self-hatred.

Seven in the morning. She threw on makeup in the work bathroom, used a bottle of disposable spray deodorant, brushed her teeth, and printed out the outline for the mock examination and waited in the conference room for Michael. He came in looking refreshed, flanked by George Dawson, the CEO of BlueCoast Bank. She had spoken to him on the phone before, but they'd never met. He didn't smile, but his face softened a bit as they shook hands. She wouldn't have been smiling, either. BlueCoast was on the hook for a lot of money.

"So, Daubert hearings?" He pronounced "Daubert" as if it were French, which made sense, but was, nonetheless, utterly wrong.

"Yes, Daubert," Jenny said, emphasizing the anglicized daw-BERT pronunciation so he'd be corrected without her having to do so explicitly. "Expert admissibility hearings. The plaintiffs moved to exclude our experts based on insupportable assumptions. Essentially, we've claimed there are no damages. They claim there are six billion in damages. So we moved to exclude their experts for the same reasons."

"Why don't the experts themselves argue for the admissibility of their opinions? If the judge is wondering about their assumptions, shouldn't they themselves defend them?"

"There could be a hearing like that, yes. Our job next week is solely to defend our position in the exclusion motions, and the judge can decide how to proceed," Jenny explained.

"Who's the judge?"

"Crystal Morgan."

"She sounds like a stripper, I know," said Michael. George narrowed his eyes a bit at Michael and pursed his lips, seeming to send a signal such quips were not his style. "Go on, Jennifer," he said, consciously looking Jenny in the eye, building a quiet alliance, shutting Michael out with subtle eye contact. Even in her sleep-deprived state, Jenny could tell George didn't like Michael. This would be interesting.

"Excluding expert opinions is a harsh sanction, but she's been known to do it slightly more often than her colleagues."

"So we should be cautious?" George asked.

"Well, the time for that has passed," Jenny said. She glanced over at Michael, whose expression was dark and hard to read. He had told Jenny to take control of prep, but he might not have known how thoroughly she'd do so. He could stop her, though, couldn't he? And he wasn't.

"Explain what you mean, please," George said. He was still a commanding presence in the room, but there was something gentle about the trust he was putting in Jenny.

"We have two expert opinions on damages. One calculates them around seventy million dollars. The other calculates them at zero. They've challenged both opinions, but their challenge of the report at zero is very strong."

"Who's the expert opining zero?"

"Chris Van Croughton," Michael piped up. "Good guy, friend of mine from Wharton."

Jenny smiled, tight-lipped. George caught her expression. "But?" He turned to her. "Jennifer, you look like you have something to say."

"I have to agree with the plaintiffs. I think he uses some baseless assumptions, and I think it will hurt our credibility with the judge. I believe we should acquiesce to the exclusion of his report." Jenny's heart was beating fast, but it felt so good to be saying what she'd been thinking all along. She almost wanted to smile.

Michael's neck became red. "We've already paid him upwards of ninety thousand dollars for the report—"

"Sunk costs," Jenny retorted. George sat back on his chair, hands together on his lap. "Should we have a broader discussion about this?" he asked.

"No," Michael said, glaring at Jenny. "The decision has been made."

Jenny turned, heart beating, feeling reckless and bold and sure all at the same time. She looked directly at Michael. "BlueCoast Bank is the client. Mr. Dawson has the final say."

Michael smiled, a little saliva coming out of his mouth as he did so. He looked deliberately away from Jenny and directly at George. "You'll have to excuse my colleague here," he said. "She was out too late dancing with my nephew."

Jenny felt like she'd been punched in the stomach. He had infantilized her and belittled her all at once, erasing the hours they'd spent that night in the very same room they were in now, stale hours in front of the computer, reviewing the damages estimates that only she understood. She looked at him and the fire of anger burned inside of her. Her own silence about everything felt crushing, and she wanted to scream.

Something else started burning inside of her. The indignation and anger solidified into something strong and small at the pit of her stomach. She was tired of caring what he thought. She knew enough that to be a good lawyer, she had to speak directly to the client. That was her job, wasn't it? Not to be Michael's lapdog, but to represent the interests of BlueCoast Bank. She had taken an oath, and it wasn't to stand idly by while her oaf of a boss made a terrible mistake.

Calling all of her power up through her body and with gritted teeth and a tightly controlled voice, she said, "With all due respect, Chris Van Croughton's report is unsupportable. I have spent hours trying to reconcile his methods and his figures, and frankly, it is impossible. The judge won't respect him, and if she doesn't respect him, she won't respect us. I don't have to point out that if she doesn't respect us, she won't respect BlueCoast Bank."

Michael looked ready to leap out of his seat, but he didn't. He tried to smile, but his dry lips stayed flat. Jenny looked over at George, who was looking down at the table. He wore a mask of professional calm, but Jenny knew he was nervous. He'd have to present their decision to his board.

"So, Jennifer, if we do it your way, then we concede that if we are guilty, we will have to pay at least seventy million?" George asked.

"Yes," Jenny said. "But we have a very good team working on the question of liability."

George took a deep breath and drummed his fingers on the table for a few beats. He turned to Michael. "Tell the judge we're pulling Van Croughton's report, that we've lost confidence in him," he said. "I agree with Jennifer."

Jenny couldn't believe it. She'd won! She'd been dancing around this issue with Michael for months, letting him know that Van Croughton's figures didn't look right, and now, finally, when she decided to say outright what she thought, the client had agreed. She wanted to whoop for joy, but she still had to maintain composure. She and Michael walked George out to the elevator bank. After they each shook his hand goodbye and the doors closed on George, Michael looked down at Jenny, eyes fixed on her. "Don't ever do that to me again."

The lack of expletives and the quiet tone made his comment even more frightening, and Jenny felt like cold water had been poured over her head. How dare she start to celebrate. She should be looking for a new job. She swallowed, hard, and turned to take the stairs three flights up, not wanting to ride in the elevator with Michael. She went straight into Lydia's office and closed the heavy door behind her.

"What happened to you?" Lydia said immediately, and Jenny, the exhaustion finally catching up with her, started to cry.

"Oh my God, you never cry. You never cry in this office. Christ, what did he do?"

"It's what I did," Jenny said, feeling like it had to be someone else's eyes welling up with tears. Lydia was right. She did not cry in the office. She was not supposed to be that cliché.

Lydia handed her a box of tissues. "Tell me what happened between yesterday and today."

"I got to the gala, and Michael brought his nephew, who hated Blake's art, and Blake overheard him say so, and I think she thought I agreed, and I didn't want to walk through the rooms, and then Blake and I sat near each other in the Vermeer gallery, and I had to go, and I called Michael's best friend a hack, and I told the CEO of BlueCoast that we should concede that damages are seventy million if the court finds liability, and Michael is really mad even though the client totally agrees with me, but now my plan better work or else it's all going to be horrible. Everything."

Lydia leaned on the side of her desk and looked down at Jenny. "I heard a lot of 'Blake Harrison' in that little speech," she said.

Jenny sniffled. Lydia opened up a bottle of the water she had stocked in her office fridge and handed it to Jenny. "Hydrate."

Jenny gulped the water down and whispered, "I'm sorry. I'm a mess."

"You're a little bit of a mess," Lydia said. Jenny smiled a little bit through her tears. "First things first. When is the Daubert hearing?"

"A week."

"Okay, so you have time."

"A little."

"The client is happy, but Michael is mad. I have that right?" Jenny nodded.

"That's not bad, Jenny. Look. Hold it together, start preparing, and then tell me what's going on with you, okay?"

Jenny kept nodding.

"You are nodding," Lydia said, looking across at Jenny, smiling a little. "Which means that something is going on."

"No, it's just—I don't know."

"Do you have some kind of crazy crush on Blake Harrison?"

"No!" Jenny barked. "That's not what's going on." Even as she said it, her voice cracked with uncertainty. Was that all this was? It didn't make any sense. She didn't actually like anything about Blake besides that Hockney room, and Blake hated her. No. That wasn't the problem. The problem was she was gallivanting around the museum and at galas when she should have been focusing on work. The thought made another little cry leap out of her throat. What was wrong with her?

As if reading her mind, Lydia patted Jenny's shoulder, and said, "Nothing's wrong with you. We'll figure it out."

CHAPTER FOURTEEN

Blake woke up in Amanda's arms. Well. Not really her arms, but Amanda's body was next to hers in the bed. She looked at her hard, trying to figure out how deep in sleep she was. Light was streaming through the window in bright rectangles, and one was squarely on Amanda's head. The nose-ring was glistening. She couldn't be too far from waking.

Blake put on the T-shirt that was balled up on the nightstand and sat up in bed, still looking at Amanda, who was breathing hard through her nose. Blake poked her shoulder with one finger. She wasn't being tender, but she tried to be gentle. Amanda rolled over and her face changed to waking. One eyeliner-clad eye popped open. She smiled at Blake, but cautiously.

"So I should probably..." Amanda said, her voice raspy from sleep.

"Yeah," Blake said, shrugging, trying to find the sweet spot between disappointed and yes-you-really-need-to-go. Amanda understood. She and Blake apparently had a lot in common. Undemanding, free-floating, casual.

Blake smiled, a little, watching Amanda uncurl herself from the bed. It had been a nice night. Blake noticed a hickey on Amanda's clavicle. She smelled good, just a faint hint of cigarette smoke. Not what Blake liked to smell all the time, but there was something about it on Amanda that worked. She closed her eyes for a moment, remembering how it felt to drink in her soft skin. Well, maybe the night had been a little better than nice.

Amanda knew her place. With a wink at Blake, she put on her clothes and stood in the doorway. "See you 'round," she said. Then, grinning, wide and bold, "I put my number in your phone."

It was only fifteen minutes later that Steve was inside her apartment instead of Amanda. "Another beautiful morning in paradise," he said, handing Blake a paper bag with a steaming-hot doughnut inside. He was early. Steve was usually early, but it wasn't even eight a.m. She rummaged for a robe to throw over her boxers and T-shirt.

"You know how much I love morning meetings," she said and softened a little as she caught the sweet scent from the bag. "What is this?"

"Some yuppy vegan doughnut. You'll like it." She went into the kitchen to make the coffee.

"Yesterday was A-plus," he shouted from the living room. His typical rating. That's what her art always got. Well, one of the early prototypes of the room was just an A-minus, but that was when one of the bulbs kept flickering out.

She sat on the couch across from him, feet up. "Rooms better than the hair?"

"Well, the hair was easier to sell than the rooms, but you're doing well. Having Amy Smith as a fan is a very good thing. She seems to like you."

"She does."

"She approached me about doing a show here in Boston. A private gallery, South End."

Blake's mood lifted a bit. "Good. That's okay with you?"

"I appreciate that she went through me first, yes. She's doesn't have a crush on you, does she?"

"No, no, she's married. She's just a fan."

"Not the tiniest?"

"No," Blake said, getting impatient.

"How can you tell?"

Blake wanted to roll her eyes. "How can you tell, Stevie? Some girl's into you or not?"

"Point taken," he said. Then, looking around the apartment, as if hunting for something, he asked, "Anyone else you want to tell me about?"

Blake sat up straight, wondering what Steve could have possibly heard about Jenny.

"No," she said slowly, trying to seem nonchalant, wanting him to share any intel.

"Well, I did see Amanda leave with you last night, you know."

Blake slumped down, unable to hide her disappointment. He was asking about Amanda. And of course he was. He studied her face for a moment. She felt herself shrink and squirm under his gaze. "You okay?" he finally asked.

"Absolutely." She smiled, trying to brush it off, but her head was clouded with thoughts of Jenny again. Blake didn't fancy herself a straight-chaser, but there she was, sinking into the memory, thinking of Jenny helping put up the walls, thinking of Jenny the first time they met, flushed with shame, but trying to hide it, looking up at her from the bottom of the stairs. She reveled in it for a moment, then tried to shift the spotlight.

"Anyone in your life, Steve?"

He shook his head. Blake knew that early on in their acquaintance, he'd nursed a bit of a crush on her. She was used to that, though, and it had faded as he got to know her. That was usually the way. A spark of attraction, and then a few too many normal conversations where Blake revealed to her admirer that she wasn't some towering, mysterious figure of the art world or any kind of rare, sensuous species, but just a hard-working aesthete.

"I don't know how you do it," Steve said.

"Do what?" Blake had a feeling he was going to ask something personal, but she pretended in her tone to be expecting a question about the art.

"I saw you leave with Amanda. You talked to her for thirty seconds, and then she's going home with you?"

Blake smiled. His tone was both incredulous and full of admiration. She tried to be cute, even though she wasn't feeling cute.

"I have a gift, that's all."

He shook his head and then opened up his nylon messenger bag, pulling out the new catalog and a few postcards and laying them on the table. She touched them reverently, amazed again to see her name on the cover of the catalog and on the back of the cards. Real museum cards. Not cheap reproductions she'd made to advertise her student show. They were thick, almost metallic, and looked like an abstract painting. A Rothko, maybe. She had chosen to focus on two walls, rather than a shot of the whole show, because there wasn't any way to really capture the light or the structure. The cards were a decent memento. She thought of saving quarters as a child and buying cards at the Met. It was retro, maybe, not something Amanda would have cared about, not Tweetable or Instagrammable. To her, though, they were perfect. Real. She could touch them.

Steve watched her look. "Pretty nice, huh?" She nodded, caught in a rush of gratitude and pride.

"Hey," Steve said, "I've got something else I want to ask you about." His voice shook a little, and Blake could tell he was nervous. "We had a weird call from a gallery in D.C. saying they were mounting a room exhibition and wanted some stills of ours. Know anything about that?"

"Rooms?" she asked, not at all following.

"Yes, they said it's like yours, walls and lights and rooms and they were asking about installation and pricing, too."

"That's weird." Blake had no idea what Steve was talking about, but it was making her uneasy. The idea of an installation of rooms wasn't exclusive, of course, and artists borrowed from one another all the time. She had been inspired by Spencer Finch, and she referred to him every chance she got. What did this gallery want with her?

Steve looked at her sternly. "You're not going behind my back, are you?"

"No. Like what? What do you mean?"

"You being represented by someone else?"

"No." Impatient again, she wanted Steve to read her mind. Represented by someone else? That would be insane. He had gotten her the Biennial, he had gotten her the Albie, he was supportive of what Amy wanted to do.

"I have no idea what you're talking about, really." She smiled, wanting to bring a bit of lightness back. But she was wondering, too. *There was one person…no.* She pushed the thought out of her mind. No one could take this from her.

Steve seemed appeased by her smile. "Okay, I'll look into it."

"That is your job, right?" She resisted the urge to tousle his hair. He was like her kid brother sometimes, and other times like an obsequious intern, and sometimes like a gregarious, encouraging aunt, and most rarely—though sometimes most helpfully—a demanding boss.

"I'm giving Amy a call in a bit," Blake said, "and taking a walk in this godforsaken tundra. Anything else I have to do for the show tomorrow?"

Steve shook his head. "Darren's folks have called me a few times. It will be a ten-minute spot to promote the museum." He looked at her with big eyes, knowing that she did not like to do interviews, especially on camera.

"Can we do a mock before?"

He nodded. "If you wish. But you don't need it."

Blake's insides started clenching as she thought about being on television, but she tried to remain cool for Steve's sake. He trusted her to handle these things, even if she wasn't graceful. He knew to change the subject. "They're saying five inches again this afternoon, you know, but it barely registers. These people are…"

"Hearty," Blake said, thinking, without wanting to, of Jenny rolling up the sleeves of her shirt to help build the walls.

"I was going to say insane," Steve said, "for living here. I guess hearty works too." He left a stack of envelopes on the coffee table. "Thank-yous for all the donors from last night."

He had already stamped and addressed them all. Blake's chest welled with gratitude. Steve jostled his keys and leaned in to kiss Blake on the cheek. She fought the impulse to wipe it off; it was a little soggy. But she didn't want to hurt his feelings. Especially not after he'd done all her thank you cards.

"You are a magician," she said.

Steve winked and took two steps down at a time.

Blake sunk into the couch, telling herself to enjoy the next few days. She would continue to forge her connection with Amy, muddle through a television interview, and finally, blessedly, get back home to her Queens studio. Onto the next project, home with her work, where she belonged.

She slumped back into the flat cushions of her rented couch and looked out the picture window at the storm already howling outside. She bit into the doughnut. Rosewater and peaches. The icing cracked against her lips and gave way to perfect syrup over flaky dough. She licked her lips. There really were all kinds of art.

Just a few more days in Boston. She'd get through it.

CHAPTER FIFTEEN

Jenny had two main goals. One was to avoid Michael at all costs until they had to show up at the Daubert hearing together. The other was to not to think about Blake at all. She told herself she was succeeding, but memories of the gala, and her brief moments in the Hockney room, kept showing up in her head, unbidden. The only good news of her week was that Michael was in Florida again—with a client or on a golf course or both, she was unsure. She was able to let his calls go to voice mail and respond immediately to his emails with nothing but a businesslike, placid tone.

And then, as he had the fateful Monday when she'd first met Blake, Davis jolted her out of the comforting silence of her office with a loud *ping* of the phone announcing his text.

Big favor. Tonight. Dinner with museum people. I need a beard.

Followed by a phone call. "Please?" Davis whined. "The Albie director—Walter—and his wife, she's a hoot—they are having me and the other curators over for dinner." He ignored Jenny's loud sigh and pressed on. "This could be good for you,"

Davis pleaded, "with all the bank connections with people on the board, right? Please? We're, like, symbiotic at this point. I need you."

Jenny sighed. Having to perform for strangers didn't sound like a lot of fun, but she was supposed to have dinner at her parents that night and was glad for a good reason to cancel. She couldn't face the rickety Green Line, which had been especially slow with all the snow. Or, of course, them. Them and their pleasantly expectant faces. The grandparents in waiting. But she wasn't ready to concede.

"Why me? Really, Davis. You don't need a date."

"You're right, you're not coming as my girlfriend. You'll be there as my friend who is gorgeous and smart and accomplished and makes me look good by association."

"Davis. Please."

"Fine. Sean cancelled. He wouldn't be as good at it as you will be anyway. I think the director of photography's husband is a lawyer. You can talk to him."

Jenny looked at the square walls of her office, the gray dimming light. She wanted to know one thing, of course, but she didn't know how to ask it. She took a deep breath. Davis answered before she had to ask.

"If you're wondering, it's museum people, not artists. Blake won't be there."

Jenny couldn't gauge her own reaction. She was disappointed and relieved at the same time. She'd wanted to apologize, but really, what did she have to apologize for? It had been a week since that stupid gala anyway. Surely Blake wasn't musing about what Brandon had said. She was probably back in New York, running her hands over the body of that pale, voluptuous assistant, working on her next big project, not thinking a whit about Jenny and the ogres with whom she kept company.

"Fine," she said.

Davis squealed. "Thank you, thank you. It's casual. At their house. Just a few people, wine, etcetera. I'll text you deets."

A few hours later, Jenny was outside Walter Smith's townhouse, banging on the pineapple-shaped brass knocker clumsily with her mittened hand. When a hired steward in a crisp, rented-looking tuxedo shirt ushered her inside, she wanted to pat herself on the back for her forethought. Thank goodness she hadn't listened to Davis. The gathering was at the director's house—that much was true. But it was more than a few people, and it was not casual. Jenny had expected that much at least. You didn't show up at a townhouse in the Back Bay, one of the ones with four levels that looks over the Orange Line pathway, in anything other than a cocktail dress and stilettos. It was cold for that, of course, but Bostonians had a trick to handle that. As she'd expected, large baskets by the door were filled with warm winter boots that had been shed like skin. Walter and Amy Smith, the director and his wife, had prepared the house impeccably. Inside, she couldn't tell it was winter. The chandeliers were plentiful and bright, casting sharp shapes on bright yellow wallpapered walls. It seemed like a spring day, everyone in their finest clothes, cocktails in hand.

Jenny made her way through the first floor, searching for Davis, and rose a few steps up to the first-floor landing to for a better vantage point. She spotted Davis from above, gesticulating and grinning and surrounded by a gaggle of admirers. When she glided to his side, he greeted her more loudly than felt appropriate for the quiet din of the room. "Everyone! My best friend!" Jenny smiled, but it was clear that Davis was in the middle of his story. He was talking about the design he'd done for Blake's opening.

"So this guy comes up to me, and he says, this looks amazing, can you do my wedding? I say, um, okay, sure, I mean, I'm thinking, he's going to pay me, right? Or does he just want to know what linens and lights I used and the LEDs on the chair. Then he gives me his card, and he's a wedding planner. He said 'his wedding' but he meant the one he's working on. For the governor's daughter! So now I'm on this wedding planner's payroll!"

Big smiles from the small crowd of colleagues. Jenny felt a surge of pride, too. "So, do you have a contract?" Jenny asked, in part because she wanted to know—and wanted to help—and also because she knew she was there to play a role, and she didn't mind doing it. Lawyer friend. Strait-laced protector.

"I do. But you can look at it." Davis said to her, smiling to the circle. "There's going to be more. I'm going to tell Walter—he's got to up my salary—because if I get five of these a year, man, that's really uncomfortably close to the peanuts they pay us."

His colleagues nodded, a few laughed. One, with glasses and a bowtie, said, "Davis, you could do it! Go out on your own. The museum would hire you to do the galas."

"I should ask for a bonus for Blake's," Davis said. The group laughed, the idea of extra money in the budget apparently a hilarious joke all by itself.

Jenny saw a woman approach the crowd from the corner of her eye, a short, friendly looking woman who was wearing a dress the same color as hers. The woman draped her arm around Davis's shoulder and said in a charismatic British accent, "What you did for that gala was magnificent." Jenny realized that the woman was Amy, the director's wife and the host for the evening. Amy beamed at Davis and the assembled guests. Her hair was gray, but otherwise she looked twenty years younger than her husband, at least.

"You're Davis's friend," she said, turning to Jenny. "Welcome, and I can see you're very good with color," she said, gesturing back and forth between her and Jenny's nearly matching dresses. Jenny smiled, liking her immediately, feeling pulled into her clear enthusiasm and grace. "I have to go check on the catering, but then I'm going to give anyone who wants one a house tour." She turned back. "Not to brag, but to show you the paintings. We get to take some from the museum! Guess who got to choose!" She pointed her thumbs at herself and made an exaggerated rock star kind of face, gleaming white teeth and scrunched up eyes. Jenny laughed. The night would be okay.

Soon they were all standing by one of the paintings on the third floor. This floor was the least austere, covered in bright angular furniture, all in saturated colors, as if a paintbox had exploded over the room. Nothing was unpainted. Even the

pillows clashed. Somehow, though, ther
The loud colors and angles didn't fight
instead seemed to dance. Jenny let her
and orange-striped side chair to a knitte
a translucent, bright red throw blanket
The blanket clashed with—no, complem
vase of maroon Gerber daisies on the y

Walter and Amy were both giving the tour, talking about a small
Derain painting on the wall, and Jenny was starting to clue in
that the bright, bold furniture was supposed to be in tune with
the painting. "Not a study in contrasts," Amy confirmed. "We
went all out on this one. Envelop yourself in crazy pops of color
while you look at this kinetic, Fauvist landscape."

"What my wife means," Walter said, "is that it is a great
privilege to live with this painting—"

"I love Andre Derain, just so we're clear, yes," Amy said,
smiling as she grabbed Walter's elbow. Jenny felt awash in their
affection for one another. She couldn't help but feel jealous. She
wanted to fit with someone so well. She wanted to banter, to be
understood. Davis seemed to sense it and put his hand on her
elbow, almost reassuringly, maybe thinking of their conversation
over drinks the week before.

Amy ushered them to the dining room. There were about
twenty of them, half museum employees, the rest plus-ones.
Walter stood at the head of the table, which extended through
their dining room and into the formal living room, another
white carpet underfoot.

He stood, adjusted his tie, and made a big show of taking it
off. "This really is the night we look forward to most out of the
year," he said. "It is our honor to show our appreciation for all
of you, our colleagues, who keep the museum running. I know
what we all do is for the love of it. Our faith in our mission
and what we bring to the city. We do make this world a better
place, because we bring beauty into it. Thank you all, and please
enjoy."

Everyone raised their glasses, a few muttered, "hear, hear,"
and Amy beamed down the table. Jenny was happy to be privy

's world and for being around all these people who
ed him. She grinned across the table at him and took a sip
perfectly chilled white wine.

The doorbell rang and Amy leapt up. From where Jenny
was seated, she couldn't see who it was. The person's face was
obscured by what she was carrying, a poster-sized folder which
had a black plastic bag haphazardly duct-taped over it. A few
snowflakes were sticking to the bag. Amy said something—
Jenny couldn't hear what—and then the person walked into the
foyer and the door closed behind them. Somehow Jenny knew
before she saw her face—deep inside her, simply by being in
her presence—knew from the jolt she felt, who was carrying the
folder, kicking off her boots, and walking into Amy and Walter's
house, toward the assembled dinner party. She *knew.*

Blake.

Jenny couldn't help it. She gasped and looked down quickly,
but it was too late. Blake had seen her. Lifting her head, Jenny
watched her move across the room. Blake's eyes settled on her
for a moment and then darted away. Jenny felt her own breath
hitch at the sudden, brief eye contact. Was she imagining it, or
had Blake's stride faltered for a moment when she saw her?

Amy gestured to a steward to take Blake's portfolio and
turned to the crowd. "Surprise, everyone, we have another
guest!" Slowly, the diners realized who was standing before
them and erupted into applause. A few stood. Jenny clapped, so
as not to look left out, but all she wanted to do was keep eating
and ignore her. She watched, out of the corner of her eye, as
Blake greeted Walter and sat in the empty chair next to Amy.

"Sorry I'm late," Blake said to the crowd, and Amy squeezed
her shoulder.

"Our last-minute addition and guest of honor, everyone."
Jenny looked down at her plate again. At least she and Blake
were at opposite ends of the table. Maybe she wouldn't have to
see her or talk to her or...anything. She would only have to be
a good friend to Davis. Make conversation with the rest of the
people at the table. Be polite, support him, and leave.

Jenny cleared her throat and turned to the gaunt man sitting next to her, who had been slurping on his wine rather contentedly all evening. "What do you do?"

"In Europe, they never ask that. They ask where you're going on your next vacation."

"Okay," Jenny said, too on edge with Blake so nearby to care how rude he was. "So where are you going?"

"Nowhere," the gaunt man said. "I can't get time off work." Jenny laughed and looked at him, expecting a smile, but finding none, turned back to her plate. Blake, she sensed, seemed to be conspicuously not looking at her. Jenny wasn't sure how well she could trust herself. Because she knew, even though she was trying not to, that her eyes kept falling on Blake. She was dressed fully in black, with a long necklace that looked like it was made of tiny teeth. On her delicate wrists were stacked orange plastic bangles. Her lips were bright red and looked like they were standing out from the rest of her face. She was joining Amy in jolly conversation that the rest of the table couldn't hear; hands gesticulating wildly, eyes bright.

Walter, for the moment, wasn't talking to anyone. Jenny leaned toward him. There were two guests between them at the table, but she hoped he could hear. "Walter, I was wondering how long you've had the Derain."

He smiled and looked a little relieved to have been engaged. "Just about two years. We're going to have to lend it to a museum in Pittsburgh in the spring, though."

"It's a truly gorgeous painting. Thank you for showing us," Jenny said, and she could feel Davis's gratitude beside her. This is what she was here for. She could do it even when Blake in attendance.

Blake interrupted. "You have a Derain in this house?" Her eyes were wide, excited.

"I'll show you after dinner," Amy said, with another propriety pat on the arm. "It's right upstairs."

Then Blake set her gaze on Jenny. She was far across the table, but somehow, when she turned, the space between them seemed to shrink and Jenny felt like they were alone, face-to-face. But not in the way she wanted. Blake was not looking at her kindly.

"I'm surprised you liked it, Jenny."

The table went silent. Out of respect for Blake perhaps? Or maybe, because Jenny and Blake were so far apart at the table, their conversation overtook the room.

"Why?" Jenny managed to squeak, immediately feeling embarrassed for squeaking. How did Blake do this to her?

"I didn't think you liked anything abstract. I mean, it's not a Hoffman or anything, but Derain is a Fauvist. Color, aggressively spread everywhere. He's pretty out there. I would think that you would like Bierstadt. Big, huge, concrete, American landscapes. The mountain looks real. You want proof that an artist is a skilled draftsman. You only like people who can draw. Am I wrong?"

The silence at the table persisted, and Jenny wondered if it was because the other people at the table could sense the hardness in Blake's voice. They hadn't been there at the gala, hadn't overheard Brandon, didn't know about the tension that kept leaping up between them. She swallowed, feeling the heat of Blake's gaze and the oppressive quiet of the dining room, not knowing how to respond. Amy smiled, so big it was enough to break the tension. "Bierstadt made everything up anyway, to call him a realist is like…Lifetime movies. 'Based on actual events…'"

Davis joined in. "I love those! Did anyone see that one about Clark Rockefeller a few years back? It was totally filmed on the Common." The other curators of the table picked up the cue, and the dining room filled with the din of voices again.

Jenny chewed her food while looking down, face hot, anger welling up inside of her. Davis had rescued her, in a sense. She hoped somehow the exchange hadn't embarrassed him. She was supposed to be supporting him, not becoming the center of attention. If anyone should be embarrassed, it was Blake. What had gotten into her? Apparently she had been mulling over what she'd heard at the gala. Apparently she was angry at Jenny, enough to speak disdainfully to her across the table.

Jenny chewed her food, knowing a purple blush was probably raging fiercely across her cheeks and neck. To think she had been considering apologizing to Blake for what Brandon had said! How could she have been regretting standing by him and Michael at the gala when Blake herself was proving to be a kind of ogre? Someone who was comfortable with trying to humiliate her at a dinner party? What was her problem?

Eventually, though it didn't feel like soon enough, the party started emptying out. The dinner plates were cleared, and dessert was being set up. A coffee urn, sparkling silver, was set up in the parlor. Jenny looked around impatiently, but she wasn't sure how to exit.

Davis squeezed Jenny's leg. "Hon, it's okay for you to head out. I think, um, I'm gonna stay?" he said with an uplift and slightly pleading eyes.

"Good," she said. "You should." She wondered if they would talk about her when she left and then berated herself for wondering. It didn't matter. Blake wasn't worth any more of her time.

Uneasy, she made her way to the door. She was about to press it open to step out into yet another snowfall when she almost bumped into Blake. She was fishing around for her clothes by the front closet, not knowing, apparently, that everything but boots had been brought upstairs. Seeing her, Blake stepped back, as if dangerously allergic to her proximity. "Sorry," Jenny said, automatically before clamping her mouth shut. She didn't want to show any weakness.

"It's okay," Blake said. She looked at Jenny for a few moments—longer than Jenny thought she would. Long enough that Jenny began shifting under her gaze. In time a glaze came over Blake's eyes, and she looked down, with something that seemed like shame on her face. Her mouth turned down. Jenny wanted to say something, but she wasn't sure what.

It seemed strange, standing in the silence. It made it seem obvious that there was something between them more nuanced than mutual dislike. Some strange fire that she couldn't explain. Just like when they had been sitting back-to-back on the bench during the gala, there was a heat between their bodies that Jenny couldn't account for. A heaviness in the silence. Maybe Lydia was right. Maybe she had feelings for Blake. She should go. Get out from under Blake's gaze, but she felt stuck.

She decided to say the plainest, truest thing that came to mind. No recrimination for what Blake had done at the table and no apology for what Brandon had said at the gala. No looking back. Just the truth. She cleared her throat and looked into Blake's eyes. "I like your art," she said.

As soon as the words came out of her mouth, she felt weak and stupid. What was she thinking? She wrapped her scarf quickly around her face so Blake couldn't see her blush.

Blake looked at her skeptically, her eyes scrunched a little, as if she were studying what was happening between them as if it was in a lab. Then, she smiled, a small smile, but one that was soft. Tiny crow's feet crinkled at the corners of her eyes. Jenny felt a rush, for a moment, a little victory. It was a beautiful smile, and her small words had made it happen.

"Thank you, Jenny," Blake said. Then she threw her shoulders back and looked down. "That means a lot," she said quietly and then looked up again. "I..." she said, and there was clearly something that was supposed to come after it. But she supplied no additional words. She just let the "I" hang, looking at Jenny.

Jenny could feel her gaze down her spine, felt the words all over her chest, felt her blush growing.

She looked at Blake. She was beautiful. She had known that, of course. Had considered it as an objective fact. Now, Jenny felt like she was seeing her for the first time. This Blake, standing before her, even though she seemed to want Jenny to rush out of the house, even though she seemed uneasy in her mere presence, was stunning. Her dark eyes were so deep with knowing, and there was a perfect curve to her cheeks and chin. Her face was regal but looked touchable, too. The slight play of the dimple on her right cheek was inviting exploration. Her spiky hair looked like it wanted to be touched, like it was daring Jenny's hands to find out what hail of goose bumps would result.

She almost wanted to gasp, but her breath felt caught in her throat.

"Good night," she mumbled, pulling her gaze away from Blake abruptly, just as she caught her pursing her lips. She closed her eyes tight, as if she was about the jump into a pool of cold water. She turned the knob of the door, flipped her hood up to guard against the wind, and launched herself out onto the street, feeling safer in the freezing, whipping dark.

CHAPTER SIXTEEN

Later that night, Blake's shoes were off and her feet were up on Amy's bright pink pouf. Walter had gone to bed, and the other pairings of curators had scurried home long ago. Blake and Davis were the only party guests left. Davis had relaxed a little bit, acting less starstruck in Blake's presence than before. The only thing missing was a cigarette, but Blake knew enough not to ask.

Blake was telling Amy and Davis about the idea of her next project. She was thinking about putting drawings in a gallery space that was lit so brightly that the paper and charcoal would fade and disintegrate over the course of the exhibit.

"I'm thinking that the piece will be like a mandala. Those are destroyed after they're made. Drawings are a bit different, though. Because with a mandala we expect impermanence. You view while it's being built, knowing of its eventual destruction. These drawings, though, you won't see them being made, but you will see them as they disappear. Albeit slowly."

Amy beamed at her and fetched a silver tray with three small gold-rimmed glasses of wine. "We can toast to your new idea!"

she said. "The caterers are almost done with the dishes, my husband is fast asleep, and I just opened a new bottle. Smell!"

"Almonds," Davis said definitively. "It smells like almonds."

"Yes. It's like Blake's rooms. What does your nose say? Do we have a glass of Vermeer or a glass of Hockney?" Amy grinned.

It wasn't very funny, but the wine and the warmth were making Blake relax, so she laughed.

"Or a Bierstadt. I think a Bierstadt would smell like pine. Maybe you should pump in some Yankee Candle Christmas scents," Davis said.

"Or the smell of buffalo fur, wet from a waterfall," Amy said.

Blake laughed again, but tensely, because Davis had brought up Bierstadt, and with it, the memory of her awkward upbraiding of Jenny. She admonished herself. Why had she butted in? What was she trying to prove? She smiled, trying to shake the memory. "I had thought about it, actually. Not the smells, but doing a landscape, like a Bierstadt or even an Inness, which can be a bit mossier. Fuzzier. Maybe I could have installed a humidifier. Pump in the thick air. Is there a sense in the lungs? Would that be touch? Or taste?"

They all sipped their wine, thinking.

Amy cut the silence. "Speaking of Bierstadt…What's the story about Davis's date, anyway? The Andre Derain lover?" she asked.

Blake's heart started pounding in her chest. Davis shot up from the chair he'd sunk into and plumped a pillow behind his back. "Jenny's my friend, not an actual date, you know that, right?"

"Of course. How do you know her, Blake?" Amy asked.

Blake's mouth went dry. She took another sip of the dessert wine, but it did nothing to help. She was sure she couldn't form words. She looked over at Davis to answer. He knew Jenny better than Blake did, after all. But he was being steadfastly silent. He seemed curious to see how she would tell the tale. The truth was, she wasn't sure why she'd said that to Jenny. All she knew was that Jenny didn't like her and somehow she kept living up to Jenny's disdain. She couldn't break the cycle. And then, at the door, before Jenny left, she had given Blake a compliment and looked into her eyes, and she had melted. She felt Jenny's gaze deep in her gut. But before she could answer or do anything to make herself worthy of it, Jenny was gone.

Blake took another sip and said, carefully, "I know her through Davis. She's a lawyer." As if that were all. As if she didn't feel unaccountably nervous in Jenny's presence. As if she hadn't fantasized about kissing her.

"She's my best friend, full disclosure, and she does pro bono for the Albie," Davis said, throwing up his hands, as if to dare Blake to say anything negative. What did she have to say, really? That Jenny's boyfriend didn't like art? Thinking about it more rationally, Blake felt embarrassed for her vitriol. There was something about Jenny that didn't let her think rationally. She just reacted.

"She doesn't think I'm technically skilled enough to be considered a real artist," Blake said finally. But she knew, even as she said it, that Jenny herself hadn't uttered the words. So, what was she expecting? That Jenny would stand up for her at every moment? She shifted in her seat, thinking of Jenny across the table, chastised, looking down, her red dress falling slightly off her shoulder. Shame overcame her. She shouldn't have been snarky about the Derain at the table, in front of everyone. When had she become such a boor?

"Since when do you care what people think? There are people who would disparage Van Gogh for the same thing," Amy said.

"I really don't think Jenny thinks that," Davis said.

"Well, she ran out of the gala after her boyfriend said I was basically a hack."

"Wow. Okay. First of all, what boyfriend?" Davis asked.

Blake looked hard at him. "The Ken doll. Thick blond hair. Sounded like he knew the older guy. Very solicitous."

Davis smiled broadly at Blake, as if he had an inside joke he was sharing just with himself. She felt a little squirmy beneath his stare. She shifted in the chair. Davis was supposed to be the nervous one, not her. Davis glanced over at Amy and back at her, seemingly unsure whether to say what he clearly wanted to. "Um," he said and fell silent again.

"Out with it," Amy said, her wide smile once again rescuing the gathering from all tension.

"A few things. That man you saw her with is not her boyfriend. Her boss, who is a horrid, overly demanding, rude, and unappreciative first class...well. You know. He was there. So if anyone said anything bone-headed about your work, it was surely him. Not Jenny. This so-called Ken doll I can assure you is not her boyfriend."

"Look, it's not like I care," Blake said, but the words came out flat. Even she knew she sounded like a middle-schooler with a losing argument.

"She's gay," Davis said, locking eyes with her, looking like he was surprised to have to say it.

If Blake had taken her pulse at that moment, nothing would have registered. Not a thump. Everything was standing still. The clocks in the room, her breath, the blood pumping through her veins. *Jenny was gay.*

Blake had known, hadn't she? Felt the spark when their hands briefly touched when Jenny had returned the drill bit. Felt the heat from her presence when they were in the Hockney room. Felt her eyes boring into her at the door. Hadn't she hoped?

"You okay?" Amy said to Blake. She realized her mouth was hanging open slightly, and she closed it.

"Sure," she said, pressing her lips together. She took a gulp of the almond wine.

"You were a little hard on her at dinner about the Derain," Amy said, but she said it gently and with a lively sparkle in her eyes.

"Yeah, sorry about that," mumbled Blake, the warmth returning to her cheeks, her breath coming back. Just because Jenny was gay, it didn't mean she'd be interested in Blake. Far from it. She probably dated women who looked just like her. Feminine, coiffed. A doctor to her lawyer. Blue eyes to her brown. Not a butch artist who frequently stayed up all hours of the night to paint in her studio and who had a penchant for one-night stands.

So, she wasn't sure why this piece of information changed anything, but somehow it did. Against all hope, she wanted to run to Jenny and apologize. Start over. Ask her out for a cup of coffee.

She had already blown it, hadn't she? Before it even began.

CHAPTER SEVENTEEN

Jenny's hatred of Michael was starting to feel like its own bloviated mass. She saw him standing by the Federal Courthouse cafeteria, looking at the white and gray landscape of the harbor, and she wanted to run. The view was stunning in all other seasons, but in the winter, the seaport district was all wind and cold, whipping her as she walked from the State Street T, mocking her with howls as she made her way over the footbridge by the Barking Crab.

Inside, Michael—hands behind his back, surveying the view, as if he owned it, said instead of greeting her, "Just three more months until my boat'll be out right there." He jammed his finger in the general area of Rose Wharf. "Right there," he repeated.

Jenny nodded, not saying anything. They walked together to the courtroom in silence. She could feel him sweating next to her as they sat waiting for the judge. They both stared intently at the briefing papers. It was all show. Michael was usually underprepared, and Jenny was always overprepared, even though there was no point. She never got to speak. Michael never let her. She was just the numbers maven, the spreadsheet girl, the exhibit curator. She knew her role. Whenever she came to court, though, she acted as if he might say, "Take it from here."

And then—today of all days—he did exactly that. The bailiff jolted Jenny from her stony, self-righteous silence with a bellowing, "All rise!"

"I'm moving your briefing schedule back two weeks to make up for the snow days," the judge said first. "Any objection?"

The plaintiff's counsel, represented by a lawyer who favored thin knit ties, said, "Thank you, Your Honor," as if the decision hadn't just delayed settlement and thus the award of their contingency fee.

"Thanks," Michael said into the mic at the table.

"Thanks?" the judge said. Her tone wasn't hostile, but it was pointed enough that Michael clued in rather fast.

"Thank you, Your Honor," he said. The judge pursed her lips and looked at him.

"We'll start with the Van Croughton Daubert," she said.

Michael looked nervously around the room and then down at Jenny's notepad. She could tell he was distracted. His lips moved a little as he scanned her outline, which was built around the concession that the zero calculation was unreasonable. Jenny fought the impulse to stretch her forearm across the page so Michael couldn't read it. But it was shared work product, of course. Nothing to hide. She had made it for him.

The knit-tie lawyer cleared his throat and stood. Jenny started taking notes, writing down most of what he said, nearly transcribing. That's what she always did. Took down the volume and parsed out the main points later.

While Knit Tie was still speaking, though, Michael yanked the paper away from her. "I'll do that. Just listen."

"Why?" Jenny whispered, ready to grab the pad back. They had already missed a few seconds.

"You're going to argue it," he said.

Jenny flushed, and her heart started beating furiously. If Knit Tie stopped speaking she was sure the courtroom would pick up the sound over the microphone.

She told herself to listen, but all she could hear was a jumble of words. She took the printed outline from its folder and clutched it in her hand. Michael looked at her and smiled. It was a small one, but it was, for the first time that morning or for several weeks—months, maybe—a break in the tension between them. It was a smile of encouragement. Of faith.

So, she summoned her courage, and when the judge said, "Counsel for BlueCoast Bank?" Jenny stood up. Not too fast, not too slow. She tried to appear graceful behind the podium. She knew what she had to say, because she believed it. Wholeheartedly, without fail. She could finally say it.

"First of all, Your Honor, we voluntarily withdraw Mr. Van Croughton's zero damages calculation." She wanted to say, "because it was a hack job," but the judge would know that was the reason anyway.

She nodded. "So, we are just wasting my time?"

"With all due respect, Your Honor, the plaintiffs also moved against the alternate damages scenario, and we strenuously oppose their motion with respect to the seventy million. If I may, I'd like to—"

"Stop, Ms. O'Toole. We should reschedule this for when the expert can defend that one himself. I was inclined to rule against you on both, but without the zero estimate you have regained some of your waning credibility."

Jenny could have screamed with glee, jumped up and down, but she swallowed and let just a small smile come through. Oh, how she would gloat later. She didn't even need to say anything to Michael; it could stay unspoken. She had won.

But she wanted to win even more. She wanted to do this herself, here, now, keep the seventy million estimate in. The expert who drafted the other report didn't need to be there. Jenny had written the whole damn thing herself, even though that was technically against the rules.

"Your Honor, with all due respect, if you'd allow me to use my allotted time to briefly overview the estimates, I think you'll see that—"

"You can do that?"

"Yes, Your Honor, if you'll permit me to approach—"

Beside her she heard the nasal, whirring sound of Michael's labored breathing. Nerves, or what, she didn't know. It was as loud as her heart. She walked to the judge with the exhibit printouts in hand.

The judge took the papers and thumbed through them faster than she could have even read the captions. "You prepared these?"

"I supported the expert in his preparation of the materials."

The judge looked down at Jenny and crossed her arms, regarding her. Jenny could sense that she suspected this was Jenny's first argument, knew that it was Jenny who'd prepared the whole report, knew, somehow, that she wouldn't leave the courtroom without winning.

"Very well, continue," she said, and Jenny was off—introducing the methodology, explaining its rationales, describing the stock drop damages with such precision even the plaintiff's attorney seemed to be listening, not just for rebuttal, but for the full explanation of the math. She was rudimentary but specific, basic but expansive. She felt like she could fly.

The light went off, letting her know her time was done, but the judge waved it off. "You're done, but I'm not," she said, and she asked Jenny a few more questions. Jenny, answering them, felt herself relax. She felt for the first time that she could excel not just in the back of the house but in the front. If there had been a jury there, she would have walked over to them, smiled, and introduced the economic issues of the case. Everything was true, so it didn't feel like advocacy. Everything was exactly as she had written.

Finally, the judge said, "Very well. Thank you," and Jenny, realizing that she was sweating a little, sat down, with a bigger sound than she meant to. She slumped in the chair, as if she had just jogged around the building. Michael didn't look over at her, but he didn't have to. She knew it had been perfect.

"We will have a short recess until we move onto the other discovery motions, but I'm prepared to rule on this Daubert from the bench. Defendant's stipulation removing the first damages calculation of zero damages is noted. Plaintiff's motion to exclude the expert's seventy-million-dollar calculation is denied."

Jenny wanted to yelp, but she swallowed it down. As she walked out of the courtroom, she felt like she had grown three feet during the hearing. She really had never been so tall. She really had never been so happy. She pushed the heavy oak door, stepping out to the blinding light of the foyer, the sloped window spanning four levels above the harbor, almost blinding her with its white, snowy view of the city. She felt like she wanted to frolic.

"Can I buy you a cup of coffee?" she said to Michael, the ultimate peace offering. She was trying not to gloat.

"No thank you," he said. "You can go home." He stretched his arms up, as if he were waking from sleep, and pointed with his chin toward the stairs to the front lobby. "Go ahead."

This was a gift. She nodded at him and walked toward the doors. She wanted to stop everyone she saw, grip their shoulders, and yell, "I just won! No, not a case but a motion. Yes! my first!"

But giddy wasn't something she was used to being, and she had no one to tell. The gray-and black-suited figures around her were all trudging to their own appointments, going in and out of their own bleak, cold days. She felt like having a mai tai on a beach. But there was no beach, no little umbrella drinks, no sunshine, and most horribly, no one to sit next to.

No one to regale the story with.

No one who would care.

Lydia would say congratulations, sure. After she explained to Davis the basic procedural posture of the case, he'd at least nod and say, "Good job!" But no one would be there at home waiting for her, ready to take her in their arms.

Then, there she was. Wrapped in layers of wool so it was hard to see her face. She was standing right in front of Jenny on the icy sidewalk, looking down intently at her phone and up again at the skyline. She seemed lost. *Blake.*

Jenny couldn't believe it. The person she most dreaded seeing and most wanted to see was standing in front of her. The coward in her wanted to turn around and go back inside the courthouse, flash her bar card, and retreat quickly into the crowd of suits.

Today was a day for victory. For firsts. Jenny swallowed, her heart beating as loudly as it had in the courtroom but muffled beneath her own winter gear. She walked toward Blake. Her strides felt slow and long, like she was making a decision.

"Can I help you?" she said. Blake looked up, her face initially furrowed with annoyance. Then, recognizing Jenny, Blake's face seemed to light up. *Am I doing that to her?* Jenny thought, feeling powerful. Not only had she conjured Blake up, she was somehow making her smile.

"Wow. Hi," Blake said. Jenny watched the puff of her breath turn into a cloud between them. Blake pointed at the courthouse behind them. "You came out of there?" Jenny nodded. Blake sighed and waved her phone. "I'm looking for the ICA."

Of course she was. Jenny felt at ease, able to help. Sort of like when she helped Blake build the walls. Somehow, being useful for Blake, in front of Blake, felt right.

Jenny gestured over at the seaport, at the skyline of half-constructed buildings and tall concrete elevator shafts. The bright red and orange cranes seemed to glow against the gray sky. Some of the cables were waving a bit in the wind. "The Institute of Contemporary Art is behind there."

Words started tumbling out of Jenny as Blake looked incredulously at the skyline. "None of those buildings were there when the ICA was built. I mean, the new building. The old one was in a firehouse. A few years ago. It was the only new building down here, and now you can't see it and it's totally dwarfed, but it still has a choice view of the harbor."

"It's on the water?

"Directly. They have a pedestrian walkway set up, I think, abutting the construction sites. You can get there from here, but you won't see it until you're behind that first building."

"You know the area well?" Blake's face was red from the cold wind, but open, friendly. Like she was interested.

The nervousness Jenny consistently felt in Blake's presence was translating into a flood of words. "When I was growing up, there was nobody here. Just warehouses. You would never come here at all. And the Rose Kennedy Greenway over there—that was like a no-man's-land. A horrible purgatory between the financial district and the North End. New buildings are popping up now like pimples. If I had a toddler, I'd be down here all the time watching the cranes."

Jenny stopped. What was wrong with her? Why was she talking so damn much? She clamped her lips together. *Pimples? Toddlers?* What the hell was wrong with her?

Blake's expression was hard to read. She looked sort of bemused. God. Or her half-smile was mocking Jenny.

"Not that I have a toddler. I mean, not that I want one. I mean, now. I mean…"

Jenny wanted to run away. She couldn't stop talking, but everything she said was coming out wrong. She had gone from abject silence in Blake's presence to full-on babble. Why couldn't she find a normal middle ground? She blew out her breath, feeling like, since she'd completely fucked up the whole interaction anyway, she might as well speak plainly. "You know. I don't rule anything out. That's all I mean."

Blake smiled, big and broad, her dimple announcing itself loudly on her face. Jenny's breath hitched at the sight of it. Blake's eyes sparkled in the gray day.

"You love this city, don't you?" Blake asked.

Jenny shrugged. "It's home." Blake pursed her lips for a moment and softened her face again.

"So you've been?"

"To the ICA?" Jenny asked. Blake nodded. Jenny closed her mouth tightly, not wanting anything to spill out. She had talked too much already, sounded like a scatterbrained Masshole. Pride in the seaport. It was probably a block of development in New York, nothing to be proud of. And she wasn't about to tell Blake that she didn't like the ICA. The building was great, sure, with views of the harbor, but the art... She had been once, yes. The huge wall in the lobby was a painting of an anime girl farting flowery clouds. Twenty-foot-tall flowery clouds. It was resolutely not her thing.

So she just said, "Yes, I've been."

Blake raised one eyebrow. "But?"

"No buts. Great museum." Jenny wouldn't give Blake the satisfaction of attacking her taste again. Making assumptions. No. She would not give her that satisfaction.

Blake sighed, just for a moment, and looked at her so directly Jenny wanted to look away. But she didn't. Blake seemed to be working up to something. The silence hung.

"Fine," Jenny said after a few more beats. "Not my cup of tea. I love the architecture. I'm glad it exists in our city. But you're right. I don't like it."

"I didn't say anything," Blake said.

Jenny was feeling worked up, combative. She wanted to explain herself to Blake and defend herself all at once. She could feel her face getting hot even though the air was frigid and they'd been standing outside so long their lips were getting blue.

"I'm sorry if that makes me unsophisticated or whatever, but—"

Blake put a gloved hand on Jenny's forearm, steading her. "I don't think that about you," she said, looking her straight in the eye. Jenny's skin burned from her touch despite the intervening layers of wool and down.

Jenny looked down. "Okay," she said, heat rising in her cheeks, aware of where they'd touched. Aware of the outsize effect Blake had on her.

Blake smiled. "I'm interested in what you like. I loved how you reacted to my Hockney room." She took her hand away from Jenny's arm, and for the first time since she'd been standing there with her, Jenny felt the full chill in the air. She craved Blake's touch again. She leaned in automatically. Blake swallowed. "I'm sorry if I gave you a hard time at that dinner."

Jenny almost gasped, but she steadied her breathing. "It's fine," she croaked, caught up more in Blake's pronouncement that she cared what she thought even more than the apology.

"So," Blake said, shuffling in her boots a bit and tilting her chin toward the courthouse. "What were you doing in there?"

"Nothing."

"I'm sure it wasn't nothing," Blake said. "A trial?"

Jenny almost laughed. Non-lawyers always thought she was going to trial. The truth was, everything settled. Even if it didn't, they'd give the trial to someone else. She was only there to calculate damages.

She had talked too much anyway. She wasn't going to bore Blake with the horrid details of her hearing. Blake, who seemed happy to be talking to her. *What was going on?*

"It was just a hearing."

"What about?"

Jenny sighed. What was she playing at? Did she really want to know? She decided to call her bluff. "I'm defending a bank. Our experts calculate the damages. We have one expert who said there are no damages and one who said there are millions in damages. I told the judge to exclude the one who said we have no damages."

Gosh, it sounded boring even to her.

Blake hadn't fallen asleep standing up. "So, you were showing the judge you were reasonable? Admitting that if you are guilty, you'll pay something?"

Jenny smiled at Blake's quick understanding. She had listened, at least. "It's civil, so we say 'liable,' not 'guilty' but pretty much, yes."

"And you won?"

Jenny nodded. "Michael even let me argue it," she said, not giving herself time to think about why this felt so natural. Why she was getting exactly what she'd been craving. Time with Blake, as if they were friends.

"Michael's the guy you were at the gala with?" Blake asked.

Jenny's blush raged furiously. Of course, the gala. That horrible night. "Yes," she said, "and I'm sorr—"

Blake cut her off. "No need. Davis told me he's kind of an ogre."

Davis and Blake had talked about her? Jenny swallowed hard, trying to maintain her breathing. She knew what she wanted. She wanted to walk with Blake to the museum, hear what she had to say about the art, take her arm, and hold her tight against the wind. Feel the heat of her body close to her.

In the silence, for a moment, she let herself wonder if Blake wanted the same thing. They stood looking at one another, their clouds of frosty breath mingling in the air.

"So I go that way?" Blake said, cutting into the silence, pointing at the harbor, where the museum would be sitting on the edge of the water, dwarfed by the new buildings. Jenny nodded, the question "Can I come along?" lodged in her throat. She stood looking at Blake, silent.

"I can't believe you found me out here," Blake said. She pivoted to make her way to the museum. She gave a wave over her shoulder.

Jenny couldn't believe she'd found her out there either. And now she was watching her walk away. Her figure disappeared quickly around the corner, and Jenny stood there, trying to figure out what had just happened and why her body was covered in goose bumps and why her heart felt like it was about to jump out of her chest.

CHAPTER EIGHTEEN

Blake wanted to get back to New York as soon as she could, but at the same time, without seeing Jenny again, she felt like she was leaving something behind. The moment she walked into her rental, she knew she wasn't going to be able to sleep. Without taking off her coat, she turned around again, feeling more comfortable in the dark cold, where thoughts of Jenny could swirl around her like the bitter wind and go unexamined.

She rode the T, sketching furiously, feeling like she was physically assaulting the paper, carving out sections of light and dark with graphite, sketching the lines of wrinkles around the eyes of sad drunks and the ill-fitting halter tops of college students looking strange and stringy under ostentatious Canada Goose jackets. Kids making out, smelling of pot, in the back of the bus. Musicians taking the T home from their gigs, stumbling in late.

At two—laughably early—the T shut down. She got off near Back Bay and walked across the Mass Ave Bridge, taking in the city. She had to admit that it was gorgeous from that vantage point. The lights of buildings were reflected on the Charles, dotting the patches of ice with color. The stillness of the night seemed to envelop the buildings and naked trees with a kind of reverence. She understood, really for the first time, that there was something to love about this city. Its quaint prettiness. Its walkability. Its water. Jenny had spoken of it with reverence, and Blake, for the first time, was beginning to understand.

She placed her hands on the cold railing of the Mass Ave Bridge and stretched her calves a little by lunging forward, taking in the skyline. Around the bend of the river she could see the Prudential Tower with a few windows lit up. She wondered if one of them was Jenny's, if maybe she was awake, too, in her office, looking out at the dark night air.

Blake's toes were almost blue when she made it back to her rental. She opened up her sketchbook to look at her night's work. It was some of her best, she was sure. It was fast and fierce, and it captured the city, the people trekking through it. Behind the scores of figures, she had perfectly rendered the wet condensation inside the busses and the unforgiving, dark cold outside. Bleary eyed, she filtered through the pages. *Yes.* This could be considered technical skill. She knew that, at least.

She fell asleep on the couch and didn't wake until midmorning, when the insistent buzzing of her phone finally jarred her. There were several texts from Steve about her appearance on Darren Rosenfeld's show that night and two texts from Amanda. The first just said *Hi*, and the second, from twenty minutes later, was a question mark.

Blake deleted them, wanting to erase the memory. She'd call Steve back soon, but first, she showered and got dressed in a fresh outfit, tight jeans and a boxy bright red sweater, and made her way to the Pru, sketchbook under her arm. She pushed her way through the mall—tourists, shoppers, and executives in suits all butting up against one another in the ugly swath of stores a few feet up from the real streets of the city. The smells from the food court and the chocolate shops were making her woozy. Finally, past all the shops was the lobby of the building. The security desk was behind a plinth of yellow marble.

"Top of the Hub?" a woman in a too-tight, blue button-down uniform asked.

"No, I—"

She couldn't remember the name of Jenny's law firm and stuttered, uncharacteristically stymied by her surroundings. Or maybe the possibility of seeing Jenny. "I'm here for Jenny O'Toole?" she said, with an uplift she thought she'd abandoned ages ago.

The woman at the desk frowned. "I need to know what business."

"Can I just leave it for her?" Blake asked, thinking it might be smarter not to see Jenny. Just leave the sketchbook, without comment, a gift of some sort. Maybe their chance meeting yesterday was the pinnacle. Maybe things couldn't get any better after that. She was a coward. She didn't deserve to see Jenny again. She had wanted to say, "Come with me," but didn't. Maybe that was the only chance she'd get.

"I'll still need a business," said the woman at the desk.

"Hold on," Blake said, fetching her phone, Googling Jenny's name and finding the firm. There it was, the first entry, Jenny's headshot showing up on her smartphone screen, "Corporate Finance." Oh God, what was Blake doing here?

"Wales, Moakley and Strauss LLP," Blake said to the security officer.

"Sit." She glared. "I need to get their receptionist to send a courier for the package."

This was more involved than Blake meant it to be. She felt itchy sitting in this lobby, this draconian system of security and pouches. She simply wanted to hand Jenny a notebook, that was all. Blake ran her fingers through her spiky hair, sitting on the leather settee of the lobby, knees bouncing up and down, second guessing everything, including, just for a moment, giving the drawings away.

She got back up and went to the desk. "I'm just going to leave it—"

Jenny's voice interrupted her. "Lost again?" Somehow, Blake's body reacted to the sound of her voice before her brain processed the words.

Jenny looked at her kindly, but also like she wasn't altogether surprised to see her, which unsettled her more. As usual, she looked gorgeous, her open face offset by piercing, knowing eyes, and somehow her lips, which Blake had thought she'd seen and understood, were fuller than she remembered, more inviting than any lips she'd ever seen. She tried not to stare and swallowed, looking quickly at Jenny and over at the figure next to her. Jenny's friend? Someone, anyway, who seemed to be Jenny's number-one cheerleader. She was smiling wildly. She put out her hand. "I'm Lydia. Pleased to meet you. You must be Blake Harrison. I'm a big fan."

Jenny, not taking her eyes off Blake, said, "Yes, Lydia is very familiar with your art."

"Jenny's a big fan, too," Lydia said, shooting her another grin and savoring the pause. "Of your art."

"Would you give us a minute?" Jenny said to Blake and turned to Lydia. Blake was relieved not to have to speak, because she feared she wouldn't be able to when the time came.

But Lydia didn't give her a reprieve. She stood where she was, looking at Blake, and back at Jenny, smiling, and said, "No need. I'll just go back upstairs. You come and find me later, okay?"

Jenny nodded and fixed her eyes back on Blake. "You're here to see me?" she said, her voice strangely high, a little shy, even. But her nervousness didn't quell Blake's.

"I have something for you," Blake said, holding the bundled-up sketchbook in front of her like a birthday cake she was afraid would fall off a platter. Jenny looked down at it only briefly, as if there was nothing more interesting than Blake's face. The eye contact was making Blake's whole body feel like it was on fire, but she didn't want anyone to put it out. How could she ever have thought Jenny was straight, even for a second?

"Take it," she said.

Jenny took the book reverently and gently and turned the top page. "You did all these," she said, not a question.

"Yes."

Jenny smiled, turning slowly through the pages, not seeming to mind the smudges of graphite getting on her hands.

"I wanted to show you I can…" Blake cleared her throat, feeling speechless again. Being around Jenny made her skin feel like it was on fire and her throat like it was ice-cold.

"You don't have to prove anything to me," Jenny said, looking at the pages as closely and carefully as she had savored the Hockney room. With focus, with feeling. Blake felt seen by her. She didn't care who else liked her drawings, who else saw them. All that mattered now was that Jenny liked them.

"You've really captured the city," Jenny said.

Blake swallowed again, blushing, feeling the whole lobby disappear, as if she and Jenny were standing on a platform and everything else had faded away.

She took a deep breath, feeling like her words were more important than ever. "You helped me see it," she said.

Jenny pulled her eyes from the pages and looked into Blake's face with her intense brown eyes, making her want to both meet her gaze and to shrink under it. Then she smiled, breaking the tension a little. "It's really fucking cold here, though."

Blake met her smile, but she didn't know what to say. Jenny looked puzzled. Blake wanted to jump inside her head, and figure out what she was thinking. What Blake wanted seemed simple all of a sudden. She wanted to take Jenny out for a cup of coffee. A can of beer. Something. She wanted to sit next to her at a counter, gaze at her, and talk. So she decided to say the simple thing.

"Can I buy you a beverage?"

Jenny's eyes lit up, and she nodded before she said, "Yes." After a beat, "Now?"

Blake almost stepped back in embarrassment. "Of course not, you're at work, I don't mean to—"

"How about dinner?" Jenny said.

"Of course," Blake said, barely letting the words leave Jenny's mouth before she responded.

"How did you like the ICA?" Jenny asked.

"I loved it. Stunning and fun and perfect. I'll tell you about it over dinner."

Blake wanted to find a way to fast-forward time. She wanted to be next to Jenny immediately. But there were still a few hours between now and dinnertime. What would Blake do? She turned hot and cold all at once. They stood looking at one another. Then she remembered that she had to be at Darren's studio for the interview at seven—she wanted to scream.

"I can't have dinner," Blake said, sounding as dejected as she felt. Jenny looked like she'd been physically hit in the gut, and Blake tried hurriedly to repair things.

"I just have to—I have to be at this thing tonight—"

Jenny seemed to grip the sketchbook more tightly, but her face softened. "Are you going to be at the Albie?" Jenny asked.

Blake nodded.

Jenny looked around the lobby, seemingly afraid for anyone to see her or to overhear her. Or maybe it was nerves. Blake didn't know which and didn't want to worry about Jenny having second thoughts. So she focused on her words.

"I've only really seen one room," said Jenny. "Can I have a tour of the others?"

Blake laughed, knowing that everything was going to be fine. She didn't know what would happen with Jenny, but she felt, for the first time, like she could go home to New York without the ache she'd been carrying. "I'll meet you back here at five. We can walk over together."

"It's a date," Jenny said. The words seemed to catch a little in her throat.

"Yes," Blake said, not knowing how much Jenny intended her words to mean.

Jenny smiled and turned to the elevator bank. Blake took a deep breath, ready to leave, when Jenny again appeared beside her. She was holding out the sketchbook.

"I can't accept this."

Blake nudged it back toward her, near enough to Jenny for the first time to smell her perfume, or cologne, or whatever it was. Rich pine. Like clean winter.

"Yes, you can."

"No. I love seeing it, and I am humbled that you wanted to give it to me, but it's too much."

Blake blanched. If Jenny felt half of what she was feeling—this magnetism, this drive, wouldn't she gleefully take the gift, run up to Lydia, and say, "See?"

Maybe Jenny was different. Didn't feel this so strongly. Blake placed her hands around the book. Jenny's hands stayed on it too, and it sat between them, its weight equally distributed among their hands.

Jenny let go, and Blake caught the weight, grabbing the book to her chest. "I'll see you later," she whispered and was gone.

Five hours later, they walked together to the museum. It was snowing a little, cold, solid little flakes accumulating lightly on their hats and noses. Blake wanted to take Jenny's hand, but didn't. Everything seemed too fragile, so alive with possibility, but still uncertain. As if someone could stop them on the street and say, "Jenny, did you know this is all a misunderstanding? Blake has a crush on you. She wants to kiss you. How funny is that?"

But no one stopped them. Jenny didn't stop either. Instead, she told Blake about Davis, their early friendship piled in with four others in an apartment in Somerville. She talked more about the bank fraud damages and her role in preparing the reports.

"So you're good at math?"

"Yeah," Jenny said. "It's not just math, it's economics. It's all these assumptions and models and trying to figure things out based on a million different hypotheticals. It can be tedious, but there are moments like yesterday when it comes together."

"Sounds a little like my job," Blake said. "Sometimes you can't see that it will add up, but it does."

They came to the Albie. It was closing in fifteen minutes, the announcement echoed through the halls from the tinny PA system. "Come," Blake said, taking Jenny's hand, the four letters cavernous with innuendo. Jenny seemed content to follow.

The gallery was emptying, and Blake relished watching the effect her art had on the visitors. Going into each room, they were chatty, alive with the chill from the city air. Walking out, after they'd been bathed in light, they seemed reverent, more peaceful, more attuned to their bodies, walking more slowly, soft smiles playing on their faces.

Blake pulled Jenny into the La Tour room, the one they had fought about at their first meeting. The light was beckoning from the far right corner. Jenny slowly walked toward it, reaching out her hands to the wall where the light was brightest. Blake felt frozen. She wanted to kiss Jenny. Needed to. The desire felt primal.

At the same time, she didn't want to change the moment. It was like drawing. A sketch might be perfect the way it was, unfinished, delicately balanced. Blake would sometimes leave it like that, but it was difficult to stop when there was more to do, more lines to render, more shades of light and dark. There was always the chance, though, that more might not be better. A light, energetic drawing could be killed in an instant from too much heavy graphite. A study on one person's face could be diluted by adding more figures. And here Blake had no eraser. One wrong move and this strange peace they'd created, this gorgeous dance of desire and comfort, would be gone.

Jenny moved toward her. She took Blake's hands in her own and looked into her eyes. "I have not been myself," she said.

Blake's heart was pulsing. Her fingers, touching Jenny's, felt like they had heartbeats of their own. "Oh?"

"I've barely slept because I was…"

"Yes?" Blake said, hoarse.

"I thought you hated me," Jenny said finally. "But I saw you yesterday. And then today you just showed up in the lobby. And now we're here." Jenny seemed to need to repeat the narrative, to make sure she'd gotten it all right.

Blake leaned closer to Jenny. At first, their lips touched drily, their bodies tilting toward each other without touching. After a moment, Blake took control and pulled the length of Jenny's body against hers. As she did so, Jenny parted Blake's lips with her tongue, and Blake moaned, quietly. She couldn't help it. She felt Jenny's hot breath fill something in her that she hadn't known was empty, and soon, they were all lips and tongue, exploring one another's mouths, pressing their bodies together, hands running up and down each other's backs. Blake wanted more, she wanted all of her, but she tried to stay composed. They were in her gallery. The museum had just closed. Who knew if any guests were still nearby? She fought the impulse to kneel down on the floor and take Jenny with her but *no*. They would just kiss. She could do that. It had only been a few seconds, but she knew that she could kiss her for hours.

Jenny pulled back for a moment, smiling. Her eyes were folding up in glee, showing some well-earned wisdom and delight.

"I can't believe I'm kissing you in this room," Jenny said.

Blake smiled, close to her face, breathing in the scent of her hair, deeply. "Why not?"

"Well, it's like you, your whole idea, your whole vision. This light is almost church-like. It's very odd. This is your creation, a part of you. It's like I'm inside of you while I'm kissing you."

Blake kissed her, deeply, even more insistently than before, feeling her own arousal mix with Jenny's as their legs intertwined even as they maintained their balance.

"Say that again, please," she said.

Jenny laughed a little. "It's like I'm inside of you while I'm kissing you."

"I'd like that," Blake said, knowing somehow they could be playful, knowing somehow they fit. Blake kissed her harder, then trailed some kisses down her chin.

"Oh God," Jenny said, cupping Blake's ass with her hands. Blake wished she had nowhere to go. She didn't want to have to go on Darren's show. She didn't want to have to return Steve's fourteen text messages. She wanted to stay right where she was.

"Let's go to the Hockney room," Jenny offered. Soon they stood kissing in the blinding blue light, their lips and tongues making unabashed sucking sounds. Jenny's hands started crawling up underneath Blake's shirt. "Jenny, Jenny," Blake said.

"Mhmm," Jenny said, planting kisses on Blake's collarbone.

"I have to go on TV."

"When?" More kisses, trailing over her shoulders. She shivered, the elation felt like a palpable thing, something she could hold.

Blake pulled her phone out of her back pocket to check the time, without letting go of Jenny's waist with her other hand. "Twenty minutes," she said.

Jenny pulled back, looked at her, and laughed, like it was the most hilarious thing she'd ever heard. "I'll get us a car."

CHAPTER NINETEEN

Jenny felt like she'd been teleported to Darren Rosenfeld's studio. She couldn't really figure out how she'd gotten there. Her lips felt raw. She hadn't made out with someone in a long time, not like that, not simply enjoying kissing and tasting. They hadn't even sat down. They had stood with their arms around each other, enveloped in Blake's light.

Now she was in the studio, leaning against a pillar near the soundstage, watching Blake get a final layer of face powder before going on camera. Jenny didn't want to look anywhere but at Blake. She would be gone in a week, and she didn't want to waste any time not savoring the sight of her.

Jenny had texted Lydia *I won't be back* and Lydia responded with a crude tongue emoji, a peach, and a smiley face. Jenny wrote back to tell her, no, she's taping Darren Rosenfeld's show. *OMG* Lydia predictably wrote back, and Jenny silenced her phone. She didn't care, suddenly, what was happening with the case or if Michael was about to fire her. All of that would be there later. Right now, it was just Blake, sitting in the makeup chair, grinning over at her.

Jenny had taken her hand. She had kissed her in the La Tour room. She had run her fingers up her strong, toned, smooth stomach. She had run her fingers through her short hair and had felt the sparks she had imagined. Her kiss had apparently made Blake moan. What had happened to her? Her shirt was unbuttoned lower than she ever had it buttoned. There was a run in her stocking. She didn't care. She felt alive.

A tall, skinny man with glasses and a cream-colored linen shirt greeted Blake and walked over and leaned on the pillar around the corner from Jenny. "I'm Steve," he said, nodding his head once but not offering a hand to shake. Jenny nodded. "Blake's *manager*," he said. Again, when Jenny didn't answer, "And you are?"

"Jenny O'Toole," she said, trying to remember to unleash her competent, commanding presence. Did he know Blake's tongue had laid claim on her mouth, on her cleavage, on her earlobe? And that instead of introducing herself she was replaying that memory with a fire between her legs?

"Blake's had a busy week," he said. Jenny looked at his face, but it was hard to figure out what he meant.

She nodded. "Great show." Unthinking, she ran a finger along her swollen lip, remembering Blake's touch. Steve seemed to look at her more closely.

"Yes," he said. He stretched out his arms and cracked his knuckles. Somehow, it didn't bother Jenny as much as it did when Michael did it.

He smiled a little more warmly. "So, do people watch this show?"

"It's local cable, but yeah. I mean, sure. My parents do."

"Are your parents likely to pay a visit to the Albus Booker Museum to see Blake Harrison's Boston debut?"

Jenny considered this for a moment. They were more likely to drive in to see a traveling Monet show at the MFA or the flower displays at the Gardner, but maybe.

"If I tell them to come, they would."

Steve smiled. "Will you?"

The question felt loaded, as if Jenny was being asked if she'd bring Blake home to meet her parents. The answer to that was a definite no. They wanted grandchildren. They had met with Jenny's announcement of her sexuality with a puritan kind of resignation. They had liked Melinda. She was nice and boring and polite and always came over to the house for dinner—not that they visited very often, but often enough—with a cake or a crumble.

What if Jenny brought Blake home to them? A volatile, occasionally butch, vegan contemporary artist? Jenny imagined them sitting next to one another on her parents' quilt-covered couch, her father offering Blake crudités. Blake's strange lipstick colors, her black bra strap showing, tunic off her shoulder. *Oh, God. No.*

"Blake is brilliant," she decided to say, dodging the parent question.

Steve nodded. "I agree. At least you didn't say 'visionary.' Girls usually say 'visionary.'"

Jenny swallowed and tried not to look as chastened as she felt. So, that was how it would be. She was just another "girl" in a series of girls, a fling for the week. She knew that, of course. From what Lydia had said, and the chemistry that Blake oozed, she couldn't think this was anything more than that. What right did she have to even wonder, anyway? All she had done was kiss Blake—*oh, she had kissed her*—in the gallery, after a few days of circling.

Fine.

Jenny looked over at Blake, who had been transformed a bit by the makeup. She looked sunny and far more feminine, her short hair angled up a bit in front in front so it looked longer. Blake smiled at her, and any care Jenny had about her parents or labels or flings faded. God, she was gorgeous. For a few days at least, she'd be Jenny's.

Steve and Jenny sat next to one another on folding chairs by the soundstage to watch the interview. Jenny was impressed by how practiced Blake's answers were. She covered her life story, ethnic heritage, and effect on the art, identity politics, and then, the questions Blake was most clearly most enthusiastic about—the construction of the rooms. Her face went from serious to bright, as she went on eagerly about the lights embedded in the walls, the filters used over the paneling to get the precise diffuse light, the meter readings of the paintings and of the rooms. "A company in Bridgewater made the light panels for the rooms," she said, giving the name to drum up business for them. "They also manufacture chemicals for the smartphone screens. Here, they made opaque screens exactly to my specifications so that the light would dance through just the way as it does in the paintings. I think it's a lot like how art has always been. Scientific exploration—like cadmium orange—have a real effect on what we're able to achieve."

When she finished, Darren took a longer pause than usual and seemed to be sweating a bit. The producer called a break and blotted his forehead. When the camera started rolling again, Darren took a deep breath and said, "Are you aware that an artist named Ned Frankenwell is mounting an exhibit very similar to yours? This was brought to our attention by a well-regarded Internet journalist this afternoon. She reports also that Frankenwell has threatened to sue you for theft of intellectual property. Can you comment?"

Blake's face lost all her color, and panic filled in her eyes. Jenny watched, helpless, as she slumped down in her chair. Her eyes darted over to Jenny and Steve—or Jenny *or* Steve, Jenny wasn't sure which. Blake swallowed, a big, long swallow.

"Darren, I—" Blake stammered. She swallowed again, apparently unable to continue. Jenny wanted to run up and rescue her, slam down Darren on to the ground, and pick her up and carry her out of the studio, but she couldn't. Everything was being recorded. What the hell was he talking about? Steve sat up straighter, too, and took out his phone, quickly, dialing a number Jenny couldn't look over his shoulder to see. She leaned forward in her cheap, light chair, afraid she'd fall off it, watching Blake breathe heavily under the hot, unforgiving lights. Then something seemed to wake inside of Blake and she managed to say, in cool, considered tones, "I can assure you it is frivolous." She sounded clear, practiced, and detached. Like Jenny, most of the time, at work. Then she said, more warmly, but with a fake edge to her words, "Can we break now?"

"Sure, sure," he said, leaning back. "Guys! Off!" Darren looked at her, nervously, like he was afraid Blake might lean over and chew his head from his neck while he was still alive and squirming. To his credit, Blake looked a little like she might.

"I'm sorry to ambush you with that, I—the Twitter account that had the news—her name was Amanda—"

Blake didn't respond, but her face looked like it had been crushed into a little ball. She stepped off the set and walked over to where Steve and Jenny were standing. "That fucker," she said, and Jenny found herself disturbed for a moment that Blake seemed to know what it was about. If she did, why hadn't she been more prepared? Who was Amanda? Who was Ned? Blake was tapping her foot, angry, angling her body toward Steve and away from Jenny.

Blake glanced over at Jenny and said, clipped, "I have to go deal with this." Her eyes were narrow, hard. Nothing but frigid cold was emanating from her body; Jenny felt wholly unwanted, like the ice would burn her as much as flame.

She nodded, dejected, wondering what was happening and how she'd fit in and immediately chastising herself for being worried about herself when she should be worried for Blake, who was clearly in some kind of trouble. Jenny turned to leave the studio when she realized they didn't have each other's numbers. "Blake!" she shouted, and Blake turned, looking annoyed. The look in her eyes seemed to erase everything Jenny and she had just shared. Jenny said quietly, embarrassed, "Here's my number." She handed her official business card to her, with her personal cell scrawled on the back.

"Thanks," Blake said and waited a beat. There was nothing behind her eyes, no warmth, no plea to stay. Jenny was shocked into silence, wondering how everything had gone from warm to cold so quickly. When neither of them said anything, Blake turned back to Steve, saying something about grad school. Jenny walked out into the frigid afternoon, feeling like, in the span of an hour, she'd both won and lost everything she'd ever wanted.

CHAPTER TWENTY

Blake walked quickly out of the studio, heart beating furiously, as Steve trailed after her. "Who the fuck is Ned Frankenwell?" was his first question.

"We were at grad school together," was all Blake could say.

They were in the middle of Allston. Blake had no idea how they'd gotten there. All she remembered, really, was sitting in the Uber driver's Corolla next to Jenny, feeling an elation she hadn't felt in a long time. An elation that had since combusted. She had told Jenny to leave. But she couldn't think about that now. She had to face this problem. Steve spun her around by her elbow. "Let's focus," he said. "What more do you know?"

"I saw the Spencer Finch show at MassMOCA with him. We were camping. Christ. Steve, can we get a beer?"

He rubbed his forehead and took a deep breath. "Go across the street, I'll smooth things over with Darren and his crew as best I can and meet you there."

In a dive ("Best of Boston 1979," it said in the window), Blake told Steve the story. She felt almost like she was talking about someone else.

"We were in grad school together," she started. "Collaborated on a few projects. Ned did video installations, strange surreal videos with people wearing animal heads. He thought the nod to Shakespeare was enough to legitimize them. Usually there was a naked woman somewhere. They were awful. Truly."

She looked over at Steve, who was listening, expectant. She remembered the videos. Hideous, grainy, crass without being thoughtful.

"We smoked pot together a few times. He was ambitious and I liked that about him. He thought about the business as much as the art. I wasn't taking notes per se, but I was taking notice. Learning. He had lunches with potential patrons. Networked our classmates, asking what everyone's parents did. If you said banker, he was like, okay, you can buy my art. If you said waitress, he was like, okay, you can't buy my art and you don't know anyone."

Steve groaned a little. Blake continued.

"As for him. He had a beard. A loud voice. He was brash and fun. We took a road trip to the MassMOCA together, had no idea what would be there, were prepared to lambast it the way we everything else, thinking 'if only we ran things,' but it was great, perfectly laid out, everything."

Blake remembered this part. More than Ned, more than anything. The candlelight. It had enveloped her whole body and imprinted itself on every piece of her skin, behind her eyes, through her whole skull. She remembered it like it was a great kiss. The memory of Jenny flashed before her. She swallowed hard, willing it to go away.

"We pitched tent at some campground in the Berkshires, a tiny two-person."

Blake stared at the bottom of her glass and flicked her wrist at the bartender for another. Only when it arrived did she continue, but now just looking down at the bar, not at Steve.

"That whole weekend we were talking about the rooms. He had no interest in installations. Just video. I was sitting in the passenger seat drawing up plans, getting excited. This was ten years ago. It has taken me ten years to do this. Alone."

Steve squeezed her shoulder. "It's rotten, Blake, I'm so sorry. We'll get through it."

"So he's doing an exhibition just like mine and suing me at the same time? How the hell does that even work? What is this gallery that's agreeing to mount it? None of this makes any sense."

"He has a crazy vendetta against you."

She took a deep breath, thinking she might as well tell Steve everything. It was going to come out eventually. "We slept together once. In that stupid tiny tent."

Steve's body shifted next to her, but he didn't say anything.

Blake sipped her beer, relieved for a moment not to be talking. Then, turning to Steve, "You have the thing—the case?"

"The complaint? Sure. Amanda tweeted it out. Here." Steve handed Blake his phone with the PDF pulled up. Everything looked strange to her. The heading, her name under "defendant." The anger was making her twitch a little as she looked at the screen. She didn't know who she was angrier at. Amanda—fucking Amanda—sharing her bed and doing this. Or Ned, coming from nowhere, trying to steal the thing she was proudest of. Or at herself. For picking up Amanda, for even knowing Ned in the first place, for not seeing this coming.

"What do I do now?" she said, swallowing a cry.

Steve put his head in his hands, elbows on the sticky bar. "I don't know."

"Did I tank that interview?"

"No, you sounded good. Professional. They might not even air that last part. I gave them a piece of my mind."

"Thanks. I can't believe this is happening."

"So, was this guy in love with you or—?"

"I don't know. It doesn't matter." She could feel Steve staring at her, with a little heat, and clued in that he was feeling something a little more complicated than she had understood, given this news. God, that old crush he had still went unextinguished. She wanted to roll her eyes or start raging against him, but she couldn't afford to lose any more allies today. She tried to put on a jocular tone, even as anger filled the whole field of her vision.

At Ned, at Amanda, at herself, and now at Steve, too. "Steve, give it a rest, okay? I'm gay. Always have been, always will be. Give me a break."

Steve chose to ignore her and said, "Go home. I'll make a few calls. We'll meet early tomorrow."

After they left the bar, Blake started wandering, too antsy to sit on a bus or trolley car and sketch. She needed to move her legs, even through the frigid air. Her breath was hanging in front of her in short bursts as she made her way up Harvard Avenue. With each step she remembered more about Ned, their ill-fated and short-lived liaison. Why had she slept with him in that stupid tent? Just curiosity, that was mainly it. Maybe boredom, and loneliness, and the feeling that nothing she did had any consequences. She was on scholarship, sure, and there were teachers who believed in her. But the whole business was so cutthroat, and she had no role models. The idea of getting paid to make art that wasn't even functional—a vase or a painting you could hang in your house to make things look more pretty— had seemed impossible. Ned had made it seem like there were no limits. He was convinced that the world needed his stupid videos. That bravado was somehow intoxicating. She was jealous of it. Maybe in that tent that night she'd thought if she had sex with him some of that confidence would rub off on her.

As it was, that didn't happen. Not right away, anyway. Not that it was altogether unpleasant. He was more attentive as a lover than you might expect someone with his ego would be. But she had no desire for a repeat performance. This was perplexing to him. She tried to explain, but he claimed it was "dehumanizing." She stifled a laugh. He stopped asking her to go to events with him. They never went on a road trip again.

After their friendship fizzled, she went back to being unaccountable to anyone. She had gaggles of friends throughout the city, her sporadically attentive mother, and a rotating cast of lovers. But no one expected her to be anywhere, do anything. It was just her and her studio. Her studio mates didn't know her schedule and were seldom at their stations in the loft they rented. She would go up alone to the roof that overlooked the

Manhattan skyline. There was an incredible freedom to being so untethered, to having nothing expected of her.

But now Steve expected something of her. His job depended on her making money. Same with Davis, the curator at the Albie. They had never even met before this week, and now his livelihood rested on her success.

But would either of them show up at her door if she were ill and needed someone to run to the drugstore? Who would? Certainly not her mother, who only called to update her when she'd found someone new to live off of for a few years. Not any of her buddies back home, too swept up in their own careers and now, some, in their own families. None of the girls she had one-night or one-week stands with from the local bar. Not even Evelyn, who floated in and out of her bed, naked, stopping by when she was back from London. Or rather, when she claimed to be back from London. Evelyn had said she called on Blake whenever she was stateside, but once, she'd seen her at the Union Square Farmer's Market on a Sunday morning, her thumb in another woman's belt loop. She never said anything. The arrangement had suited them both fine. No need to mention it.

Now this lawsuit. Who did she have to call? She didn't want to tell any of her friends. It was embarrassing. They'd believe her, she was sure. But it wouldn't take away the sting of shame. She didn't want anyone to worry. This was hers, hers alone to bear. That felt, for the first time, unbearable.

She drew a ragged breath, choking on the cold air. She wanted to cry. That's what she wanted to do—needed to do. She looked for a warm spot, but saw only a Gap and gastropubs that weren't open yet. Then there it was, right in front of her, a jubilant painted mural wall almost obscuring the name. *Zaftigs Delicatessen.*

She knew who she wanted to call. But that would be impossible. She had ordered her away, turned from her coldly, embarrassed about the whole thing for a host of reasons. Her survival instinct had kicked in. *Flee. Do not share. Solve the problem.* Only she didn't know how to solve this problem. And she just wanted Jenny to tell her it was going to be okay.

If Blake called her now, Jenny would think that she was being opportunistic. Working the connection to try to get legal advice. No. She'd screwed everything up, quickly and efficiently. Sure, she hadn't been kissed like that in years. Maybe ever. It had been so long since she had let herself go, tasting tongues and lips and skin, for the sheer fun of it. My God, it had been fun.

But now it was over. She would be back in New York in a week. Steve would figure out what to do. And Jenny would find someone else. Someone with less drama. Someone she deserved.

CHAPTER TWENTY-ONE

Jenny trudged back to her office by default—she wasn't sure where else to go, so she sought the familiar sounds and smells of the cube where she spent most of her time. Her window was fogged up again; just a few dotted streetlights from below were forcing their way through the glass. She'd spend yet another long night there, in its stale comforts. Could it really have only been the day before that she had won the motion in court? It seemed like years ago. She felt like she was years tired, for sure.

Her email inbox showed 130 unread messages. She started clicking through them. Each one was just another line in the parade of boredom and pointlessness. Chatter back-and-forth about admissible evidence. "In search of" emails from other lawyers for contacts at the U.S. Attorney's office, divorce lawyers, complaint samples. Endless subpoena requests and corrections. Jenny could feel her head starting to spin, the pressure of her job squeezing her temples. Then, around unread message number 117, one from Lydia. *You okay? Saw Blake's getting sued.*

Jenny opened up the email. Lydia had included a link to the public complaint. She was pulled in immediately, reading the lines. This Ned character was suing her for damages, for her earnings. He claimed to have drawings he did of the rooms, years before Blake had made them real. Jenny saw holes in his arguments already, ways to combat it. A few drawings did not mean that he had come up with the idea. And were the drawings really his? How would the documents be verified? She found herself coming to Blake's rescue already. She took a notepad down from the shelf, started scrawling questions and counterpoints.

"Jenny?" Lydia, standing in her doorway.

Jenny looked down at her pad, wild with markings, and then up at Lydia, head tilted and eyes wide with concern. Jenny raised her hand toward her head, feeling like she had food on her face and didn't know it. Well, actually there was something like that. Her knit wool hat was still there. She had lost all her bearings. How embarrassing. She had been cast aside, and here she was taking notes on the case. She covered over the paper with her forearm as Lydia approached and leaned on her desk, peering down at Jenny over her glasses.

"You look like hell. Are you okay?"

"Fine. Blake's getting sued."

"I saw that. You want to tell me what happened?"

"Nothing."

"What I saw down there in the lobby wasn't nothing. There is a force field around the two of you. It's powerful. Like I've never seen you before."

Jenny looked down. She knew Lydia was right. Not that it mattered.

"Start from the beginning, Jen. She shows up here with art for you. Her art! As a gift! Then you go to the gallery. You're watching her tape Darren Rosenfeld's show. And then what?"

"Darren asked Blake why there is this person—Ned, the plaintiff—why he claims he thought of the idea first. Blake got upset and cold. She shut down, told me to leave."

Well, that wasn't exactly it, but it might as well have been. Jenny swallowed, to keep herself from crying. When had she become a crier? When had she become the kind of person who forgot to take off her own hat?

"You looked at the complaint?"

Jenny nodded. "Thanks for sending it."

"Well, I looked into it—"

"You what?"

"I looked into it. It's pretty much in my wheelhouse, intellectual property, you know. There's incendiary language in the complaint, and he's playing the press, but there's a lot of weakness his allegations. I think we could win a motion to dismiss. The standard for that is extraordinarily high, but he doesn't even fully allege—"

"Stop," Jenny said. "She doesn't want my help."

"You don't know that."

"I do. She told me to leave. She didn't even have my number. I had to give it to her on my business card like an idiot."

Lydia sighed, seeming to debate what tack to take. "Cut the crap," she finally said. "You've been mooning over her for days. She needs your help now, but it's like you're shutting yourself off. I don't get it. If you don't want to call her, I will."

Lydia reached for Jenny's cell phone. Jenny wasn't sure she'd really make the call, but she snatched it away and made a big show of tucking it into the inside zipper of her briefcase. Lydia held up her hands in defeat.

"We kissed," Jenny said a moment later, looking down at her desk so she didn't have to register the cascade of expressions she imagined would cross Lydia's face.

"Oh, Jenny," Lydia said, but she was interrupted by the viscous sound of Michael clearing his throat from the doorway.

Lydia jumped and stood up straight, smoothing her blouse and skirt. She clamped her lips together and looked at Jenny, waiting for her to say something, but Jenny stayed silent.

"Jenny, can I have a minute of your time?" Michael said. The way he said the words—a little more high-pitched than normal and uncharacteristically warm—made Jenny's spine go cold. It smacked of self-satisfied pity. She could smell it. Her victory the day before notwithstanding, she'd been out of reach, ignoring his emails, like she had all the others. Was she about to be fired? Lydia scampered out, but not before giving Jenny a sympathetic scowl. She closed Jenny's office door behind her, apparently thinking better of making dirty hand gestures over his head the way she normally did.

Michael sat in the guest chair and scooted toward Jenny's desk. His knees hit the side. No feet up today. Jenny felt numb. This day really couldn't get worse. And it was essentially the same day as yesterday, because she hadn't slept.

"So," he said. "We should discuss something."

"Just do it," Jenny said, her newly discovered brashness jumping out.

Michael lifted his chin a bit, regarding her. "Do what?" he said slowly.

"Fire me."

"You think I'm here to fire you?" Jenny didn't respond. Michael continued, looking at the wall to his right, covered in Jenny's diplomas, rather than at her face. "Why would I do that?"

Jenny stifled the automatic "I'm sorry" that threatened to bubble out of her mouth. Instead, she just nodded, looking at him, trying not to look scared.

"You won yesterday. You did well. I called the client. I told him about your performance. He was pleased. Where were you, by the way?"

The memory of Blake's hands and hot lips came rushing back to her. Her cheeks turned red, her limbs went on fire, just thinking of it. The kisses. The kisses in that light. If Michael noticed, he didn't say anything. She couldn't speak.

"Whatever differences we've had, the client is very satisfied with our work. Your work."

"I'm glad," Jenny managed to squeak out. Was he really praising her? "Thank you" hadn't been said yet, but it was nearly there, bobbing on the surface.

"Again, I did not appreciate the tone during the initial meeting or the way the whole thing unfolded."

"I understand. And I appreciate the opportunity to present the argument."

Michael looked at her. His chapped lips smacked together for a moment. "You're different lately," he said.

Jenny felt ready to lunge at him. How dare he. "What do you mean—" she started to spit, but he waved his hand to cut her off.

"Different. You are speaking up." He said it neutrally. He was neither condemning her nor praising her. He took a deep breath, and his eyes softened a bit. With a grunt, he said, "I understand that you may have been giving me the message about Van Croughton for many weeks now, but that I was unprepared to hear it."

Jenny kept her mouth shut, but she had to work to keep her jaw from dropping to the floor. This was the closest Michael had ever come—would ever come probably—to a mea culpa. And it was coming today, of all days. This interminable mess. She didn't smile, but she looked at him less sternly as he stood.

"Thanks," she finally whispered to his back as he walked out of her office. He didn't indicate if he heard.

CHAPTER TWENTY-TWO

Blake decided to call her ex for support after all. Evelyn was a lover-turned-friend who, after a pint, reliably threatened to maim anyone who dared cross Blake. She played the part nicely, shouting into the phone, "I'll go down to D.C. my bloody self and see these goddamned copycat rooms and then light them on fire!" Blake held the phone close to her face, taking solace in the comfort of someone else's anger on her behalf.

"Where are you, anyway, Evie?"

"Staying with a friend in Philadelphia."

Blake's heart didn't quite sink, but it felt a little heavy in her chest. "A friend?" she tried to say playfully.

She could hear the smile in Evelyn's reply. "Actually, yes, just a friend, not that it's any of your business. How are things up there? Nab any Irish Catholic Puritans?"

Blake's stomach tightened even more. *Yes*, she wanted to say. *Yes, and I lost her.* She was glad, at first, that Evelyn couldn't see her face; she really would have known something was up. But her pause gave enough away.

"So that's a yes. I can read between the lack of lines," Evelyn said quietly. "What happened?"

"Nothing," Blake said. Because it was nothing. A few kisses. That was it. But she couldn't even lie to herself about it. It was far more than a few kisses. It was the most glorious, flourishing session of kissing she'd had in years. Maybe ever. It was fun, and tasty, and playful, and finally having her arms around Jenny made her fingers burn and her body heat up so quickly it felt like she was falling in—*No, it couldn't be.*

Evelyn was waiting for her to elaborate. "I met someone, but she's not my type," Blake said finally.

"What is your type?" Evelyn asked.

Blake swallowed for a moment, thinking of Steve's assistant, Liza, Amanda, and Evelyn on the phone. What did they all have in common? No expectations. They all let her go. They understood who she was. The sort of woman to flee in the middle of the night because she needed to go restring bulbs. The woman who had a different date for every opening, who didn't want to have to be anywhere in case she wanted to be in her studio.

"You are," Blake said, finding it easier to flirt than to be honest.

"I wasn't fishing for a compliment," Evelyn said. "I meant to ask what you're measuring this girl against."

"Well, she's serious and smart and thoughtful and very intense. Laser-sharp focus. And she has this chestnut reddish hair that cascades. It's like these silken ropes of hair, so shiny, and these pale brown eyes that seem to change with the light."

"She a good shag?"

"I don't know, Evelyn."

"You don't yet know! Well, this may be a first."

"Stop it. I've had a hard day."

"It's better to talk about this girl than that Ned character, isn't it?" Blake couldn't argue. It was true, and she felt a tug of gratitude for Evelyn.

"Maybe a little. Thanks, Evie."

"But?"

"I screwed it up. They ambushed me on TV, and I barked at her, and I told her to leave. There's no going back. She's..." Blake swallowed, trying to figure out why it felt so foregone. Evie sighed, a welcoming, comforting sigh. They agreed to speak again soon, but when Blake clicked off she felt emptier than she had before.

Why would Jenny even want to speak to her now, after she'd dismissed her so readily? Her artistic triumph had been cut down too, now that she was embroiled in this legal quagmire. She had no idea how to make things right again, and it was driving her mad, and all they had done was kissed.

What did it say about her that the only person she had to call was her decidedly not-girlfriend? Her stomach rolled. And Steve texted, not making anything easier.

I put in a call to Walter, but you should stop by Amy's. Make nice. Make sure they're not thinking about pulling the show.

Got it, she responded dutifully, worried again for Steve's job. She hoped she hadn't screwed up anyone's life but her own. That somehow seemed easier than giving Ned the power to make her worry about herself.

Snow had started to fall, but it was only flurries and would barely register. The Prudential stop was the closest stop to Amy's, and when Blake emerged from underground, bitten by the wind, and looked up at the building, her heart started feeling pretzel tight. Jenny's office was way up above. Where was she? Looking outside or down? Could she see Blake below if she looked hard enough? Or maybe she'd run into her on the street outside, dusty with snow. What would she do if she saw her? Apologize? The memory of kissing her was seared in her mind. Her lips felt hot simply thinking about it. The kind of kiss she'd never get again.

When she reached Amy's townhouse, she paused, gathering up strength before ringing the doorbell. The museum wasn't going to be pleased with any controversy. They had to know it wasn't her fault. She'd fight it, though she wasn't yet sure how.

Amy answered. Blake couldn't quite smile, but she tried to look somewhat warmly at Amy through the cold and the snow.

Amy lit up. "Oh, Blake, honey, thank goodness! Come in!" she said, her arms gathering in Blake's shivering body.

"Walter!" she yelled. "Blake has come for a visit!"

Walter walked in and looked at Blake in the doorway. His lips were in a flat line, and his eyes pierced her from across the foyer. His mustache seemed more unkempt than usual and decidedly unfriendly. "It's not true, is it?" he said, as if her answering the question was the price of entry.

"Absolutely not," Blake said, relieved to have him be so forward. "I stole nothing. He stole from me. And I'm sorry for the bad press."

"Enough," Amy said, her arm protectively around Blake. "Pour us something dark and strong, Walter, and we'll talk this through."

Amy and Blake sat in the first-floor drawing room with an Eakins staring down at them, a woman in a white gown, looking pained. *I feel like she does*, Blake wanted to say, but it was too much of a joke, too light for how serious everything had become. Why did they have an Eakins anyway? Eakins was so creepy. His women were so unhappy.

Amy seemed to read Blake's mind. "I hate that painting," she whispered, as Walter walked in the room with three crystal tumblers of whiskey on a silver tray.

He sat near Blake, looking at her much more softly than he had when she came in. "Tell us what happened," Amy invited.

"First I want to apologize. I know you took a chance on the show, and I apologize that any controversy is now attached to it."

"We'll live," Amy said, meaning more than her and Walter. She meant the institution. The whole Albie, all of its patrons, all of its workers. Nervous Davis, who had championed her from the start.

Blake smiled crookedly. "Please tell everyone."

"If it's how you say," Walter said, his voice low and rolling, "our general counsel said we can hire some outside help to get a counterclaim. I am well out of my depth here. She'll be back from Turin in a few days, and we can talk. In the meantime—"

"That's not enough," Amy said. "We have to counterpunch now. Can you get that Tweeter person who interviewed you at the gala to write a story about your side?"

Blake blushed, beet red. Amy seemed to pick it up immediately and smacked her lips together. She looked over at Walter and then at Blake. Blake felt the heat of embarrassment roiling in her body, compressing her chest. She was so severely off her game that she'd given everything away, just by her expressions. She tucked her knees up to her chin, letting her stocking feet rest on the edge of the chair, thick socks making static on the upholstery.

"Walter, honey, can we have some girl talk?"

He looked relieved and stood. "Good of you to come, Blake," he said, and Blake wanted to feel like he meant it.

"You know Amanda?" Amy said when he was out of the room, the "know" filled with meaning. Amy understood. Blake nodded, not wanting to verbalize her own stupidity. "Understood. Before or after she broke the story?"

"Before," Blake said. "I think."

"So maybe she is not a horrific traitor, and it's a bad coincidence and she's just discourteous for not calling you first."

Blake smiled, crooked. There was such an easy "or."

Amy supplied it. "Or she is truly heinous and had it off with you knowing that she was going to release a story about this crackers person suing you and she didn't say anything while she was with you."

Blake nodded. She felt tears welling up.

"So, if you were with this Amanda character, what happened with Ms. Derain from the other night?"

Blake's cheeks flamed up again, and she looked over at Amy, who, again, could read her face instantly. "Oh, you've had an entangled week," she said.

"Just an entangled two days," she corrected, weary. Amy was right. When she said it out loud, it was ridiculous.

"So why aren't you with Jennifer right now?" Amy asked. It was a decent question, Blake thought. Yes. That's where she wanted to be. But it was impossible.

"She was with me when I got ambushed on TV. And she basically left. Or I pushed her out. I don't know. She probably doesn't even believe me. She probably thinks I'm a plagiarizing hack. In addition to being an overly dramatic bitch."

"She doesn't think any of those things," Amy said simply.

"How would you know?"

"I saw her looking at you that night. There was fire in her eyes across the table. Real fire. The epitome of smoldering looks. Blake, you have to know that people enjoy looking at you. But this girl. I saw her, and I thought, 'Wow. She has it bad.'"

Blake took a gulp of whiskey and felt it burn down her throat. She hoped it would extinguish the anguish she felt in her body about how much of a mess she'd made of everything.

"I've got it bad, too," she said to Amy.

Amy smiled. "Well, go get her," she said.

The trouble was, Blake had no idea how to do that.

CHAPTER TWENTY-THREE

The next morning, Jenny took the Green Line out to the suburbs for her scheduled Mom-and-Dad brunch. For a while, she'd gotten them to come to downtown Boston and take her out. When it became clear, though, that the parking situation downtown made her father need to take extra blood pressure medication and that meals out had too much sodium in them anyway, she decided to go to Newton. Sometimes when she walked through the doors to her old brick childhood home she thought she could still smell the wafts of cigar smoke, even though her father claimed to have quit years ago. She opened the door without knocking, as usual. Her mother, as usual, seemed to sense her presence, acknowledging it even before she crossed the threshold.

"Honey!" but the "honey" was for her dad. "Honey, Jennifer's home!"

Home. That's what her mom always called it, even though she hadn't slept over in years. Her father gave her a strong hug. *Hmmm.* That cigar smell was pretty fresh.

"Jenny Penny," he said. "Your mother made a new strange egg concoction, and I ordered a tart."

"Smells good, thanks," Jenny said, remembering reading about Blake's father, and immediately feeling happy that her folks were still together, still here, still themselves. Feeling grateful to be there, in the same house she'd always known. She felt embarrassed by her good fortune, almost, ready to wrap her cold hands around a mug of hot coffee and enjoy their company. She wasn't exactly forthcoming with them most of the time, and they always said something to annoy her, but they were there, weren't they?

Her mother emerged from the kitchen, an old-fashioned apron tied around her waist. She had never cooked when Jenny was young. There was no way to work full time and get dinner on the table. Now, in retirement, she enjoyed it, trying recipes from *Martha Stewart Magazine* and food blogs and chef cookbooks and TV shows. She smiled, clearly proud of today's offering.

"This is Turkish stew for breakfast. Do you know that Boston is one of the best places for upscale Turkish? There are about seventy-five ingredients, thirty of which I'd never heard of and had to look up online." She smiled. "Oh, Jenny, you look tired."

"Whenever someone says that you look tired, they just mean you look like shit," Jenny said.

"Not true!" bellowed her dad, turning from the chair by the fireplace. "You always look beautiful. And today you look beautiful and tired. A mother knows. Also, watch your language."

Jenny stood beside her mother in the kitchen and started tearing tarragon leaves. Her mother patted her hand, as if offering sympathy for some unspoken tragedy. Before Jenny could make sense of the gesture, her mother explained it, saying, "We heard about Melinda."

She could almost feel her father awkwardly stiffen in the next room, but he stayed quiet.

"She seems happy."

"You saw her?"

"Yes, Mom, I ran into her, actually—Yes."

"Oh. Well. Send her our regards."

"I'm not going to see her again," Jenny said, the words falling out almost mechanically, not giving herself time to digest how awkward it was that they were speaking about Melinda. Today of all days. Right after what she'd been through with Blake.

Her mother said nothing else, and Jenny stood beside her, still handling the herbs, both of them in silence. Her father cleared his throat. "Anyone else special in your life?" he shouted from the other room.

"Nope," Jenny squeaked, hoping her parents didn't hear all the layers and uncertainty and regret in the word.

They sat at the table, spread with too much food—the fancy eggs drowned in tomato her mother had made and also bagels and lox and the smoked whitefish spread from one of the delis near Jenny's. The spread was given a platter of honor at the center of the table. There they were again, just the three of them, as they always would be. Jenny relaxed, a little, examining herself for any more unease about Blake. One good thing had happened, she decided. She had realized how much she wanted to be with someone. Anyone. Maybe she would let Davis fix her up with someone. Or take Lydia up on her offer to start an online profile. Even her father was asking if she was single. It was time to change.

They clinked their orange-juice glasses and ate in silence except for the chewing. The silence felt comfortable. Until her mother ruined it by saying a little too loudly, "I heard you were at the Albie gala." Her eyes were sharp across the table, so intent. Jenny stared at her, noting for the first time that her mother's eyebrows had gone gray. Was that common? She had never noticed that on anyone before.

"I was," Jenny said. It felt like so long ago.

"With a man?"

Jenny wanted to laugh, but she could see her parents were serious, inquiring. What had they heard? Before she could spit out a halfway amused denial, she went cold, suddenly understanding her parents' questions. They thought she'd gone straight again. That it was just a phase after all. That at thirty-three she'd seen the light. Anger boiled up in her. Someone had spied her at the gala with Brandon and tipped her parents off? Melinda was pregnant, and they heard about the sighting and gotten their hopes up? What the hell was going on?

"I was there with my boss," Jenny said, gritting her teeth, "and his nephew. It was not a date, and I did not have a good time."

Her parents exchanged a look. Jenny saw it in an instant and thought about ignoring it, but instead speared a soft-boiled egg out of the gravy with her fork, held it up, said as flippantly as she could muster, "I'm still gay," and popped the whole egg into her mouth.

Her father grunted. "Just want you to be happy," he said, and for a moment, looking across the table at her mother, who was staring intently into her plate, and at her dad, whose rosy cheeks from how hot the thermostat was lent his face a kind of joviality that didn't really match his mood, Jenny believed him. Maybe that was true. It might as well be.

"Thanks," she said, finally. "Please don't spy on me."

Her mother smiled at her, tight-lipped, concerning. "The Marshes from down the street were there. Casual conversation. That's all."

"Very casual, I'm sure."

"Well, how was the art?" her father said, trying to change the subject, not knowing that he was failing completely and that Jenny cared not only about the art, but also the artist, more than her father could possibly know, and she was sitting at brunch thinking about Blake, and how coldly she'd been dismissed, and how she wanted to help but couldn't. Shouldn't. Thinking she needed to let Blake go.

"Magnificent," Jenny said. She shoveled in a few more bites of food.

"I saw an interview with her," her mother said, oblivious, like her father, to the effect the direction of the conversations was having on her. Jenny's knees were bouncing up and down, she was sweating, eating more and faster than she meant to, gulping the coffee.

"It's too bad about the lawsuit," her mother said.

Jenny swallowed, but the piece of bagel she had in her mouth was too big. She reached for the water glass, but too fast. She knocked over the pitcher. Her father leapt from the table to clear it, Jenny hunched over, trying to swallow, and her mother gripped the sides of the table as if to hold it steady while she figured out what had happened and why everything had gotten so tense.

After a moment, Jenny could talk again and a towel was on the tablecloth soaking up the mess she'd made.

"Blake didn't do anything wrong," she heard herself saying, impassioned. The clink of the dishes as they spooned themselves more food sounded very loud. She tried to slow her breathing. She knew, at least, at last, what she needed to do.

"Excuse me." She walked up to her childhood room. Her mother had converted it into a place for gift wrapping but kept the bed with its magenta skirt. She pulled her cell phone out of her bra and called Michael. Uncharacteristically, he picked up on the first ring.

Jenny said, "Am I generally in your good graces?"

"Yes," he said, not needing to ask who it was, even though Jenny was speaking out of turn.

"Enough to ask you a favor?"

"You can ask."

Jenny took a deep breath. What Lydia said about there being a force field around her and Blake felt true. Maybe Blake didn't want her for anything more than a little fling, but Jenny had quickly come to care for her. There was no use pushing that aside. If she could help her, she would. "Can we take on Blake Harrison as a pro bono client?"

"So that's who you and Lydia were talking about calling when I was standing in your office?"

Jenny blushed, trying to remember precisely what they had been saying and what Michael had apparently heard. "Yes," she said finally. "Lydia would like to help, too."

"We can. Tell her to come in tomorrow at nine. Get a conference room. Me, you, Lydia, and Greyson."

"Thank you. Really." Greyson was one of the firm's managing partners. He focused on intellectual property, but even Lydia hadn't worked with him very much. His time was worth $1,200 an hour. And Blake would get his services for free.

Jenny still didn't have Blake's number, so she called Steve, getting his number off the business card he'd flicked to her while they were watching the taping of the show. He picked up right away.

"Wales, Moakley and Strauss would like to help Blake," she said, as professionally as possible, though her heart was pounding. It wasn't even Blake on the phone, but her manager, and she was nervous as she'd ever been. She had it bad.

CHAPTER TWENTY-FOUR

Blake's knees were knocking together as she sat in the conference room. The day had become clear. They were looking down at the Charles River, where water and ice were glistening in the bright winter morning sun. Steve seemed mesmerized by the view, too. Sure, they'd each seen their share of dramatic New York City skylines, but there was something almost pastoral about this cityscape that made the view especially captivating, especially in contrast to the soaring steel and glass windows and walls of the white shoe law firm in whose care they had somehow become ensnared. Under other circumstances, she would have wanted to sketch the view. But she couldn't. Her fingers felt frozen and her throat felt sore.

Her knees kept bouncing under the table. "Where are they?" she said to Steve.

"Jenny said nine. It's only five-of. We were early. No thanks to you."

After Jenny had called Steve the night before, he tried calling Blake several times. But she hadn't answered her phone. She had been curled up on her bed, drunk from Amy's good whiskey, caught in a storm of anger and regret. She couldn't draw, she couldn't talk, she was just blank, staring at the white wall of the rented bedroom, wanting to go back in time, to when she had been kissing Jenny in the gallery. All that was gone, thanks to Ned and this stupid lawsuit and thanks to her ordering Jenny out as if she meant nothing to her. Steve pounded on her door this morning, telling her they had an hour to get downtown for this meeting. Blake threw on black slacks and a turtleneck, hoping it was professional enough for Jenny's office, feeling like she was a kid who was caught without clothes for a funeral. She hoped the meeting wasn't going to feel like a funeral. She hoped, at least, she'd see Jenny and have the chance to apologize for how she'd dismissed her. She'd be here for another week. Maybe, at least, even if Jenny didn't want to see her again like that, she could at least buy her a cup of coffee. Dinner. Something.

Blake cracked her knuckles, an added layer of impatience.

"What's with you?" Steve said, standing by the window and craning his neck to see a brave kayaker making her way through ice floes on the Charles.

"Just nervous."

"To see the girl? Or about the case?"

So, he was a mind reader as well as a manager. Blake looked down and started picking at her cuticles. She was supposed to be together, powerful, graceful, incandescent. That's what *The Globe* had said: "In addition to the luminosity of her rooms, Blake Harrison herself is an incandescent presence in the Boston Art Scene." A mouthful of a sentence, but she liked the sentiment. Only now, here she was, in wrinkled clothes, spiky hair, picking at her fingers, being sued by a vindictive ex-whatever, mooning over a lawyer who probably never wanted to see her again.

Except…except she had called Steve. Except she was doing Blake this favor.

Two tall, suited goons walked in first. One was the man she'd stood behind at the opening, the one who had denigrated her art. Michael, the boss Jenny hated, Blake presumed. The other man was shorter and more wrinkled, but the lines around his eyes made him look a little kinder than the boss. Standing beside him was Lydia, the woman Blake had seen with Jenny in the lobby. The fan. And finally, Jenny, wearing a perfectly tailored green wool sheath, a color that made her hair look like it was almost glowing. Blake couldn't help but stare at her. The need to touch her was almost overwhelming. The conference table was planted between them, though, and it was long. The men came over to shake Steve's hand, then Blake's. Jenny circled, too, saying to Steve in her professional-sounding voice, "It's nice to see you again, thank you for coming."

Then she put out her hand to Blake and looked her square in the eye. When they shook, the whole room seemed to spin. Blake felt the power of their touch almost instantly. A current ran through her body so strongly she was sure it would electrify the rug she was standing on and then travel up everyone's feet; there wouldn't be a person in the building without a crazy fan of static electric hair. Jenny felt it too. She had to. When they touched, Blake thought, her lips had parted, just a bit. When their hands dropped, Jenny took a seat across the huge table. Blake felt like melting, or hiding behind the frosty corporate blinds by the window, or getting sucked up by the air vent with the fake office air. She needed to be with Jenny alone, not with all these suited goons. Since that was impossible, she felt like she needed to flee.

"I'm Kit Greyson," said the shorter attorney. "I've been doing intellectual property cases for forty-five years. I took a look at the complaint. We have some thoughts."

Lydia slid a binder across the table to each person in the room. Blake opened it, trying to concentrate on the words on the first page, but all she could see was a jumble of letters and numbers that somehow spelled "Jenny" over and over again.

"He clearly hired someone good, but we have a strong motion to dismiss and several counterclaims. Ms. Harrison, a few questions?"

Blake nodded. Jenny gave her a quiet, tight, almost encouraging smile. *Maybe she doesn't hate me. Not completely.*

"First, let's talk about what's true. Dates you were in school together? The trip he alleges you took? You first saw the Spencer Finch piece with him?"

Blake nodded. All true.

"And is it possible that he does have drawings of the rooms? Initial prototypes, drawn up by him?"

"Not possible," Blake said.

Lydia, who had been writing furiously, looked up. "Not possible? How can you be sure?"

"He can't draw," Blake said. "He does video. Or did. Drafting of any kind was never in his toolkit. We took life drawing together. I just know—he can't draw."

"Can you?" asked Michael. Blake smirked. Wow, this guy really couldn't leave that alone. Blake was about to say, "Yes," when Jenny said, more loudly than was warranted, "She's incredibly skilled, Michael."

He put his hands up in a gesture of surrender. Blake noticed that Lydia was smiling down into her paper as she jotted the notes. Blake felt gratitude overtake her. Somehow, Jenny saw her fit to defend.

More questions from Kit. "Where are your earliest prototypes?"

"I'm not sure," Blake said. It was true. She'd tried to locate them. She had texted her studio mates when she was on the T this morning, asking them to look through some of the files she kept under her desk, but they weren't up yet. Steve didn't have any drawings from before 2006. That meant that Blake might have destroyed them during one of her performance pieces. She might as well come clean.

"I might have eaten them," Blake said.

"Excuse me?" Kit shifted in his seat.

"I did a performance piece where I shredded some of my own art into tiny pieces, really pulverized it, and slowly ate the paste."

Michael looked like he was about to vomit. Just what she would have expected and hoped. Lydia looked intrigued. Jenny's expression was harder to read, but Blake certainly had her attention. That was something.

"It was called 'Consumption of Evolving Ideas,'" Blake continued. "I ate pages from the Bible and *New York Times* Op-Ed articles too."

Everyone remained silent. "It won an award," Steve said, as if that justified or explained anything.

"So the earliest evidence of use in this case you've…eaten." Kit didn't sound amused or disgusted. He just sounded like he needed to get the facts right.

"I'm still looking," Blake said, "but that could be the case. I think, though, that the sketches he says are his were probably mine. How can you date those anyway?"

Lydia piped in, eager to help. "We can have a forensic analysis done, and expert testimony about handwriting—"

"That sounds expensive," Steve said.

Jenny waved her arms, asking Steve to stop speaking. "The firm is handling everything."

Michael grunted at his end of the table, not realizing how loud he was. When everyone looked at him, including Jenny, he jammed his finger into the air and said to Blake, "You have her to thank." Jenny and Blake locked eyes for the second time that morning, and even without their hands touching, the electricity started up again, coursing down Blake's neck into her back and into the upholstery of the chair, down to her feet, to flood the whole room. She swallowed slowly and mouthed across to Jenny, "Thank you." Jenny just smiled. Blake saw Lydia hit Jenny's leg under the table, but Jenny didn't break her composure.

"This was an ex-boyfriend of yours?" Kit asked next.

Blake shook her head. "No. A friend."

Lydia seemed to pause in writing her notes. Jenny appeared to be blushing, but she was looking down into her binder, as if she wanted to reference something before speaking. Only silence came from that side of the table, however. Finally, Lydia said, half-looking at Jenny, "It's important that we know, um—"

Blake gripped the sides of the table and looked straight at Jenny, willing her to pick her head up and look her in the eyes. "Let's just call it an ill-fated experiment," she said. Jenny looked up. Blake smiled at her, hoping she'd understand the transmission, gay girl to gay girl. *Jenny, it was an experiment. A phase. A mistake.* And most importantly, *I want you.*

Jenny smiled at Blake, full of knowing, and all of a sudden, there they were, alone in the room, it really seemed. Alone in their understanding, alone in their shared urgency to end the meeting, ignore all the consequences, and leave together, fingers laced. Blake felt giddy. She didn't care about the lawsuit, didn't care about the fact that she was returning to New York in a few days. She just wanted time with Jenny, time with this exacting, confounding, profoundly intelligent woman who somehow, improbably, seemed to want to spend time with her.

Kit had more questions. An hour's worth of questions, as it turned out. They went through everything. The first room Blake made, the plans, which carpenters' union she contracted for the walls. Steve fielded the financial questions, which apparently would bear on potential damages. Blake kept looking over at Jenny and was rewarded with glimpses of a blushing neck that clearly showed how hard she was trying not to look over at Blake or with her eyes, which got steamier as the hour wore on.

Finally, Kit called the end of the meeting, said he and Lydia would work together on an answer, counterclaims, and a motion to dismiss, adding that Blake had to sign the official engagement letter. She was gracious in saying "Thank you" but couldn't wait to get to the corner of the room where Jenny was packing up her binder and notebook extremely slowly, apparently on purpose, waiting for Blake to walk over to her.

"Thanks," was all Blake could think to say. She was overwhelmed by Jenny's generosity. After what she'd done, her willingness to put so many resources behind her—call in so many big favors—was extraordinary. Most of all, Blake kept thinking how lucky she was that Jenny believed her. That was the true gift.

"Can I take you to dinner?" Jenny asked. Her voice was small, squeaky, not at all like the commanding tone she'd used in the meeting or the first time she'd introduced herself from the bottom of the stairs.

"I'd like that," Blake said. "Yes."

"Where should we meet?"

"I'll be at the museum," Blake said. "In the gallery."

"All day?" Jenny's voice was low, almost a whisper. Her hands seemed to be shaking. Blake could see them gripping the binder and the side of the table. She wanted to kiss her, so badly, that it was almost impossible not to. But the walls were glass, and Michael was lurking outside, looking at them.

"All day. Waiting for you. Drawing."

"What are you going to draw?" Another whisper.

"You," Blake said, and as she said it, she knew it would be true. She would draw Jenny. She would sit in silence and gratitude, drawing Jenny.

CHAPTER TWENTY-FIVE

Jenny found Blake hunched over her drawing pad, the same spiral bound hardcover Blake had presented to her in the lobby the day before. The memory of their kiss in the La Tour room suffused her. Her lips felt bigger than they were, slowly pulsing, the closer she got to Blake. Blake was focused on her page, lost in it. Jenny walked toward her, enjoying the privilege of gazing at her without her knowing. She could move slowly, and she let her eyes travel the length of Blake's right arm up to her perfectly round, smooth shoulder. Her tank top was billowing out a little beneath her collarbone. Jenny wanted to kiss all along her bones, taste her décolletage, nibble on her earlobes. That moment in the La Tour room had made everything come alive. She knew, seeing Blake sitting there bent over her pad of paper, fingers scribbling wildly, that there was no turning back.

She had made a reservation at a small vegan place in Somerville. It was intimate but casual. White tablecloths but bright. She had wanted to strike the right mood—this was going to be a date, utterly and completely, but they were still getting to know one another. They had already kissed, sure, but at the end of dinner, she wanted to be able to walk away. Take things slow, if that's the direction they seemed to be heading. Even though, cruelly, they only had a week before Blake moved away.

Seeing Blake sitting cross-legged on the floor, hugging the pad of paper to her chest, Jenny felt a surge of nearly uncontrollable desire. She wasn't sure they'd make it to the restaurant at all.

Only when Jenny was standing over her did Blake look up from her pad of paper. Jenny could see the pink rush to her cheeks. "Hi," she said, just as Jenny said, "Hello," and they both said, "Oh, hi," again. Blake didn't move toward Jenny, though, or make any motion like she was intending to stand. Instead, she intently clutched her pad of paper. She didn't seem nervous, exactly, but guarded. Jenny wondered for a moment if she had been wrong about her interest.

Then they locked eyes again, and Jenny felt her insides lurch and knew she wasn't alone.

"What are you drawing?" Jenny said, her voice coming out even huskier than she meant it to. Blake was nervous too, it seemed, all blinking eyes.

Blake kept the pad close to her chest. "Nothing. No one," she said quickly, as if embarrassed about something.

Jenny laughed, feeling uncharacteristically in control. Aware of what she was doing to Blake, she sat on the floor next to her, with only a little space between them, and said, "Let me see."

"Really, it's nothing."

Jenny gently placed her hands on Blake's, which were clutching the edges of the sketchpad. Her pencil had fallen by her side. When they touched, Blake gasped in air. Jenny did, too, but kept her breathing controlled, lifting Blake's fingers away from the paper, one by one. She felt like her fingers were burning, amazed at how the simple act of touching the tips of Blake's fingers could make her whole body feel like she was stepping into fire. Blake let her arms fall limply at her sides. Jenny took the sketch pad from her and placed it on her own lap. Blake looked at Jenny's face, not the paper. Jenny looked down, flipped over the first page, and saw a drawing of a woman. Carefully rendered, like the ones Blake had shown her of people on the bus, full of splashing thick lines and well-controlled thin ones, a fire and energy leaping off the page. The woman was sitting on a chair, completely naked, looking off to the side of the page. And the woman's face, though half in shadow, was unmistakably Jenny's.

Jenny gasped in a little air. She couldn't help it. She wanted to laugh, and grin, and kiss her ragged all at once. Blake had been drawing naked pictures of her? Had anyone *ever* drawn a naked picture of her?

"Guilty as charged," Blake said into the silence. "I'm sorry." She smiled a little, the sides of her mouth turning up a bit mischievously, and Jenny laughed.

"That's me?"

Blake nodded. "I know, I'm like a fifteen-year-old boy."

Jenny picked up the pencil from the floor, leaning over Blake for a moment to do so. She smiled, wide, and narrowed her eyes, feeling playful and extremely turned on and serious at the same time. "We have a problem," Jenny said, in mock reproach, but again, her voice was lower, huskier than she thought it would be, so every syllable came out like an erotic invitation. Blake didn't say anything but just continued to stare at Jenny.

"My breasts are actually bigger than this," she said, pressing the pencil into Blake's hand. She looked at her, eyes wide. Jenny clamped her fist around Blake's hand and guided her onto the page. "If you are going to try to draw me naked, you should be more accurate. My nipples are also a lot darker than you've made them here." She tightened her grip around Blake's hand and felt her flinch. They were both sweating. Jenny guided Blake's hand and pressed down hard on the pencil, commanding her to draw thick, dark lines around the areolae.

"That's better," Jenny said. Blake was breathing loud and heavy. Jenny was coming apart inside, dripping wet, with the ends of her fingertips and toes feeling red hot.

She put her mouth close to Blake's ear, still moving the pencil across the page with her hand, tracing the firm ab muscles and strong thighs Blake had drawn for her. "Come home with me and I'll show you the real thing."

Jenny had never said anything so forward in her entire life. But something about Blake made her feel brave. She was terrified and exhilarated that she had somehow become a person—or rather, realized she was a person—who could whisper something like "Come home with me" in Blake Harrison's ear.

Still in command, she got up before Blake could answer or try to kiss her and grabbed Blake's coat from off the hook by the gallery entrance. "Here," she said, holding it open and guiding her arms in.

Blake said nothing, seeming to know that Jenny was enjoying the dynamic immensely. And Blake seemed to be enjoying it too. She looked at her with big, watery eyes and licked her lips quickly before following her down the steps. Jenny walked slowly, deliberately, enjoying the effect she knew the delay was having on Blake. When they reached the door, she made sure not to touch her as they walked out. They said nothing while waiting for the bus and nothing on the bus, where they sat together, but barely touching except for their upper thighs. Jenny thought a hole would burn through the fabric covering their skin, they both felt so hot, fiery, breathing in and out, nearly heaving. She couldn't think about what she was doing—bringing this woman—this volatile, famous, completely inappropriate woman—back to her apartment with no pretense whatsoever. But she had never in her life wanted something—someone—so much. She had never been so reckless. And so sure.

CHAPTER TWENTY-SIX

If Jenny had suggested they ride the bus all the way to Maine, Blake would have done it, hot with anticipation the whole way. After seven stops, Jenny said, "Here," gently taking Blake's forearm and guiding her off the bus at the next stop. As Jenny opened the door to her apartment, she fumbled for her keys a bit, breaking the spell just enough for Blake to lean in and slip a hand underneath her coat, around her waist. Now it was Jenny's turn to gasp. As she turned the doorknob, Jenny whispered, "That bus ride was the most erotic twenty minutes of my life."

They stumbled through the door, and Jenny kicked it closed behind her. "Until the next twenty minutes, and the twenty after that," Blake said. They kissed, finally, hungrily, pouring everything they'd been feeling since the kiss in the La Tour room and on their silent, charged bus ride, into each other's lips and tongues. Jenny had one arm around Blake's waist, and Blake did the same, slipping her palm behind Jenny's shirt to feel the hot, smooth small of her back. Blake's tongue explored every crevice of Jenny's mouth, and Jenny pulled her in for access, resting her other hand on the back of Blake's head and pulling her close so that their mouths would smash together. They were each groaning, not knowing who was making which sounds and not caring.

"Slow," Blake said, breaking the kiss for just a moment as Jenny's hand moved toward the front of Blake's jeans.

"I can't go slow," Jenny breathed. "I need you."

Blake needed her too. She needed to be inside of her, on top of her, she needed every inch of their skin to touch. But they each had their coats on and their boots.

"You can have me," Blake said, pulling away a little. She looked Jenny in the eye and said almost firmly, "You have to get undressed first. You were going to show me, remember?"

Jenny gasped, seemingly aware, now that she was on the receiving end of it, how erotic her command must have been.

"I remember," Jenny said, stepping away from her. And then, almost solicitously, "Would you like to sit down?" Blake nodded. She took off her coat but left the rest of her clothes on, even her boots, and sat on the couch. She was shaking and dripping wet, feeling as if she had entered into a parallel universe where she would get everything she wanted.

Jenny stood across from her and unzipped her coat, making eye contact with Blake. Blake wasn't sure how she could make unzipping her bulky down winter coat sexy, but she knew that everything she did, everything she thought, in Jenny's presence, had something erotic about it.

And indeed, she was squirming as Jenny unzipped the coat. The collar of her shirt was wide enough to give Blake a glimpse of her black lace bra when she leaned down to pull off her boots. Jenny looked straight at her as she unbuttoned each button of her shirt. Soon she was wearing only her pencil skirt, stockings, and bra. Her nipples were hard and long, almost showing over the top of the demi cups of her bra.

Blake, fully clothed, stared up at her and licked her lips, just slightly. Jenny walked toward her, implying that she was going to offer Blake her breasts, before turning at the last moment and saying, "Zipper?" Blake's fingers fumbled as she unzipped her skirt. It fell to the floor. Jenny didn't move. Blake reached up, fingers still hot and fumbling, and undid her bra. Jenny still did not turn around. She ran her hands down the sides of Jenny's ass, her perfectly smooth, pale skin, and took down her pantyhose and her underwear with them.

Blake had never shook so much with need, looking at and feeling the perfect body in front of her. The perfect woman in front of her. She ran her hands up and down Jenny's toned thighs, wanting so badly to go straight to her clit and make her moan, but wanting to savor her even more. Kiss her. Taste her mouth before tasting her juices. Jenny seemed to agree. She turned and, cupping her breasts, looked down at Blake, who was still sitting. "See? I look a little different than in your drawing."

"You are more beautiful than any drawing. I could never capture you. Ever. You are so, so beautiful."

Jenny smiled and then crouched down in front of Blake. Her breasts hung from her frame, inviting and full. Blake wanted to suck on them fiercely, but there would be time for that. Jenny leaned down and pulled off her boots and rolled down her socks. Blake gripped the fabric of the side of the couch to keep herself from falling. With her clothed and Jenny not, Jenny's confidence was overwhelmingly erotic. She was stark naked, undressing Blake, either knowing she was perfect or knowing that Blake wanted every inch of her no matter what. Or both.

Jenny pulled Blake's arms up a bit to pull off her sweater, and as she got closer, Blake could smell her arousal. Blake moved to kiss her once the sweater was above her head, but Jenny put a finger on her lips, as if to say, "Shhhh." Blake went limp, not sure she could hold out much longer, feeling an orgasm beginning to build even though they were barely touching.

Jenny lifted Blake's hips and maneuvered off her pants, so that both of them were naked. Then she straddled her on the couch, pressed their breasts together, and kissed her, hard, needy, and it felt as if their entire bodies were locked in a kiss. Blake could feel her large nipples against her chest. She could feel her wetness on her upper thigh. Both of them were groaning, loud, without censor. Blake could not wait any longer. She moved her hands down Jenny's body, toward the core of heat, and, finding her wetness, slipped two fingers inside of her and found her clitoris with her thumb. Jenny's whole body lurched back. So, she was as close as Blake was. She felt Jenny contract around her fingers. "More," Jenny said, whispering, but insistent, in Blake's ear. She put a third finger inside her, still working her clit with her thumb. Jenny was grinding on her hand, one hand massaging Blake's compact breast and the other propping her body up on the arm of the couch.

"Oh God," Jenny said, as her body enveloped Blake's knuckles.

"You're so beautiful," Blake said, looking straight at Jenny, whose cheeks were bright red and whose eyes were clear, looking at her. She shifted her weight a bit and sucked on Jenny's nipple. She looked up for a moment, seeing Jenny's pupils widen, and mouthed, "Is this okay?"

"Yes, oh God," Jenny said, and she threw her head back as her body contracted tightly around Blake's hand and her juices gushed over Blake's fingers and thigh.

Blake grabbed the back of Jenny's head and pulled her in for a fierce kiss as the orgasm ripped through Jenny's body. She kept her hand inside of her until she gently tugged on her wrist and extracted it. Straddling one of Blake's legs, she guided her dripping hand up to Blake's mouth, just as she had done when she was holding the pencil.

"You taste me and I'll taste you," Jenny said. She sank down on her knees, licking slowly and indulgently between Blake's legs. Blake's body responded quickly. Jenny used her fingers to spread Blake's labia and began sucking on her clitoris. Blake closed her eyes, savoring the feeling, until she started shaking. She looked down at Jenny, whose hair was tousled a bit and whose perfect back arched between her legs. "I'm going to come," she said to Jenny, as if Jenny couldn't tell. As she did, Jenny joined her darting tongue with her fingers and entered Blake. Blake's body rolled in an orgasm as Jenny groaned and pressed her mouth firmly between her legs, flicking her tongue back and forth along with her fingers, as Blake's cries subsided.

"Come here," Blake said, when she caught her breath, helping Jenny to her feet and then cradling her so they were lying side by side on her couch, overcome by their chemistry and how brave and bold they'd been with one another. Unafraid, vulnerable, playful, strong. Delicious.

There was too much Blake wanted to say, too much she wanted to think and express; it was starting to scare her how much she wanted to jump off of the cliff in front of her, holding Jenny's hand.

"So," Blake said, holding onto Jenny, tasting her on her lips, running her fingers through her thick chestnut hair. "This looks like a really nice apartment."

"You want a tour?" Jenny laughed.

"Not really," Blake said. "I want to stay right here." Out of caution and self-preservation she swallowed the last word of that sentence—*forever.*

CHAPTER TWENTY-SEVEN

Jenny woke up to find her arm was asleep, lodged under Blake's back. Or maybe she woke up because her arm was asleep, all pins and needles, wresting her from what must have been a pleasant dream. Waking up to Blake, naked in her bed, sheets tangled up around her, could yield nothing but pleasant dreams. Blake's head was sideways on the pillow, her strong profile against the blinding white sheets.

With the tip of her finger, barely touching her so she wouldn't wake her, Jenny traced the perfectly curved line from the top of Blake's head to her shoulder and then to the curve of her breasts, to where the sheet met her skin. Blake shifted a little but was so deep in sleep that Jenny had free rein to look, gaze, worship, and consider the beauty lying there in front of her. In her bed. Jenny had gone from starkly alone in that bed to being consumed in it by the fire of Blake in no time at all. Her life had changed completely.

It would have to change back, she reminded herself. Blake would be gone in a few days. This was just a wake-up call. A big adventure to jolt her out of complacency. Fun.

Jenny could see the faintest hairs above Blake's upper lip. There were only a few—Blake must groom them fastidiously—but Jenny could gaze at them now as much as she wanted. The intimacy of that shocked her for a moment. She assumed Blake wouldn't want her to notice the hairs. Maybe she'd see them in the mirror later that morning and wonder if Jenny had noticed them while she slept. But after yesterday, how could they be embarrassed about anything? They had been so raw with one another, so needy, demanding, and playful. They had been overwhelmed by their own freedom.

Maybe that's how Blake always was with her lovers. For Jenny, last night was a little different than she was used to. Oh, who was she kidding? The last person she had sex with was Melinda, and by the time that relationship was over, sex was both rare and uninspired. No. Blake was something different. She brought out something fierce in Jenny.

Jenny rose from the bed, telling herself to let Blake sleep. She navigated the piles of underwear around her condo, the bra on the kitchen chair, Blake's bag by the door. With every clank of the dishes, turning the water on, she expected Blake to come out of the bedroom with a T-shirt on and say she was sorry and she had to leave. But she didn't. She kept sleeping.

Jenny looked out the window. More white, a great big swath of it. The snow had fallen on top of yesterday's by only a few inches, but everything was white again. She thanked her good sense, again, not to own a car, to be landlocked in the city. NPR was talking of delays and power outages and saying that the T was shut down again.

What fortune. Caught inside her apartment with Blake. All day. *Perfect.*

Jenny turned on the coffeemaker, but the immediate beep let her know that she hadn't set it up the morning before. That was a first. She found herself humming, some bland pop song she had heard through the tinny computer speakers from Lydia's office.

Blake's voice chimed in from the doorway to the kitchen, quiet, humming along. She was singing the tune but butchering the lyrics adorably. "I wanna sex you up. Sexy sex you up. Hot stuff, hot mess. Sexy sex sex!"

Jenny turned around, grinning at the goddess in front of her. "That is *not* how it goes."

"Close enough." Blake smiled and stretched, so that the T-shirt she was wearing rose a little over her pubic hair. She hadn't put on any underwear. Jenny felt herself going faint again with arousal and turned back to the coffeemaker.

Blake slid her hands around Jenny's waist and linked them. "You make coffee, too?"

"And I defrost scones." She pulled a frostbitten bag from the freezer, with a piece of masking tape that had a date written on it from the previous spring. Blake looked at it suspiciously and back at Jenny.

"They are vegan, flaxseed, raspberry something," Jenny said, reading Blake's mind.

Blake smiled. "You were planning this since last spring? Lying in wait for a vegan to sleep over? And you have the scones to prove it?"

"My mom made them."

Blake looked at her, arched eyebrow.

"She went through a pretty intense vegan baking phase," Jenny explained, speaking quickly, finding herself embarrassed and somehow exposed. "It was not my favorite. So…"

"Well, they will be perfect, I'm sure." Blake turned on the oven. When she bent down and opened the door, again, she flashed her ass at Jenny, who felt ravenous in a way she never had before. "If you don't put on some pants…" Jenny said.

Blake spun around and grinned. "You'll what?"

"Come here," Jenny said, her voice husky. She hadn't even had her coffee yet, and she had more energy than she was used to. Ravenous, craving energy. She felt like she was in someone else's body. But it was hers, blessedly. All hers.

Blake walked over to her and put her hands proprietarily on her waist. Jenny leaned in and kissed her, with no pretense of chasteness, her tongue lapping and saliva spreading across their lips. "Back to bed," she said, and Blake almost ran, gripping her hand and pulling her into the room. They lay on top of each other on the already tangled and crumpled sheets. Their breasts were smashing together, nipples hard, rubbing raw up against each other's chest.

Jenny kissed Blake with her eyes open, looking at her perfect face. Her left hand was rubbing Blake's head, the short crew cut hair, soft and prickly at the same time. Blake slowed her breathing a bit and snaked her hand down between Jenny's legs. Jenny didn't need to wait, didn't need to kiss her anymore. It was like she was living in a constant state of arousal. She parted her legs, just enough to invite Blake's fingers in. Blake took the invitation and began gently rubbing her clit. Jenny moved her hand down to Blake's center and matched her movements. They kept kissing, shaking the bed with their rhythm. "You're close," Blake said between kisses, with her eyes closed. She knew. She was not asking.

Jenny bit Blake's lip in response, groaning. She put two fingers inside Blake, and Blake did the same to her. Their forearms were smashed together between their legs, and they wouldn't let go. Blake began shaking and became slick around Jenny's hand. Jenny inserted a third finger inside of her, and then a fourth, and then, as Blake groaned in encouragement, her thumb. Gently, she pushed, and her whole hand was inside of Blake. Blake's hand had slipped out of Jenny as she surrendered to her own need, but she kept rubbing Jenny's clit with her thumb. Jenny started coming, just as Blake did.

"You're doing it," Blake said. "You're kissing me while you're inside of me." Jenny almost laughed, but instead it came out like a "Whoop!" which was joined by the insistent beep of both the coffeemaker and the oven timer.

"Good morning," Jenny said, laughing, as they caught their breath and slowly, considerately, drew their limbs back to themselves, and kissed one another on the forehead.

They sat together at Jenny's table, eating the warm scones her mother had made months ago and drinking strong black coffee. The scones were a little dry, but much better than Jenny had expected. They oozed the juice of macerated raspberries and coated her tongue with inviting crystals of sugar. She could smell Blake on her fingers as she brought the coffee cup to her lips.

My God, how my life has changed. She smiled at Blake. "So, tell me something I couldn't learn from Googling you."

"You've been Googling me?"

"Yes."

"Well. That's mutual, summa cum laude, dean's scholar, First Circuit Clerk, author of 'Potentials and Pitfalls of Visualization of Economic Models at Trial' in *Securities Litigation Quarterly*. That was a good one. Extremely riveting. Right up there with *Lolita*."

"Quite good. But really. How about this: If you weren't an artist, what would you be?"

"Well, I wouldn't be me."

"No, I mean, would you be a fireman or what?"

"I really mean I wouldn't be me." Jenny looked at her silently, and Blake shifted in her seat, apparently trying to be patient.

"I'm not being obstinate. Or at least I don't mean to be. I think there are a lot like me, and some just aren't as lucky. They can't actually make art. If I did something else, I'd draw at night. I'd draw on the way to work. I'd draw at work. I did. You should see my sketchbooks from when I was a clerk at a shoe store in high school. Stilettos, oxfords, sandals, boots—drawings I did in the storeroom on break. It's a compulsion."

"And now you get to make a living."

"I never thought I would be able to. I mean, I was always thinking I could scrape by with a day job. And only intermittent opportunity to actually do what I wanted. This is intense." Blake looked up at the ceiling and let out a puff of air that would have sent bangs sailing if she'd had any. She looked back at Jenny, as if to ask if she'd answered the question.

"If you needed a day job, then, what would it be?"

"Something mindless to leave room to make art."

Jenny slumped back in her chair, in defeat. "You are really not answering my question."

Blake smiled back at her, mischievously, like she knew something Jenny didn't.

Jenny felt foolish, like a child who had been invited to a party full of popular kids and she wasn't sure if she was there because they liked her or because they were making fun of her. She pulled her robe tighter. "Should we talk about your case?"

"Really?" Blake sat up and straightened out her shirt. "Now?"

Jenny walked over to where she'd stashed her iPhone on the counter, checking to see if Lydia or Michael had written about a contingency plan for the office for the day. She needed to get back to work, not talk to Blake anymore. She couldn't be faced with Blake's body across the table. She was losing track of herself. "My office is closed, but it might make sense, just to get a few things in order. We can work here, and then—"

"The whole city is shut down. I heard the news too. We can't go anywhere. We are going to stay right here. You are going to give me a tour of your apartment and tell me who every one of those people are in those pictures on the wall, and then I'll make you something for lunch."

Jenny softened. She wanted to know about the pictures? Really? Walk through the family tree? They would be inside together all day. Wasn't this exactly what she'd dreamed of? Why couldn't she relax? She looked around at her kitchen, registering that there was a dearth of food in the fridge or the cabinets. She smiled sheepishly at Blake.

"Peanut butter and jelly is vegan, right? Also I think there's an avocado somewhere."

"Yes. And tell me something." Blake looked at her with lusty eyes.

"What?"

"Vegans taste better, right?"

Jenny laughed and leaned across the table to kiss her, the blush rushing wildly, plainly from her shoulders to her neck. She didn't care. "Yes," she said, and then "Yes," again.

CHAPTER TWENTY-EIGHT

Blake made something even better than peanut butter and jelly for lunch. She was hungry, in so many ways, and wanted to feed Jenny. She grilled frozen sourdough bread in Jenny's cast-iron skillet with olive oil, and topped it with the ripe avocado, caramelized onions, lemon juice, and a generous pinch of sea salt.

"Oh my God," Jenny said, biting into it, and letting some of the avocado glob down her chin. "This is like—"

"The second coming of Christ himself, in sandwich form?"

"Exactly." Jenny smiled, and the fact that her smile was one of appreciation for what Blake had done—made her almost swoon.

Jenny looked at her apologetically across the table. "I think I might have to do a little work after all," she said. Blake nodded.

"Can I draw you?"

"While I work?"

"I won't bother you. I won't say anything. I'll just draw you while you work."

Jenny acquiesced, setting up her laptop at the kitchen table. Blake could see her go into concentration mode very quickly, her posture quickly slumping as she hunched over the computer.

Blake pulled conte crayons out of her bag, knowing she'd need thick lines and saturated colors to capture her this morning, postcoital, filled with sensuality and lust. Drawing Jenny, she fell into a trance. She felt grateful. She had admired Jenny and it had apparently been mutual. She had wanted her and she got her. And here she was, in her condo, making her lunch, being allowed to just gaze. She felt like a kid, barely believing her good fortune. She had snapped her fingers, it seemed, and finally got what—*who*—she wanted. It was magic.

Jenny pulled a piece of wavy hair behind her ear, and predictably, Blake felt a jolt between her legs. She wanted to kiss her again. On the neck. On her lips. On her breasts.

What did Jenny want, though? She told herself not to worry. Just enjoy. She'd be leaving soon. This case would be resolved. Jenny said so, and Blake believed her. She'd brought the firepower of the expensive lawyers into the room, and they'd all pledged to care for her.

After she drew a few pages, Blake circled Jenny again, looking for the right angle. She considered the light and how it fell on her limbs as if she were a sculpture in a museum. Walking behind her, Blake saw the green border of an Excel spreadsheet pop up on the screen. Jenny was absorbed, looking at the numbers, opening up new windows, letting her eyes fly over the screen, while at the same time tapping out messages on her phone.

Jenny was doing work that Blake couldn't even contemplate. Her eyes blurred seeing the rows of numbers and Jenny's tightly controlled way of working. It was incredibly fast, but there was a focused precision to it. She recognized that concentration. She could see the same focus in herself. Jenny's mind was different, her commitment different. She was so…what was the word? Dutiful. More dutiful than Blake could ever be. She wanted to live here, in Boston, probably. She wanted to have dinner with her parents. She wanted to have babies. She wanted her nine-to-five job and a dutiful wife, defrosting scones.

It occurred to Blake then that Jenny might not even be out—not really. She couldn't handle the scandal of Blake. She couldn't be with Blake, not if she had to go back to work at that law firm while Blake was painting enormous nudes on walls and eating pieces of paper and making enormous vagina sculptures. *God, no. This would never work.*

She kept drawing, to keep herself from getting worked up. No need to worry about the future. *Just enjoy her now*, she told herself, capturing the arch of Jenny's neck, her long arm resting on the table, the way the blue glow of the computer screen lit up her face. She kept sketching, tracing the lines of Jenny's legs and how they were crossed under the table. Outside, the snow was continuing to fall in a thick blanket. Occasionally the whips of wind outside the window made it look like it was snowing up into the sky rather than down. The swirls of white circled around them, even as they sat, warmed from the inside out.

Be glad, Blake told herself. *Be glad you get this much.*

Jenny closed the top of her laptop. "We really should talk about your case," she said. Blake had been lost in the sublime, and Jenny wanted to bring her back to reality. She couldn't think about it because the rage would consume her. And she wanted to be consumed by something else. Jenny.

"Let's just ignore that for a little while longer. Will that be all right?" Blake said, her heart pounding.

"How can you?" Jenny said.

Blake sighed. The calm she'd felt drawing Jenny was being replaced by a terrible kind of tension. The anger was flooding back. So was the panic. She could feel it rushing in like a wave, and the sensuality of their morning was being pulled offshore.

"I feel helpless," she said finally. "Helpless and mad. I'm not his first victim, you know. He stole a drawing of my friend Claudia's right off the wall, about four years ago. We saw him lurking around, no one had seen him in a while, and we were all kind of on guard. Later that night one of her drawings was missing. We never reported it and could never prove it, but we all knew. We all got freaked out after that. Looked for him at every opening. This is bigger and meaner than anything—"

She felt tears emerging from behind her eyes, so she stopped to swallow. Jenny turned to look down at her, sympathy emanating from her gorgeous face. Blake felt her pulse slow.

"I'm so sorry," Jenny said simply. Blake looked up at her, dazzled by her beauty as though she was seeing her for the first time.

"I remember seeing you at the bottom of the stairwell," Blake said, finding joy in the memory.

Jenny smiled, straddling the chair backward, looking down at where Blake was sitting, drawing, cross-legged on the floor.

"I remember that too."

"I couldn't stop looking at you."

"I'm sorry I called you a diva," Jenny said. She swung her legs over the chair. Blake watched her. Arousal started replacing her anger. She licked her lips as Jenny locked her eyes. Jenny started unbuttoning her shirt, maintaining eye contact, her eyes smoldering.

"It was 'fucking diva,' if I remember correctly. And you were right," Blake said, only able to muster a whisper.

"I was not right. Can I make it up to you?" Her shirt was off. She let it drop to the floor.

Blake smiled at the woman in front of her. The woman she did not deserve. "God, yes," she said, and stood.

CHAPTER TWENTY-NINE

"Let's go for a walk," Blake said. It was after dark and nearly zero degrees outside. They had ordered Indian food in and tipped the delivery man double the cost of the meal because they felt so guilty making him come outside while they were nestled cozily in Jenny's apartment. They had spent all afternoon looking at one another, enjoying the sights and sounds and smells of each other. Learning how to give one another goose bumps.

And now Blake wanted to go for a walk. "Yes," said Jenny. She had discovered something about herself in the last few hours. She was willing to say yes to anything Blake asked. But there was something that felt a little impatient about Blake now, something restless. Jenny had seen her looking at her phone.

"Let's hold hands through our coat sleeves," Jenny said. "We will be like a two-person winter bundle."

"That sounds lovely." Blake kissed her, and Jenny could taste the curry on her lips and the excellent bottle of red wine she decided to open for just this occasion. And faintly, her own breath lingering in Blake's mouth. They had become conjoined.

They each put on their coats. Jenny slipped her hand into the end of Blake's sleeve, as she had suggested. It didn't quite take. They laughed, drooping their naked wrists from the failed experiment.

"We need a muff," Blake said.

Jenny giggled, continuing for a beat until Blake heard the joke she'd made. "Not that kind," she said, and stepped closer. The nearness of her made Jenny's core start throbbing again, even though she had almost assumed there was nothing left in her. No more blood to rush there. No more senses to overwhelm. She thought she needed a break. But she had been turned on for hours, it seemed, ever since she'd been in Blake's presence.

"I think I have to kiss you again," she said. Blake leaned into her, a tacit invitation. They became serious, caught in the strength of their magnetism. Their tongues started their own lovemaking session, wrestling each other. Jenny slipped off Blake's coat, and it fell to the ground. Jenny cupped her hand between Blake's legs, and Blake let some of her weight drop into it. With her other hand, Jenny started unbuttoning Blake's pants, but she pulled away. Not too abruptly—gently—but she pulled away nonetheless.

"Not now, let's go." Blake kept one hand on Jenny's hip and leaned over to the side table to get her gloves and handed them to Jenny. Jenny tried to hide her disappointment with a sly smile.

"You don't want to stay?" She tugged at Blake's nipples through her shirt. She couldn't understand why Blake wanted to go for a walk when the cold was so unforgiving. She had just started to relax into the debauchery of their evening, and Blake hadn't even put back on her bra.

"I need to get cold so you can warm me up again," Blake said.

Jenny reached quickly for her hat, feeling the fire between her legs burn anew. "That sounds good."

When she turned, Blake was looking at her phone, her face in a frown. When she saw Jenny glimpsing her, she shoved it back in her pants pocket. Jenny started to ask who it was and whether anything was wrong, but she could see on Blake's blank face that the topic was closed for discussion. Blake didn't owe her that kind of news, she reminded herself. She didn't owe her anything.

The South End was deserted, which was helpful because about a foot of snow had fallen, and there was nowhere to walk but the middle of the street. The snowbanks were piled up high, turning gray, but in the dark air and the occasional spotlight from a streetlamp, the snow looked white and bright. And a little eerie, like the world had been encased in marshmallow icing.

"I've only seen one storm this bad," Jenny said. "When I was in high school. We didn't have school for a week, and I was so disappointed."

"You grew up here, right?"

Jenny nodded, trying to bat away the feeling that her answer made her inadequate. Not good enough for Blake. "About twelve miles west. My parents still live there."

"Do you see them often?"

"The occasional Sunday dinner or brunch, yeah." Jenny took Blake's mittened hand, trying again to imagine her sitting on her parents' couch. She couldn't. The image just didn't fit.

Blake took her arm from Jenny's abruptly and looked at her phone. Jenny saw the bubble of a text message, but looked away, not wanting to pry. They had been inside all day, together. Who was trying to reach her? And why now? Why hadn't she left the phone back at Jenny's condo?

Blake gave her a half-smile, made a big show of clicking the lock button, and put the phone back in her coat pocket.

"Is there something I should know about—"

"No!" Blake's admonition came quickly, but she tried to soften it with a smile. "Just something—"

"If it's about the case, we should call Lydia, she can start a file of—"

"It's not that," Blake said, blowing a puff of breath into the air above them. Jenny felt like she was talking too much, not playing it cool. She wanted to be quiet, but she was curious and nervous for Blake and couldn't stop talking. And what else? A slimy feeling was crawling up her back. Slime that wouldn't let her shut up.

"So, who's texting you?"

"None of your business," Blake said. Her tone could have been mistaken for playful only by someone who was emotionally remedial. Jenny knew there was no actual mirth in it.

"Sorry," Jenny said. But the slime was overtaking her, and she couldn't resist asking, "Your manager's assistant?" She smiled, the same kind of emptiness on her face that Blake had in her tone.

"No," Blake said, looking at Jenny with cold, gray eyes. "Amanda. The one who broke the story."

"Oh," Jenny said. And then the slime on her back turned to ice, and her whole body curled up into a snowball and she understood. Blake had slept with Amanda, likely just a few nights before.

Jenny really meant nothing. That's how this was done, right? She had done it too. Slept with Blake, knowing she would go back to New York. She wasn't about to rent a U-Haul. Still, it felt like she'd been frozen. Her fingertips, which had been flaming from touching Blake, had gone cold.

Blake kept walking. A little straighter, a little quieter, not giving anything away.

"What does she want?" Jenny finally said.

"To apologize. I don't know. I'm not sure she knew about Ned before..." She trailed off, jiggling the phone in her pocket.

"Check it if you want to," Jenny said, trying to talk herself into feeling better, back into the rhythm with Blake. It didn't matter who she had been with a few nights ago, she told herself. It mattered that they were together now.

They kept walking. Blake was targeting the freshest snow piles with her boots, making the drifts crumble.

"So..." Blake seemed to be feeling around for the syllables, trying to pick up the thread of the conversation again. "You think your parents are going to come see the show?"

"We're back to them?" Jenny was beginning to think the walk was a big mistake. She longed for the cocoon of her condo again, the warm sensuality of it. Out here, it was gone.

Blake stopped under a streetlamp. "I'm just trying to figure out what you want from this—"

Jenny puzzled over Blake's face. She could feel her picking a fight and wasn't sure why. She felt indignant, like she was being accused of not knowing herself.

"Is there something I've said—what are you—?"

"It's none of my business. I'm going to be gone in a few days anyway. I just—"

"Just what?"

"I just want to make sure I'm not going to hurt you," Blake said. But it sounded condescending, not caring, like Jenny had become a nuisance. Jenny looked at her through narrow eyes, her unease building.

Blake's mouth made a straight line, and she said, "I mean, do your parents know you're gay?"

"How could you even ask me that?" Jenny's tone was somewhere between pleading and biting. She wasn't sure which. She couldn't figure out what Blake was saying or why, and the anger was starting to ignite. Jenny had been so forthright with her body. How could Blake think that she was suppressing anything? What was this about?

Blake took a step back and tried to soften her face. "Look, I just—"

"Just what?" Jenny stopped walking and yanked her arms from inside Blake's pockets. Rage burned inside of her. First she had to keep reminding her parents that she was really gay, and then Blake had to ask her if she was even *out*? She couldn't win. What the hell was this?

"Look, your boss doesn't know. He's utterly puzzled. I wasn't even sure for a while," Blake said. "I mean, now, it's clear." Blake pulled down her scarf and smiled. But Jenny saw it as shallow. She felt angry, defensive. She wasn't about to let Blake's smile melt her all over again.

"Just because I'm not sleeping with everyone I meet, including *men* and a goddamned Twitter influencer who calls herself a journalist, doesn't mean I'm a closet case," Jenny said.

The moment became as frozen as the sidewalk. She watched Blake's face crumple in slow motion, and she wanted to take back the words. She had sounded more disgusted than she meant to. More judgmental. She wasn't sure she could take anything back.

"Wow," was all Blake said. Her silence was biting. She readjusted the scarf across her lips and nose and stared down the street.

"Blake, I—" Jenny moved toward her, wanting to take the words back, but Blake stepped aside, avoiding her body.

"No, don't. You don't get to judge me. I don't have to answer to you. I don't even know you."

Her last sentence froze Jenny in her place. She started regretting everything, wishing she were back to a week ago, when things were predictable. Waking up alone. Answering emails from Michael. Seeing nothing but her spreadsheets and the gray view outside the window.

"That way is the Charles?" Blake asked, gesturing to the street, which looked like a valley of snow-covered cars.

"Yes, but—"

"That's all I need to know. Thanks," Blake said, and she walked down the street, hands sitting tightly in her pockets.

"Wait!" Jenny yelled, without thinking, without planning ahead what she wanted to say. She ran a few steps. Blake had stopped short in the street and was looking at her, a stern challenge on her face. Hurt, too. The combination was reminiscent of the expression she wore when she had looked down at Jenny from the top of the stairs when they first met.

"Wait," Jenny said, more quietly. "It's freezing and…I want you to…"

Blake looked up at the sky for a moment and then cast her eyes back down to Jenny. "I don't think I'm what you want," she said.

Jenny went limp, helpless. A plow rumbled by them, spraying snow on the sides of their jackets, the sound drowning out the panicked beating of her heart. Blake turned, and she watched her go, feeling like she swallowed a rock that was slowly making its way down her throat and into her stomach.

She walked back to her condo, which felt even emptier than it had before. There was a tangle of sheets in the middle of the living-room floor. The half-drunk bottle of wine sitting on the kitchen counter, mocking her. She saw Blake's teal bra, slung over a dining room chair. She took a shower, rubbing Blake's smell off her body. She tied on her terrycloth robe and looked around her empty apartment. She was exhausted, but sleeping was not an option. She was afraid of what she'd dream. And she could not sit on the couch, not where they'd just made love. It still seemed to be shaking in tune with her body.

Jenny let her eyes dart around her apartment. The lonely crevices. The nooks behind piles of mail, the umbrella stand, the piles of boots and wet socks by the doorway. And there, on the entryway table, Blake's notebook. The one she had tried to give Jenny, held closed with a binder clip. Jenny reached for it and sat on the floor. She opened it up slowly, and looked at drawings she hadn't seen at first, examining the hairy wrists of old men as they gripped subway bars, the erotic swell of breasts Blake seemed to find on women, even as they were bundled into down coats. The large, lolling head of a baby in a carriage, and another nursing under a cover, pudgy feet in view on its mother's lap. And then, improbably, Jenny saw Melinda's face staring at her from Blake's notebook. Unmistakably Melinda, resting her hands contentedly on her belly. The woman next to her was her fiancée, the woman Jenny had seen in the pictures online. Melinda was wearing the same look of adoration and contentment Jenny had seen on the wedding website, but somehow, captured by Blake and not a camera, the look was all the more passionate and alive.

It was a look that Jenny had never given Melinda. She hadn't ever felt it. But it was a look Jenny now knew well. Very well. She knew it was how she looked at Blake.

And there, sitting cross-legged in her robe in the middle of her apartment, while Blake found her way back to Somerville in the freezing, unforgiving night, Jenny knew. She was in love with Blake Harrison. Unmistakably, hopelessly, passionately in love.

CHAPTER THIRTY

The fucking Boston T wasn't operating. A few inches of snow and it had shut down again. Blake started walking down to Mass Ave and across the frigid footbridge again. This time, she wasn't looking across at the Prudential for Jenny. She knew just where she was and where she'd left her.

Blake reviewed why she left. Her phone had been blowing up with texts from Amanda, apologizing and wanting a comment on the story and wondering if she was free. Blake was tired of feeling the vibration during their cold walk, every communication worrying her, making her feel like a pariah, a diva surrounded by drama. And that made her feel like she didn't deserve Jenny. So she pushed and pushed until Jenny lashed out. She wasn't seeing it so clearly as it was happening, but now, in the frigid, razor-sharp air, without Jenny next to her, it seemed obvious.

Jenny hadn't taken much pushing to say something petty and cruel, though. Yes, she had slept around. Wasn't she doing the same thing with Blake, enjoying her body just as a fling?

Jenny had said herself, several times, that Blake would be gone in a few days.

Blake's face fought the wind over the Charles and the rush of the occasional speeding car over the bridge. She heard a beeping plow in the distance. The sights and sounds felt oppressive, like every gust of wind was clouding her brain, making it harder to think. *What do you want?* The question was teasing her mind, mocking her. She wasn't sure how much longer she could walk. When she was about halfway over the bridge, her phone buzzed again. She fished it out of her pocket, both dreading and hoping at the same time that it was Jenny texting her *Come back.* Instead, it was a text from another number she didn't know.

It said, *I'll settle.*

Blake froze and gripped the phone tighter. *Ned.* This was a shakedown? Really? She flipped off the top of a mitten to reveal her fingerless gloves and typed quickly,

Please don't contact me at this number again.

$$ = show gone, Ned wrote. If it really was Ned.

She wanted to tell someone, ask someone's help. After the fight they'd just had, she couldn't call Jenny. She felt so alone, so helpless, that it felt insurmountable. The cityscape stared back at her. Never had she wanted to be back in New York so badly. But she couldn't get a train, or even a bus, until the next morning. And she had to clean out her apartment, and do a few more guest lectures at the local colleges, even though she was worried that with this lawsuit, no one would even want her.

Blake decided to call the one person she'd met, besides Jenny, who seemed likely to be awake at midnight in the frozen city.

Davis walked into the bar fifteen minutes later. "The Miracle of Science? Really? That's all you could come up with?"

"I was nearby, and it's warm and open," Blake said, kicking out a barstool for him. "Thanks for coming." Of course, she had figured he would. He was still starstruck.

"You okay?" Davis asked, simply, like they were old friends.

Blake looked at Davis's expectant face for a moment and considered lying to him. Not breaking the veneer of her composed celebrity. But she couldn't. She needed to be a normal person in a bar. She needed a friend. And he'd do.

"I'm freaked out, because I got this," she said and passed him the phone. He read the short exchange with the no-name number.

"That's the guy who—"

"Is suing me. Yes."

"You need a lawyer," Davis said.

"I have one. Four, actually."

"That's a relief."

"I haven't shown them this yet. It just happened. And it's one in the morning."

"Well, I think they'll tell you that this is some kind of blackmail, right?"

"Well, that's what I get, right?"

"No," Davis said, very quickly, his spine straightening and his shoulders shooting back as if he were about to make a speech. Blake imagined that all the queer feminist blogs he was accustomed to reading were about to be brought to bear. "This is not your fault. He's some asshole who is trying to steal your idea. He's not the first. Only unlike others, his own stuff isn't even good."

"What do you mean?" Blake asked.

Davis sighed, twisting a bit on his bar stool. "Rodin stole from Camille Claudet. And then you have the married couples. Who the hell knows who was really doing the art? Robert Delaunay stole from Sonja. Willem De Kooning stole from Eliane."

"I am not anywhere near the caliber of any of those women."

Davis looked at her adoringly. She found herself feeding off his admiration, comforted by it. "You might be. And Ned's *definitely* not any of those men."

"Well, I'll drink to that," Blake said. She waved the bartender for a beer, taking a moment to organize her thoughts. "I don't blame myself for what he's doing now. But something seems karmic about this. I did not expect this level of success. I dreamt of it. Even if I don't sell another piece and don't get another museum show, I've made it more in the establishment than most of my peers. It's come on quick. I've been waiting to be called on it. My art is good. People like it. I get that. But all along, I've been waiting for someone to say 'No, not you.'"

"That's bullshit. If I have one good date, I don't expect the next one to be bad. Or Jenny wins one case, she doesn't expect to lose the next one."

Blake's throat went dry at the sound of Jenny's name. Davis seemed to register Blake's silence.

"I think she likes you," he said. "She's my friend, and I'll deny it if you say it came from me, but I'm giving you a nudge. I think she likes you."

"We're past that," Blake said.

"And not in a good way?" Davis said, searching her face.

"In a very good way for some time, and then, as of just a couple of hours ago, not in a good way. I'm not sure what happened. I'll be gone in a few days anyway."

"Do you want to tell me about it?"

"You're her friend. I can't—I wouldn't—"

"That's why you called me, isn't it? To talk about Jenny, at least a little bit?"

Blake sighed. *Yes,* she wanted to say. *Of course. Thank you.* She looked down at the paper coaster and started tearing it into little pieces as she spoke. "She helped me. Got people in her firm to help me. We kissed. I thought that I screwed it up, but I hadn't. So we…Now I think maybe it is over. Before it began. I don't even know what it is. And…"

Blake trailed off and then considered the beer she'd drank. It wasn't so much that she was willing to be so candid, but it was enough that she could use it as an excuse to herself if she regretted it later. "I'm a bit lonely," she said.

Davis smiled and let out a little laugh. "Well, Holzer said as much. To Kiki Smith, actually. Verbatim it was 'I suspect you've noticed that making art can be lonely.' So don't get too down on yourself. I think it's an occupational hazard."

Blake managed a little smile, still tearing at the coaster, appreciating Davis's manner. "So what's the occupational hazard for a museum curator?"

"I'm not sure," he said, with his initially cautious smile getting a little bigger. "Maybe it's getting calls from lonely artists who are secretly in love with their best friends?"

"Another beer?" Blake asked, not bothering to deny it.

"Absolutely," Davis said.

CHAPTER THIRTY-ONE

Jenny had been avoiding Lydia all morning, but Lydia found her in the office cafeteria. She put two fists on the table and looked down at Jenny. "You're my friend, so you want to explain to me what the fuck is going on?"

Jenny chewed on her half-frozen, iridescent piece of watermelon and shook her head.

"How am I supposed to help you if I don't know what's happening?"

"What makes you think I need help?"

"You're eating cafeteria watermelon, for starters, in the middle of January."

Jenny looked up at her, mouth clamped shut.

"I've been trying to reach you all last night and all this morning."

"My phone is off."

"Why?"

Because she was tired of checking it to see if Blake had called or texted, and for a few hours, the answer to that was no. So she decided to shut it off, because she knew she wouldn't be able to sleep if the phone was on so that she'd keep checking it. She was waiting for her apology. When it looked like she wouldn't get one, she decided to not even wait. But that was too much to explain to Lydia. And knowing Lydia, she would figure all that out eventually anyway. So Jenny said, "I just wasn't taking calls."

Lydia looked at her, head cocked to the side. She opened her mouth to ask another question and then seemed to decide against it. "So you haven't heard from Blake?"

Jenny shook her head. "No."

Lydia sat down next to Jenny. "Listen, the firm got an email last night. Our IT people intercepted it, but it was going to go to everyone. Another demand letter, this one with more ramblings about how Ned invented the rooms. A whole bunch of bullshit, but he's disseminating it widely."

Jenny felt her heart constrict. *Poor Blake.* She turned to Lydia, and Lydia seemed to see the complicated reaction on her face. "Weirdly, though, it shows him to be a psycho, so it's better for the case. But it's really fucked up. And we can't reach her."

"Can we get him for harassment? Or isn't there some claim? Extortion?"

"Maybe. We have to see if he's contacted her asking for money."

"He didn't," Jenny said. Lydia's eyebrows lifted a bit.

"Really?"

Jenny nodded. "Really. I was with her all day."

Lydia couldn't help but smile. "In your condo?"

"Yes."

"You weathered Snowmageddon in your condo with Blake Harrison. Jesus, Jenny, you do surprise me sometimes."

Jenny couldn't quite smile, but the memory made her want to.

"You had a fight?" Lydia said.

Jenny nodded, tears beading in her eyes. She wiped them away quickly and tried to grin. "It was a fun affair!" she said, too brightly, too loudly, so her voice landed like a thud in the quiet cafeteria. She looked around and smiled and buried her head in her hands on the table.

"I've never seen you like this," Lydia whispered, lips close to Jenny's ear as she covered her head in embarrassment. "You're off-kilter. It's different."

"Thank you for being my friend," Jenny muttered. She felt queasy, because it wasn't real sleep she'd had; it was twisting and turning, upset and embarrassed, cold and lonely. She had Blake's body next to her for only one night and already couldn't stand its absence.

Lydia rubbed her hand on Jenny's back in a small, kind circle. "Hon, I think you two will patch it up, hear me?"

Jenny let out a small whine. "She's going back to New York anyway."

"That's not too far. Who knows. Okay?"

Jenny picked her soggy face up from the table. Lydia looked her square in the eye. "We do need to find her, though, for the case. How can you help?"

Jenny could help, even with the hurt coursing through her body. They went back to Jenny's office, and Jenny called Steve. He gave them the address of her apartment in Inman.

"How the hell are we going to get there?" said Lydia. The T was still not operating and no one had gotten an Uber in days. They both knew the very disappointing answer was that they had to walk.

"Start from the beginning," Lydia said, as they started on their journey. It was about three miles. The Mass Ave Bridge was covered in a sheet of ice, with only a few cars going by. They clutched the bridge's banister, feeling glad that even if they plunged into the Charles, they might survive because they'd land in a few feet of soft snow on top of ice.

"I don't know how to talk about it," Jenny said, even as she began doing so. "It was amazing. She is amazing. But then she said she thought I was closeted, and her phone kept beeping, and then I basically called her a slut."

"That's terrible. Why would you say that?"

"I don't know. I'm scared, Lydia. What if I never find someone?"

"Wait, is this about existential loneliness? Or about her?"

Leave it to Lydia to ask the most important question. They walked in silence with the wind whipping them, making their way across the bridge and into the bowels of Somerville. "I'm getting us coffee for the next leg," Lydia said. She peeled off to go into a Dunkin' Donuts, both of them keenly aware that Jenny hadn't answered her question.

Jenny replayed her memories of Blake. They felt physical. When she conjured up Blake's body, she could feel her lips burn. Her hips circle. Her core heat. No one had ever made her feel the way Blake did. Free, fierce, fearless. She had never wanted anyone as much as she wanted her.

Lydia came out of the Dunkin' with two coffees and a bag of munchkins, bless her, and stopped to look at Jenny, seemingly able to tell that she had come to some sort of conclusion.

"Let's just find Blake," Jenny said, "and make sure she's okay." Lydia smiled, and squeezed her gloved hand, appearing to hear the layers of Jenny's answer.

They stopped twice more for coffee, and, as the roads seemed to clear a bit, Jenny finally was able to get an Uber—at only 3.0 surge!—and they got to the apartment before eleven. Jenny's heart was pounding as they pressed the buzzer. "Yes?" A woman's voice. Not Blake's. Jenny wanted to turn and leave. She couldn't bear it if Blake had just gone home with another woman. After what they had shared—

Lydia grabbed Jenny's arm, sensing Jenny's resolve weaken. "We're here for Blake Harrison."

"Regarding?" said the voice.

"We're her lawyers." After a pause, the door buzzed, and Lydia and Jenny clomped up the stairs, trailing snow as they went.

The door to Blake's apartment was open, and inside was Amy, wearing a tasteful St. John suit with a host of bangles that must have been cold in the snow.

Amy introduced herself to Lydia, and her eyes fixed on Jenny, who was still standing back in the doorway. A smile came on her lips, wide and knowing, and her eyes crinkled almost with a little laughter. "Hello," she said and her head turned to the opposite wall. Jenny followed her and saw Blake, who was standing in the small galley kitchen in the dark, her body half blocked by the doorjamb. Taped all along the wall were sketches of Jenny. Bold, sensual, gorgeous sketches of Jenny, some clothed, some not, all reverent, taking great care with her features and limbs and light. Blake was looking at her, but trying not to be seen, nervous.

Jenny made contact with the one eye that was visible and smiled. She couldn't help herself; she was, as always, drawn to her. She could feel the force field building around them again. She wanted to run to her and take her hand and look at each picture on the wall.

Instead, she sat down in the chair next to Lydia, trying to guard her own heart. Lydia must have noticed that every drawing was of Jenny in various states of imagined undress, but she didn't let on. Instead, she looked right at Blake and spoke for them both. "We're going to fight Ned with all the power of our firm," Lydia said. "Tell us what's going on."

CHAPTER THIRTY-TWO

Blake couldn't believe that Jenny was in her apartment. Jenny, with her perfect condo of clean lines and steel appliances and white marble, was sitting next to Amy and Lydia in her little Somerville rental. Somehow, seeing her, all of Blake's other problems seemed trivial. All that mattered was that Jenny and she would talk and make up. She needed to apologize. She ran a finger over her skull, retracing the lines where, just a few hours before, Jenny's fingers were mapping her follicles, making her skin tingle, her breath short. She wanted to go back to that moment. Too much had happened since then. She wanted to go back in time.

Blake had spent the night drinking stale coffee, frantically drawing portraits of Jenny. She had shut her phone off, and she was afraid to turn it back on because of Ned. Amy had shown up at her doorstep at nine in the morning, a cranky livery driver with a town car stuck in the bank outside her doorstep.

"We have to talk," Amy had said, before telling her that the museum's email server had blown up with messages. That was two hours ago. Since then, Amy had been regaling her with stories of her husband's tenure at the museum and some of the worst behaved artists they'd had come across, keeping Blake's mind off the extortion. Or her heartbreak. Or both.

"Is that the Derain lover?" Amy had asked, seeing the drawings hanging on the walls.

"Yes," Blake said, because she didn't know how else to describe her.

Amy, politely, sipped a cup of tea she'd taken the liberty of making herself and said, "Exquisite drawings."

And then Jenny walked through the door. Blake sat down as Amy talked to her guests.

"I open my husband's email," Amy said. "That sounds odd, but I do. He gets invitations to things I want to go to, solicitations for book manuscripts and signatures, and fan letters. I answer some, or I filter them to our secretary. It's maybe old-fashioned, but I take care of the social calendar. I like it. So this morning, there's one with a strange address with the rantings and ravings of a madman."

"They were sent to our firm today, too."

"That fucking bastard," Jenny said suddenly. Lydia smiled and then looked down. Blake felt a wave of gratitude wash over her, happy for Jenny's indignation on her behalf. She tried to search Jenny's face, but she was still looking down. She could tell by her posture she was tired. It must have taken her a long time to get here. Blake had done it again. Made her life more difficult.

"Yes, it's awful," Lydia said. She sighed, seemed to gather herself, and said to Blake, "Did he threaten you in any way? Did he imply that you could have avoided this?"

Blake felt hopeful. Maybe there was a way out. "He texted me he'd settle. Yes. It felt like extortion. Is that the word?"

"Yes! Good!" Lydia smiled, encouraging. And then, gathering herself again, "Extortion is not good, obviously. But we can use the threat against him." She dove into her briefcase. "Let's write down every time he's contacted you, and the number, and everything."

"I shut my phone off, it was so much." Blake took a deep breath. "He texted me yesterday, after I was walking home from Jenny's."

"Why didn't you tell me?" Jenny asked, speaking to her directly for the first time.

Blake blushed. She felt horribly nervous, wanting everyone in the room to go away just so she and Jenny could talk.

"I didn't want to worry you after we—after I left," she said. Amy and Lydia seemed to shift in their seats.

"Lydia, darling, it is Lydia, isn't it?" Amy said. Lydia nodded. "I'm wondering if you'd like some tea."

They got up and walked into the kitchen. Blake and Jenny looked at one another across the room and didn't break eye contact.

"I'm sorry," they both said at once. Blake smiled over at Jenny a bit sheepishly.

"I was out of line," Blake said. "I think maybe I picked a fight—it was stupid—I didn't want to drag you into anything so I just lashed out. I really apologize. And you are right. I'll be gone."

Jenny cocked her head and looked at her. Blake's body trembled from the deepening eye contact as she resisted the urge to crawl over to Jenny on all fours.

Jenny spoke slowly, as if wanting to know how her words would be received before she got them all out. "I'm sorry for what I said. I shouldn't judge you at all." She took a deep breath, and added, "I don't."

Blake felt like crying, like letting it all out. Laying it at Jenny's feet. But she had left last night because she didn't want to do that.

"I don't want to burden you," she finally said. And as she said it, she realized it was incomplete. It was more than that. She had grown so terrified of how she was feeling that she had started to push Jenny away. It seemed easier.

"Are you angry?" Jenny asked. Blake swallowed. She had been coughing down her own tears, so the lump in her throat was almost painful.

"I'm somewhere beyond anger," she said.

Jenny smiled, a little, her eyes lighting up, apparently wanting to comfort Blake. After everything, she still had generous eyes.

"I'm surprised I don't see you shouting, fuming, turning red, destroying things in your apartment, and giving vengeful interviews about male privilege."

"My stoicism is scaring you?"

"I'm not scared, no," Jenny said. She stood and walked toward the drawings. "Something occurred to me," she said. "What if none of this matters anyway?"

Blake watched her as she slowly looked at each drawing. Jenny kept walking, slowly, as she talked, pausing in front of the naked pictures of herself. Her voice was wavering a little bit. "I mean, you haven't seen what he's tried to do. He could have copied your piece exactly and failed. I could try to repaint a Derain or a Bierstadt, and it would come out like crap. People would know. They wouldn't care whose idea it was. They would just put mine in the trash and keep the real art. Yours is the real art."

Gratitude washed over Blake again. Her skin tingled and she felt her chest expand. She wanted to run across the room and kiss Jenny again, go back to bed, kick everyone out of her apartment, and listen to Jenny say, "Yours is the real art," over and over again. She began to ingest the substance of Jenny's words. The words traveled through her body, filling her limbs with Jenny's voice. It was true. Blake had been so caught up in the legality of it and the feelings of betrayal that she had forgotten the singularity of what she was able to do.

"These are me, huh?" Jenny asked, still not turning to face Blake. Blake didn't respond; she felt like she hadn't been invited to. "Well, now everyone's seen me naked. Not just you." Jenny continued. Blake wished she'd turn around so she could read her face.

"I'm sorry," Blake said. Jenny turned, her hair cascading around her shoulders and her eyes sparkling. She smiled at Blake, and Blake's breath caught in her throat. *My God, she's beautiful*, she thought, not for the first time, wanting again to run across the room.

"Don't be sorry. They're gorgeous," Jenny said. She spoke so plainly that what she seemed to be saying was the absolute truth. Blake wanted to kiss her until they were both crumpled in a pile on the floor. She was too tired and too grateful to say anything.

Blake heard Lydia and Amy's footsteps coming back. "I'm glad you're here," she said softly to Jenny, because that's all she knew to be true. She wasn't glad they had to talk about Ned. She was embarrassed for the drama. She was glad Jenny was in the room.

Lydia sat back down on the couch and looked back and forth at Jenny and Blake. There was a smile playing somewhere in her eyes, but she seemed ready to get down to business. She blew out a puff of air and made a little whistle.

"We're good? Good. Look. This fucking sociopath is committing crimes now. Perversely, that's good for us. It's going to work out. Amy, the museum needs to put out a statement unequivocally in support of Blake. And Blake, where's your manager? He might have gotten the emails, too. We will fix this. Jenny and I will fix it."

CHAPTER THIRTY-THREE

The press conference was set for noon the next day. Jenny didn't have to do anything to prepare. Her colleagues had taken over. Kit Greyson would be speaking to the press because he had the gravitas Blake needed, it was decided, even though Lydia had become most well-versed in the case. Jenny and Lydia had both scoffed at this, of course, because gravitas and gender always seemed to be so intertwined. That was a battle they could fight another day. This was about Blake and restoring her reputation.

Jenny and Blake hadn't been alone together since their few moments in her apartment when Lydia and Amy left the room ostensibly to get tea. Soon after that, Steve arrived, and Blake and he together had spent a long time talking, asking Lydia a few clarifying questions. While they talked, Amy and Jenny quietly packed up Blake's drawings in huge vellum folders. It was strange for Jenny to be handling so many images of herself, thinking about the feel of Blake's fingers on the page. On her body. It felt like the same thing. Now it was a memory. Jenny couldn't see how or when it could happen again. Blake was going back to New York after the press conference.

Amy's driver dropped Jenny back at the office. Jenny wasn't sure how she'd spend the night, and she wasn't even sure if she'd go to the conference. Blake needed to focus on her career, not on her. Jenny hadn't checked her email since the day before. She rode the elevator up to her floor with a sense of abject dread. Here she was again, in the vertical prison, ready to be confronted with thousands of messages, demands on her time from Michael and clients and colleagues. Her time with Blake had woken her up to something. It's not that she hadn't known she was unhappy. It's that she hadn't cared. But now, she did.

She looked around at her office. On her chair there was a handwritten note: "Where are you?—Michael." He had written "11:09 a.m." at the top. She crumpled it into a tight ball and threw it into the trash and sat on the chair starting blankly ahead, not quite ready to boot up her computer.

"You're back," came Michael's voice from the doorway. His face was not as angry as the note suggested it would be.

"I'm back," Jenny confirmed.

"I haven't seen you in two days."

"Sometimes weeks go by and you don't see me." It was not something she would have said even just a week ago, but there was a boldness to her. A readiness to unleash.

"Not when I'm in Boston."

"True."

"What are you doing, Jenny?" he said, leaning on the doorjamb in a way eerily similar to how Blake had, surveying her from across the little room.

"Editing the damages estimates."

"Okay. But you're not yourself. Haven't been, by my count, for about two weeks."

Jenny looked at him, wondering how they'd worked together for five years and still had such a limited way of interacting. He was so seldom kind, so seldom casual. The gala had been a landmark event for them. A chance to connect. He had sullied it by inviting his nephew. Or maybe Jenny was the one who had sullied it. Maybe she was the one who was hard to read and hard to reach. She might as well start now with some truth telling.

"I'm gay," Jenny said. She looked hard at him, waiting for some reaction. He looked down into his paper cup of coffee and stirred it with the wooden stick and tapped it on the side.

"So, you won't be calling my nephew." He looked up and smiled, pink lips spreading wider than she'd ever seen.

"No."

"Sorry about that."

"Even if I wasn't gay, that was out of line."

"Point taken," he said, nodding, looking down into his coffee again. Jenny realized for the first time that she had some power in the conversation. Slightly, subtly, it had shifted. He needed her. She could feel it.

"Anything else?" Jenny said.

"Do you like your job?" Michael asked. Jenny looked at him, thinking she misheard at first. When had that ever mattered?

She thought about saying no, immediately and bitterly, but decided the truth was better, even if it wasn't as clear. "Sometimes," she said slowly, watching his reaction. The word seemed to please him.

"I hope so." He coughed a little into his sleeve. "One hell of a winter this has been, huh?" Jenny saw him then, not as a demanding ogre, but as someone who, like her, was just trying to figure out how to live his days. Ward against loneliness. Make his way home in the snow to a warm house and a warm meal. He hadn't been trying to cause her pain. Her unhappiness wasn't all his fault. It was hers.

She smiled. "Wicked bad winter, yes."

"You're going to the press conference tomorrow?"

She nodded. "That's what I've been prepping for all morning. Sorry." She gestured to her trash can, figuring he'd seen her chuck the note.

"Kit told me. I know. It's okay." He rubbed his temples. Still, Jenny seemed to be making him nervous. It wasn't the lesbian thing, she didn't think. He seemed to have taken that in stride.

"The art's grown on me, I should tell you," Michael said.

"I don't believe it." Jenny smiled, feeling herself lighten, wondering if she'd have a chance to tell Blake. If everything was steady between them, she might. "Which room is your favorite?"

"The Hockney," he said. "That one. Bright, cool. Makes me think it's not winter here. Takes me away."

"I was swept away in there, too," Jenny said, and they eyed one another almost companionably.

"Sorry again about Brandon," Michael said. "He did like you."

Jenny wasn't sure how to respond, because she wanted the strange warmth between them to remain.

"He seemed nice," she finally said.

"So does the artist," Michael replied, and before Jenny could respond or even just let her mouth open in surprise, he stepped rather lightly out of her office and back down the hallway.

CHAPTER THIRTY-FOUR

Blake bought a Red Sox cap at South Station as a disguise. It was all she needed. Seven hours and one-half of a sketchbook filled later, she was stepping off the Amtrak at Union Station to test Jenny's theory. She glanced disdainfully at the Capitol building for a moment before heading northwest on Massachusetts Avenue—same street, different city. She needed to see for herself if Ned's rooms were anything to be afraid of.

The gallery space was in Adams Morgan. She had never heard of it or the people who owned it. There were only a few explanations for the show being open at all. The gallery owners could be oblivious to what Ned was doing, but that was unlikely, being that he was relying on their publicity. They could have somehow been duped into believing him or were the kind of scum that fed on the publicity whether they believed him or not. The third explanation was the most likely. Ned set up the gallery and was answering only to himself. This was his stupid vendetta. He alone was trying to take her down.

Washington, D.C., was warmer than Boston, though the people there didn't seem to know it, because they were bundled up in down coats like their brethren to the north. She walked quickly through the empty streets, enjoying the feeling of being able to put one foot in front of the other without worrying about slipping on ice. After more than an hour, she was there, face-to-face with the gallery door. Ned's name was etched in the frosted glass window. She tried peering in but couldn't see anything. She hadn't told anyone she was making the trip, because they would have advised against it. Lawyers, she knew, advocated distance.

She thought of Jenny, then, not touching her that morning, even though the space between them had felt thick and warm. Jenny looked at the drawings of her own naked body with some kind of deliberate distance. She tried to shake the thought and stay in the moment. If she glimpsed Ned, she would leave, hopefully undetected. If she could see the rooms without seeing him, she would.

Blake saw a heavily pierced, young, lithe man with leather pants and plaid topcoat walking to the gallery. *Thank God, not Ned.* He carried a jangling circle of keys. Blake stood closer to the curb, trying to look like she was busy wrenching a free paper from one of the stands on the corner. The pierced man opened a series of locks on the front glass door and turned on the lights. The bright glow from inside filtered out to the sidewalk. Blake waited a few moments and then wandered in after him. He nodded at her from behind the gleaming white front desk as she entered. She kept her head down and pulled the Sox cap further down over her forehead and walked through the gallery.

It took her only a few seconds to know that Jenny had been right.

The rooms were smaller than hers, but it wasn't the size that mattered. They were clumsily lit, bright in all the wrong places, with a strange unevenness to them. He had chosen different paintings. First was a Monet, and just as Blake had known, it didn't work. The light felt simply dull. He had put up a lavender filter, but there was no joy in it, no playfulness. Nothing that enveloped her. The brightest room, which was apparently modeled after a different Hockney, wasn't hot or evocative. It was just bright, so blinding she shut her eyes. The light made her want to back away into the street, rather than walk through.

It was awful and she was overjoyed. She stayed for a few minutes, wondering why it had taken her days to know that visiting was the right thing to do. There was nothing to be afraid of. Ned could steal all the ideas he wanted. He couldn't make the rooms alive. She wanted to teleport herself back to Boston, rush to Jenny's side, and envelop her in a wave of grateful kisses.

Instead, she walked out of the gallery, careful not to look the attendant in the eye as she wrote "Fuck you" in the guestbook.

After an Acela red-eye back and just a few hours' sleep, Blake was standing inside the lobby of the Albie wearing her slim fitting pantsuit and long dangly earrings, trying to look serious and composed. It was the outfit Amy had suggested, and Blake agreed it was the right one. Flanking her were all the people who, over the last strange week, had come to be in her inner circle. Steve, of course, but also Davis, Lydia, Amy, and Kit, the partner at the firm, with his thin tie and gravelly voice. She was being well cared for. Ned couldn't get to her. Lydia had already filed a restraining order. They had told the museum security guards to look out for him. Even though his brand of aggression wasn't physical at this point, that did make her feel safer. She hadn't told anyone about her visit to his gallery.

The only person missing was Jenny. Blake scanned the small scrum of reporters for her but didn't see her. She looked to the right, outside the small press room, at the few audience members who were listening in, but she wasn't there either.

Deep breaths. Amy squeezed her hand. Kit spoke first.

"My client is filing a counterclaim for extortion against Ned Frankenwell. We expect criminal charges will be pending once he is located. We have already made an emergency motion to dismiss the civil suit against my client, as it is so clearly one of the instruments of Mr. Frankenwell's extortion. That is all we have to say as a legal matter. It is my pleasure to work with Ms. Harrison and if anyone has questions, please contact me afterward." He smiled at Blake and gestured for her to come forward.

She looked down to the paper that Amy and Lydia had both written for her and read it. She wasn't sure she could do much better than a mechanical recitation, because as she'd said over and over, this was not her strong suit. What did they expect? Public speeches were not in the job description of an artist. But she was trying to be a good sport.

"Thank you all for coming. Unfortunately, my story is not uncommon. Women are often accused of not being the genesis of their ideas. In this case, there is no basis to believe that I stole anything from Ned Frankenwell. It is clear, and we can show, that it is the other way around. He took the idea from me and has failed to execute it. Ultimately, the law doesn't even matter as much as the experience of an artist's work. My rooms found their spark with Spencer Finch. I have gone one step further. I can't patent the idea of a lit room. I can execute it and I have, and the visitors of the Albie seem to agree. I'd like to especially thank the museum, Davis, Amy, Lydia, Mitch, and of course, Jenny, who has made my time in Boston better than I ever could have imagined."

The last sentence was unscripted. The name Jenny got caught in her throat a little; she wondered if anyone else could hear it. Jenny wasn't there, but at least Blake would have done her best to say goodbye.

At the end of the press conference, Amy told Blake the car was waiting outside. "We're getting another eight inches tonight," she said, "so you should really go."

"I have to walk through the rooms again," Blake said, and Amy, understanding, nodded. Blake walked up the steps to the gallery. It was after open hours, so it was closed, and the lights had been shut off. All that was remaining of her masterpiece were the walls, painted in the chosen colors and glosses, illuminated by the track lighting from above. It was dark, eerie, flat, like a maze. And then, through one of the doorways, she saw half a silhouette. A woman, looking at one of the walls.

Jenny.

Blake stepped in the rom. It was the Vermeer room, but you couldn't tell. It was dark. The magic was gone.

Jenny turned to Blake. "Kind of strange without the lights on."

"Really nothing to write home about."

"It's amazing to see it so naked, actually. Shows what a full world you created."

"I thanked you," Blake said.

"For what?"

"For everything. The legal help. You know."

"The legal help." Jenny turned around, let out a little air, mock laughter. "Well, you're welcome for the legal help."

"I didn't mean it that way—" Blake protested.

"I know," Jenny said. It sounded like she wanted to say something else, but she didn't. She looked at Blake in a way that made her feel as naked as her rooms.

"I'm sorry," Blake said.

"Why are you apologizing? We had a great night."

"And day." Blake smiled. Jenny did too, but it felt a little weak.

"And day," she repeated. "So that's it?"

Blake wanted to scream. *No, that wasn't it. It couldn't possibly be.* She had been thinking about no one but Jenny for days. She had been drawing no one but Jenny. Her whole mind was centered on Jenny. She was seeing the letter "J" float in front of her eyes. She wanted to go back to New York so badly, except for one reason. Jenny wouldn't be there. Jenny wouldn't be sitting beside her in the car.

"You were right," Blake said.

Jenny looked at her, puzzled. "About what?"

"The rooms. I saw them. I went to see Ned's rooms, and they were terrible. They did nothing. He can't get to me, no matter what."

Jenny's smile was all the reward Blake needed. It stretched over her whole face. "I'm glad," she said. And then, her mouth in a small circle and eyes narrow, "As your lawyer I have to advise you that wasn't a good idea."

"It's okay. I was in disguise."

Jenny smiled, her mouth tight. She looked almost wistful.

Blake took a deep breath. "Friends?" she said.

Jenny's smile was still taut around the edges. "Yes." Blake put her hand in Jenny's to shake it, and time seemed to slow again. The blood rushed from her face, her hand felt like it was on fire. She gripped Jenny's hand tightly, afraid to pull away, and Jenny tightened her grip, too. So in a few seconds, they were not shaking hands, but holding hands, looking at each other, alone in the dark gallery.

"What is this?" Blake asked.

"It's something," Jenny replied, in a whisper. Their hands were still clasped, and their eyes still locked, but they hadn't moved any closer together.

"Can I call you?"

Jenny nodded. "Please."

"I have to go," Blake said. She wanted to say, "Come with me," but she knew Jenny couldn't. She'd have to get back to work. Back to that boss of hers, back to her numbers and her condo and her suits and her life. Blake had to get back to cleaning up her own mess. A mess she had already saddled Jenny with too much of.

"Goodbye," Blake said.

"Blake, honey!" Amy's voiced echoed through the gallery, bouncing off the walls. Jenny moved back to a corner of one of the rooms, in shadow. Blake let her hand drop, slowly, and watched Jenny slink away.

"I'll be right there," Blake called to Amy, and she turned and walked away.

CHAPTER THIRTY-FIVE

In the weeks after Blake left, Jenny fell into her routine again. Answer to Michael's demands. Work. See her parents for brunch or dinner. But she felt like there was a new kind of courage inside of her. She started leaving work a little earlier and taking long walks around the city. She visited the new food trucks in Copley and when she rode the T she looked out the window instead of down at her phone. She was spending more time with Davis, too. Leaving the office at five for dinner one Friday, she ran into Lydia on the elevator.

"You're getting to be more like me!" Lydia said, smiling and punching her playfully in the arm. Singsongy, she continued, "Leaving work, loving life, don't let the man get you down, down down." She turned it into a song, gyrating as the sliding doors closed. "Baby are you down down down down down. Doooooown, dooooooown. Now the elevator goes down, down down down down." Jenny couldn't help but laugh.

"What are you doing tonight?"

"The boy and I are making dinner, then we are going to see a play at the ART. Something with music and strange costumes. I can't remember what."

"Well, you seem very cheerful about it."

"Yes, ma'am," Lydia said, practically skipping out of the elevator. "Spring has sprung."

And it had. Jenny was feeling it, too, the warmth in the air, the long thaw after the collectively suffocating winter. Little buds of green were popping up everywhere, and the whole city seemed to be ready to burst into color. All the arms and faces that had been covered up for so long were visible. Flesh seemed to be everywhere.

Jenny wondered how Blake would draw everyone's transition to spring. She wondered what she'd think of the painted electric boxes popping up all over Somerville, wanting to know if she would have been as moved by the da Vinci show at the MFA as she'd been. It seemed cruel that she had been here in the winter, missing how people splayed themselves out along the banks of the Charles in a modern day Grand Jatte, goose poop be damned. She wondered if Blake was claustrophobic and if the Porter Square stop would bother her. No, probably not, she was a gritty New Yorker. God, how provincial Jenny must seem to her.

She met Davis outside a ramen place on Mass Ave. There was a line twenty-deep, but the place wasn't even open yet. "We're too old for this," Jenny said, looking ahead at the hipsters in front of them, all eyes down on their iPhone screens as they salivated over the bowls of pork belly they'd eat while crouching on the sidewalk. "If you say so," Davis said, and he took her hand and led her to an Italian place a few blocks away, filled with gray-haired couples—Jenny saw an author and a U.S. Senator—eyeing each other in the candlelight. Jenny found herself thinking of Blake again.

"What's up with you?" Davis asked finally, after they had toasted their martinis in uncharacteristic silence.

"Distracted. Sorry."

"Well, I have news, so pay attention. I'm getting a raise!"

"Congratulations!" Jenny grinned.

"Thanks! I'm also getting a title change. They are dropping 'assistant' to my 'curator' because there was never a non-assistant curator in my department anyway. And, drumroll please—I am on contract to do the designs for the museum gala for the next five years!"

"That's amazing, Davis. Congratulations, really."

"Thank you, my lady. And don't worry, that's a separate contract, nothing to do with my museum raise. It's a whole other freelance thing. Yes, I will make sure I get my taxes professionally done with that kind of income."

"Good. So you are paying for dinner?"

"If we had stayed at the ramen place, yes, but now that we are here…"

"…I still make twice as much as you, so I'll pay."

"Precisely."

Jenny clinked his glass again, trying to quell her unease. She was happy for Davis, and she didn't mind paying for dinner. It was something else. It was just that she wanted to be at dinner with someone else. With Blake.

Davis, prescient once again, said, "Have you heard from Blake?"

"Sort of. I sent her the sketchbook she left at my place."

"And?"

Jenny looked down. "She texted to say she got it, but that I should have kept it."

"That's it?"

Jenny wasn't sure she wanted to answer. There was more. Blake texted once a week, sometimes twice, all kinds of pictures, and Jenny tried to find hidden meaning in them. Blake sent photos of stacked-up trash bags covered in an inch of snow, looking like a snow man leaning over offering passersby a cup of tea. An errant piece of graffiti, somewhere under a tunnel near Central Park; it looked to Jenny like a "J" or, once, a "Jennifer." A picture of two fire hydrants, one red and one blue.

Jenny wasn't sure what to make of the messages, but they felt like love notes. She wrote back, usually immediately. Something bland, always just along the lines of *Thank you*, or *Hello to you too*. Nothing more. Jenny thought about taking her own pictures. She walked by a snowfield a few days ago. It was so dirty it was brown, but the snow was melting from the bottom through the street, and it was reflecting the light in a dizzying way. She tried a few times to capture it, but couldn't, and was instead left with twenty different muddy pictures on her phone. It was her attempt at art and at communicating with Blake, but they weren't good enough to send. She couldn't bring herself to delete them either.

"So she texts?" Davis said again, jolting Jenny out of her meanderings.

"Just pictures," she said.

"Nudes?" Davis said.

"No, and that's not funny."

"Sorry," he said, chastised. And, more gently, "You seem to miss her. Or something."

"I do."

"Why don't you call her and tell her that?"

"We didn't leave it as anything. We just left it…she's on the phone with Lydia twice a week about the case anyway, so maybe when that's over. I don't know."

"Well, do you want me to help you set up an online profile, get back out there?"

"Out where?"

"To find someone."

I did find someone! And she's gone, Jenny thought. That's what it felt like. She had been given a few days, and she had lived them fully, and now they had been taken away.

"Maybe later. Sure. Thanks."

A high-pitched beeping sound came from her phone. The special ring for her father's cell phone, for use only during emergencies. She fished it out of her bag quickly and gave a panicked, "Hello?"

"Everything's fine, your mother's iPhone is just out of batteries."

Jenny felt her heart slow down. "Thank God."

"We're at the Albie. The last day for those rooms you said you liked. Free Fridays! Want to meet us?"

Davis mouthed, "What?" at Jenny, but she waved him off. "I'm not sure. I'm here with Davis, but—"

Her mother's voice shrieked through the phone. "He can give us a tour! How is he?"

"Hold on, Mom," Jenny said, pressing mute and setting the phone on the table for a moment. Then, to Davis, "So. They're at the museum."

"Let's meet them. I haven't seen your parents in ages. Not since your mother's Indian food phase."

"It's the last day of the rooms."

Davis sat forward in his chair. "Oh," he said. "So they're there to see that."

"Yes," Jenny said, lips pursed.

"How do you feel about that?"

She smiled, trying to brush it off. "Always good to revisit the site of one of the most passionate kisses one has ever had, is it not?"

"That's the spirit," Davis said.

Her parents were both in Bermuda shorts, even though it wasn't quite warm enough for that. Everyone who had survived the winter was a little overeager with their summer wardrobes. They were standing on the steps of the museum, waving at Jenny and Davis before they were within earshot.

Jenny followed her parents up the stairs, the same stairs she'd walked in her tuxedo dress, the one that sat sullenly in the back of her closet, limp now like it knew it wasn't allowed to live up to its true potential. She remembered the glitz and glamor of that night, of Davis's gorgeous arrangements, and it felt so far away.

They stepped into the gallery. Despite the crowd, the rooms felt silent as ever, the reverent tone that Blake was able to create rushing over all the visitors, making them have an experience that was about sound and sight as much as anything else. Jenny watched her father, who was not an art lover by any means, wade through the Vermeer room. When he came out, he was moving more slowly, a play of a smile across his face. Peace and some childlike wonder. Her mother stayed in the La Tour room for quite a while, and when she emerged she was almost prayerful, seeming to carry the candlelight with her in her palms. The light had stuck to her.

Davis pointed at the Hockney room. "You're not going in? It's your last shot."

Jenny joined the line and walked slowly in, feeling again the flash of blue light, just as she had the first time, sensing the heat of the sun on her face and the heat from the pool tiles radiating through the soles of her shoes. It was as magical as the first time she'd seen it, alone with Blake after she returned the drill bit.

Jenny's mother interrupted her daydream. "This one is very summery!" she said, gleeful, putting her hands up to the sky. "It's like an anti-SAD lamp."

Jenny laughed. "I guess."

They converged at the top of the stairs again.

"We really didn't plan for you to be our hosts. We just were trying to be spontaneous," Jenny's father said, a little embarrassment showing on his face.

"Spring has sprung, you know, what better way to celebrate than calling your daughter and saying 'meet me at the museum!'?"

Jenny smiled at how Lydia had said "spring had sprung" earlier the same day. "Sure thing." She smiled, delighting in them. She hadn't seen her parents this jovial in a while, and the mood was catching on.

They started walking down the steps of the museum.

"Your father and I are getting a new car," her mother said. "One of those tiny smart car things."

"Mom, test drive it. I'm not sure Dad can fit."

"It's me with my heels that's the problem! After this winter, we said, we need a car that can fit in the shed and also one that can park in tiny, tiny spaces."

"It's terrible in the snow. Rethink this, please."

"Well, maybe I will. I was just making conversation. Ever hear from that artist?" Jenny's mother said, quietly leaning in as they clip-clopped down the marble.

"Blake?" Jenny almost choked on the name.

"Yes." Jenny's mother paused and looked at her for a moment and back down at the stairs. "I heard her thank you in her press conference."

"You watched that?"

"I did." Jenny didn't say anything back to her mother, wondering how much she understood. When they reached the bottom of the staircase, the banner of Blake's work flying overhead, her mother said, "Now that I've seen her art, I would love to meet her in person."

Jenny tried to picture it, as she had once before. This time she found, strangely, that she could.

On cue, Jenny felt her phone vibrate. She pulled it out of her bag. A picture from Blake, no text. Two red roses, stuck in a crevice between cobblestones on the sidewalk. Jenny felt a wave of warmth through her body, as if Blake were right there, holding her hand. She needed to make that happen.

CHAPTER THIRTY-SIX

It would have been a good spring if not for the lawsuit. That's what Blake kept saying to herself, moping around New York. It was this fucking lawsuit. All Ned's fault. She had to update Steve on the progress of everything, the motions filed, the impending court dates. He was checking with Blake's insurance in case they actually had to go to trial or if they decided to pay the fucker off. Everything was moving more slowly than she would have liked.

Blake talked to Lydia at least once a week. Lydia rattled off the next fifteen things on the "to-do" list until, she always said, "You can put this all behind you, Blake, just put this all behind you." But it seemed too unfair that anyone had to think of it at all. Because there were many other things Blake wanted to think about instead.

One was her next project. The decomposing drawings, the faded pencil, the light disintegrating the page. How would she do it? Which drawings would she use? Was it going to be about seasons? Memory? Love? All of the above? She woke up in the middle of the night thinking about the project, so she knew it would work. She could not rest.

The other thing she wanted to think about instead of the lawsuit, of course, was Jenny. She knew Jenny sat in her office just a few doors down from Lydia. Blake wondered if she might be straining to hear their conversations, crowding into Lydia's door afterward, asking, Blake imagined, "How did she sound?"

Blake worried, too, that Jenny might have forgotten her. She sent her photos, and Jenny responded to the texts quickly, but not especially warmly. Blake wondered if she'd ever get back an image of her own or a phone call. Just something that meant *I'm thinking of you. I miss you.*

But no. Jenny seemed determined to forget.

Blake busied herself with the documents. Lydia needed records of everything that Blake had used to plan the rooms. They weren't in the "discovery" phase of litigation yet—Blake had learned, too fast, and unwillingly, that "discovery" is when your whole life is up for grabs, gutted. They wanted to find the smoking gun for settlement purposes, if there was one. She was pretty sure she'd eaten the drawings, but maybe there were some left in her sketchbooks.

Blake had to document everything for her counterclaim, too, all her interactions with Ned, the creepy texts he'd sent sporadically over the past few years. She didn't have the texts, of course, but she did have a few postcards, a letter, one voice mail that somehow had ended up as an audio file on her computer. That was fortunate. It referred to "Your rooms" as in "Blake's rooms," making his later claims seem obviously frivolous.

Then, mercifully, on a Tuesday, Lydia called her early in the morning, sounding giddy. "He's been arrested for drunk and disorderly and attempted robbery of a gallery—not one with any of your art in it—and we're going to swoop in now!"

"What?" Blake rubbed the sleep from her eyes. She had been up for a few hours in the middle of the night experimenting with chemicals that decomposed graphite that she might spray on the drawings to speed up the process.

"The asshole. I had my friend who's a public defender keeping an eye out for him, because I know bad meat when I smell it, and sure enough. I have someone from our New York office at the ready to call him, tell him to drop it, or we'll make a big deal out of this. He's toast."

Blake felt sad, for a moment, that Ned had sunk so low, and seemed to not be well. Then she remembered what he had done to her and shook off any sympathy.

"What do I do?"

"Wait. I know that's not the easiest thing to do. Wait."

So Blake did, for two days. Working furiously on the faded drawings, running science experiments in the studio with different kinds of paper, acid, and bright lights. Disappearing ink. She considered and reconsidered, eventually deciding that the pencil drawings had to be standard pencil drawings on normal paper. Nothing tricky, just speeding up the process of decay. The lights could be bright, or even blinding, as long as over time, they made the paper crumple, yellow, and the drawings disappear.

Lydia finally called. "Voluntary dismissal. We got him to sign it. He was working with a firm, you know. They seemed to think he was as nuts as we did, but they were politic enough not to say so."

"Thank you, oh God," Blake said, feeling like she wanted to cry; all the tension and stress and fear was finally letting itself surface. She choked a little sound into the phone.

"Are you all right?" Lydia asked.

Blake couldn't answer. Another little sob.

"This is a totally normal reaction," Lydia said, clinically, but comforting at the same time.

"Thanks," she said again, feeling her hands stop shaking, just a bit, not knowing how the cloud of relief, happiness, grief, and gratitude all could go together.

"So that's it?"

"Yeah, we pulled out all the stops. Showed his lawyer the texts and some of your drawings and threatened a defamation suit on top of all the other stuff. It was not pretty. It was fun, though."

"I'm glad," Blake managed to say.

"Well, so seldom there's a clear good guy."

Blake smiled. She hadn't thought of herself that way; really, she was thinking victim. "Good guy" sounded better. More proactive. Empowering. Like it was a fair fight. And the idea that other people saw her that way gave her such relief. She allowed herself the thought, for a moment, that maybe Jenny saw her that way.

She stood up from the pile of papers, looking around the room. Many of the drawings were of Jenny. Even the ones that weren't, or weren't supposed to be, had something of her in them, or at least something of the way Jenny made her feel.

"Blake?" came Lydia's voice, a little tentative through the receiver.

"Yeah?" Her breathing had slowed, the tears in her voice subsided.

"Hold on." She heard a rustling of the phone, women's voices, a beep, silence, and then another click. Her heart was beating faster with a daring hope... *Was it Jenny?*

Sure enough, it was. "Blake, hi." Jenny's voice was low and it resonated in Blake's body. She could feel it meeting up with her bloodstream and thumping, drumming throughout her limbs, playing her whole body like it was an instrument made out of a hollowed-out gourd.

"Hi," she managed to croak, her sense of relief and nervousness about both Jenny and the case mixing and mingling into too many emotions to parse.

"I'm so happy for you," Jenny said. Blake imagined her, perched on Lydia's desk, stockings on, legs crossed, a stiletto heel dangling off her toe, perfectly cut suit, thick hair falling down around her shoulders.

"Thanks, me too." They sat in the silence for a moment.

"Well, Lydia did an impeccable job," Jenny said, sounding a little businesslike, but out of nervousness, not because she was trying to push Blake away. *Right?*

"I hope you've enjoyed the photos I've sent," Blake said and seesawed back to nervousness herself, aware that Jenny was speaking from Lydia's office, and perhaps the door was open, and perhaps she wasn't dangling her feet from the desk, but standing nervously, wanting the conversation to be over.

"Yes. So much. I keep wanting to respond in kind, but I don't know how. I just…"

"They're just my way of saying hello," Blake replied.

"Well. Hello," Jenny said, with an uplift of flirtation in her voice. Blake could hear it and felt her confidence return. She needed to see Jenny. She felt giddy, all of a sudden, ripe with possibility.

"I'd like to see you," she said, plain and true. It felt like the easiest way to go. Might as well lay her cards on the table.

"I'd like that too," Jenny said, just as bare, and again, the sound of her voice traveled through Blake, making her feel charged and alive. "I've been wanting to call, but…"

Blake nodded, and then realized that she was nodding and Jenny couldn't hear her. "That's okay. Me too. We'll talk soon, okay? I'll call you, and we'll talk, and figure out…"

"What this is?" Jenny said, completing the question.

"Sure. Good. Excellent," Blake said, uncharacteristically redundant, chatty, enthusiastic, offering three words when one would suffice. *Yes.* Yes is all she needed to say, wanted to say. *Yes, Jenny. Yes.*

CHAPTER THIRTY-SEVEN

Since Jenny had won the argument about the BlueCoast Daubert, Michael had given her a wider berth. She hated him a little less, because she felt free. She had decided to leave her job and was thinking about becoming an economist. An economic *expert*, in fact. She could design the analyses that she cobbled together for litigation. She would actually write the reports and defend them during depositions and at trial. Grad school brochures were strewn across her kitchen table. It would be a long road—GRE, master's, doctorate. More school, yes. But it finally felt right. And she figured law school hadn't been a total waste, since she first had to get her law degree to know the field existed.

Thinking about the next phase of her career was also meant to take her mind off Blake. Since they had last spoken, Blake sent occasional text messages. Just *Thinking of you*, and more photographs. A Manhattan street with the sun setting just at the end of it, over the Hudson, between the buildings, a glowing orb shooting shards of light across the buildings. A broken traffic light with both the red and green blazing at the same time. The texts only came once every few days and Blake said nothing else, nothing more about visiting, or how things were at home, or wanting anything from Jenny other than what she'd already had.

But that phone call in Lydia's office was different than any text. It was awkward, and halting, but had a certain fire to it. That phone call was Blake's voice, with its low tone, its slow pace, the pauses between words that Jenny had found so erotic. Blake said they'd talk and figure it out. Whatever "it" was. But Blake didn't call. Not for two whole weeks. Until she did.

Jenny watched her phone light up on her desk, the name "Blake Harrison" blinking across the screen. Her finger hovered over the answer icon. Then, as if she were jumping into the cold rough ocean, she picked it up quickly.

"Hi, I—"

"Hey, so—"

"It's been a while." Jenny's voice broke through the overlap. It had been two weeks and one day since they had spoken in Lydia's office. Yes, she'd been counting.

Blake's silence filled her ears.

"I'm coming to Boston," she said, after a few breaths. Jenny couldn't tell if she had more to say. They had become so awkward with one another.

"Why?"

"To see you!" she said. Jenny smiled into the phone, wanting to relive their night together, became giddy that she'd get the chance.

"I'm so glad," she said to Blake, but just as she did, Blake said, "So also, actually—" and stopped.

"What?" They started talking over one another again. Finally, Jenny said in a firmer voice, "'Actually' what?"

She heard Blake breathe in. "I'm going to see Amy, too, about a show."

Jenny blushed, embarrassed that she hadn't realized Blake was kidding when she said she'd be coming to see Jenny. Why had she jumped to that conclusion? She was both feet in again, with no assurances from Blake. She had to be cautious.

"Okay. Well, have a good time," Jenny said.

"Back up," Blake said, with a trace of smile in her voice. "I want to see you. Amy was going to come here, but I suggested Boston because of you. Got it?"

"Yes." Relief flooded Jenny's chest. Maybe she wasn't swimming alone.

"So can I?"

"What?"

"See you? Take you out to dinner? A proper date." Jenny closed her eyes and could see Blake's lips as she formed the words. Her nervous smile around each sound.

"I accept." She hoped Blake could hear her smile, too. "When?"

"This Friday."

"Can I pick you up?" Jenny asked quickly. "Where are you staying?"

Now it was Blake's turn to stumble a bit. "I thought—"

"With me!" Jenny's foot was shaking nervously, like it was trying to fly off her leg. She blushed furiously, embarrassed again. They were one stroke together and one stroke apart.

"I didn't want to presume," came Blake's voice, a little quiet, chastised, too.

"Presume away. Okay. Yes. Fine. Okay." Jenny was sputtering now, amazed, Blake just announced she'd be there. With no pretense, dinner and a fuck.

Blake laughed. "We're better in person I think."

Jenny just nodded, and Blake somehow was able to take the silence as goodbye, and hung up. She held on to the phone in her palm, even after it had gone silent and Blake's name was no longer on the screen.

Three days. She'd be seeing Blake in three days. She sat back in her desk chair and swiveled to look out the window. Spring was inching along. There were a few green dots in the landscape. Jenny wondered again if Blake had ever seen Boston like this. Not half-dead. She smiled at her translucent reflection in the window, not quite sure she recognized who it was, but liking what she saw. Just letting this be what it was going to be. Welcoming Blake to town, to her bed, gleeful at the thought.

Jenny stayed at work late on Thursday, wanting to finish all her work for the weekend so she'd be able to leave early on Friday and spend the weekend with Blake. It was late, around eleven, and the office was empty. Her eyes were starting to protest about still being open, but she still had a few more lines of the spreadsheet to optimize.

Her phone beeped. A text from Blake.

Hi. Can't wait to see you.

Jenny wrote back immediately, too tired and too excited to start worrying about the composition or editing her thoughts.

Me too.

Where are you now?

Office.

You work so hard.

You sound like my parents.

I certainly don't want to sound like them.

Jenny waited a few moments, and Blake wrote again. *You need to relax.*

Jenny waited another beat and Blake wrote again, *I'd like to relax you.*

Well, that was a little flirtatious. Jenny smiled, getting excited for the next day, for Blake's presence, for their magnetism to be in person again.

You excite me, you don't relax me, Jenny wrote, feeling bold.

Can't I do both? came Blake's reply, immediately. Jenny's face felt flushed. She wanted to look around the office, make sure no one else was there. She was feeling turned on. She couldn't believe that Blake's power over her was so intense that she could be sitting on her desk chair, in front of a green spreadsheet, feeling turned on from a few text messages, which were pretty innocent, but she was.

What are you wearing? Blake wrote.

Seriously? Jenny replied. Then, quickly, *Navy suit. I was wearing it the second time we met.*

Good

So Blake had dispensed with any punctuation. That was interesting.

How about you? Jenny wrote, trying to keep it light.
Nothing
Really?
No. Black leggings and a red T-shirt
Jenny smiled, picturing Blake perched on a stool in her studio, surrounded by pads of paper and buckets of pencils. She had sent a picture of the studio once, and Jenny enlarged it on her tiny phone screen so she could see every pixel of Blake's world.

Jenny was about to write back some piece of that thought, but Blake wrote again before she typed it out.

I wish I could kiss your neck
Jenny flushed again, suddenly cognizant of a nearly overwhelming need to touch herself. This was too much. She had to get home, relieve the tension there, in bed, with or without Blake texting her, and get ready for tomorrow. This was getting absurd. She was in her office, for God's sakes.

You can kiss my neck tomorrow. Jenny texted, with the proper punctuation. She couldn't be feeling turned on in her office. She needed to let Blake off gently and go home.

But I want to now, was Blake's immediate reply. Jenny couldn't deny she wanted to know where this would lead. How far was Blake going to take this? She banished rational thought and decided on a different approach. Playing along. Her breath was coming up shallow.

I want that too, she wrote, leaving the ball in Blake's court. She squirmed in her seat, waiting for her to reply. It seemed to take a long time.

I want to do so many things, was all she wrote.

She decided to ask, to take it to the next level. Fuck it. She was turned on, it was late at night, she would play this game if Blake wanted to play.

Oh yeah? Like what? Jenny wrote.

I want to suck on your nipples, Blake replied, quickly.

Jenny's breathing became heavier. She got up quickly, opened her door, and looked down the hallway.

No one. Not a light to be seen. She was alone. When she turned back to her phone, Blake had already sent a few more messages.

I want to take off your skirt
I want to climb underneath your desk
I want to lick you, taste you
I want you to hold my head
I want to make you moan

Jenny couldn't hold back. She slid her right hand inside the waistband of her skirt and her underwear and started rubbing her clit, her mouth going dry with Blake's texts.

Jenny fumbled as she texted back with her left hand, *I'm so wet.* She couldn't believe she was doing this, but she couldn't stop. She needed Blake. And if she couldn't be there with her, this would have to suffice.

I am licking you & taste so good, Blake responded. When Jenny didn't respond right away, too busy panting, Blake wrote,

Take off your underwear. Jenny noticed the punctuation.

Ok, Jenny wrote.

Put two fingers inside of you. Blake's next instruction.

Jenny complied, rubbing her clit with her other hand. She couldn't text back that way, with both her hands occupied, so she waited for Blake's next message.

Now suck on your fingers.

Jenny did so, feeling her body nearing orgasm, not caring that she was splayed open in the middle of her office, her work timer still clicking by.

Taste good?

Yes, Jenny managed to type back.

I want a taste, Blake wrote.

I wish, typed Jenny.

Blake's next message was a picture. Jenny opened it up and couldn't figure out what she was seeing at first. A door, a glass wall…then she realized. It was the elevator bank on her floor.

Jenny sat up in her chair, yanking her fingers out of her body. What did this mean? Her top button had come undone.

She buttoned it, smoothed her skirt, and gingerly approached her door, opening it softly, knowing that anyone within a few feet of her would be able to smell sex. She looked down the hallway. Still dark. No one there. She walked past the coffee station to the elevator bank. And there, behind the glass wall, behind the door was Blake. She was pressing her breasts up against the glass, and her eyes were hooded with heavy lids, lust jumping through them. It seemed almost cruel, the glass, and then funny, and then, in Jenny's state, urgent beyond all measure that she pull Blake through. Touch her. She pulled her I.D. from her belt clip and waved it at the scanner. The door didn't open. Blake started laughing a little bit, Jenny could see her chuckle but couldn't hear her. Finally, the door beeped open, and Blake almost fell through.

They kissed before they said anything, tongues moving so aggressively Jenny thought they were trying to mold their mouths together. She had been so close to orgasm, and now, with Blake here, it was like she was in a state beyond orgasm, on some other planet where nothing mattered but her body's pleasure. She was barely human anymore; she was just desire. She didn't care that she was right outside the elevator bank in the hallway, without underwear, wetness dripping down her legs. She didn't care that she had just been masturbating on her leather office chair, and now Blake was here.

"I need you," she finally said, in the middle of their kissing, and it felt so true and raw she was overwhelmed by it. She pulled back, panting, to look at Blake.

"Can I take you home?" Blake asked, almost demurely. Jenny took her hand, and they walked down the darkened hallway, into her office, their fingers interlaced. Jenny resolved, as she walked, that for the weekend—for however long they would be together—if she could see Blake, she'd be touching her. Blake's skin felt like it gave her energy. Completed some endless cycle of need.

She pulled her into her office and kicked the door closed. "Take me here," she said, "and then you can take me home."

Blake didn't hesitate. She pinned Jenny against her desk, wrenching her starched shirt out of her waistband, yanking down the cups of her bra and undoing the back strap in almost one motion. She sucked on Jenny's nipple and put two fingers inside Jenny as she leaned on the desk, and then three, pumping in and out with a primal kind of force.

"Please taste me," Jenny said, almost wanting to cry, she was so happy and so needy all at once. Blake pushed Jenny's ass up onto the desk, and Jenny scooted herself back, toppling a few binders in the process. Blake laughed, and became serious again, kneeling down and attaching her mouth to Jenny and licking, slowly at first, and then faster, as Jenny circled her hands around Blake's neck and thrust her body forward into Blake's face.

"Oh God, oh God," was all she could say. Blake seemed to be agreeing, moaning herself, with her hand down her own pants. Jenny looked down at her beautiful face, but all she could see were flashes of light, shards and shadows. Sparks. Then, through the cacophony of colors, Blake's eyes, fixed on her, watching her writhe in pleasure, with an expression so pure Jenny recognized it as adoration.

Blake was looking at her adoringly.

She came without embarrassment, without holding back. Her body exploded in pleasure, the orgasm rolling through her and warming her to the tips of her fingers and toes. She pulled Blake's face away, and grabbed her shoulders, hugging her close. Blake rested her head on her chest, and Jenny stroked her cheek.

"I missed you," she said, and Blake squeezed her tighter and said, "I just couldn't wait." She looked up at her with a serious expression, but then let her face smile. "I wanted to surprise you in your actual office," she said, "but I couldn't get past the damn glass door."

Jenny laughed. "How did you even get onto the elevator at all?"

She fished a card from the pocket of her shift and showed it to Jenny. "My old pass from the meeting about Ned—I just changed the date."

"You could get in trouble for that," Jenny said.

"Well, we could get in trouble for a lot of things," Blake said, tracing along Jenny's cleavage with her damp finger.

Jenny looked at her, feeling like her whole life had changed, and she had changed along with it. "When I'm with you," she said, "I don't seem to care."

CHAPTER THIRTY-EIGHT

When Blake woke up the next morning, it took her a moment to remember she was in Jenny's bed. She stretched, and it felt like she was swimming in silk. High thread-count sheets had never meant anything to her before now. When she turned over, she almost gasped when she saw Jenny, whose skin was as smooth as the sheets. She looked more beautiful than Blake could imagine, let alone capture in a drawing. The line from her neck, down to her shoulder, down to her elbow, was somehow both angular and soft. Strong and still inviting pampering. Her whole body, wrapped in the sheets, looked so perfect it was almost untouchable, godly, pure. At the same time, she was one of the most sensual, alive, and embodied women Blake had ever known.

She thought back to Liza. Yes, she'd made that mistake when she got back to New York. A quick, pleasant, but somehow shallow fuck on Liza's couch, and Blake didn't want to stay the night. Didn't want to see her sleep. Didn't want to inhale her smell, surround herself with Liza's things. It was like she didn't really want to touch her. Not really, not wholly.

When she was in Jenny's presence, all Blake wanted to do was fuse their bodies together. In the middle of the night, even as they turned away to get a little more of the bed to fall asleep, Blake made sure their toes were touching. This morning, watching her sleep, she rested a hand lightly on Jenny's back. She needed her skin to touch Jenny's. It was like she needed it to breathe.

She didn't want to move, but she had to pee and put on coffee and get something for breakfast. Not seem like a freeloader. Cook this hard-working goddess a good meal. She needed to call Amy, too. Tell her she was going to be late, maybe by a few hours. There was no way she was leaving Jenny's apartment anytime soon. She wanted to stay in their cocoon of love and sex and pleasure.

Blake gently removed her hand from Jenny's back and rolled out of bed. She pulled out a long red Henley from her bag. Split neck, just at the clavicle. She felt graceful in it, and she wanted Jenny to think she was beautiful. She felt beautiful. The way Jenny touched her... She took a deep breath, shivering, remembering. It made her feel gorgeous. Jenny's reverence for Blake's body somehow amplified Blake's reverence for her own.

She crept quietly into the kitchen, put the coffee on. She wanted to present Jenny with breakfast, but it didn't feel quite appropriate. She was in Jenny's house, and they weren't at the point that Blake could start whipping through cupboards and dirtying dishes, were they? And even if they were, what did Jenny have that Blake could eat? The frozen vegan scones were no doubt gone.

She should have brought something. She should have gotten them a hotel room so they could order room service. Suddenly, her calling Jenny and inviting herself over didn't seem fun or gamine, but gauche. Jenny deserved room service. A proper date. Blake had been too casual for too long, stuck in some other kind of life of crashing on couches and staying up all night working and rolling out of bed to get a bagel. Jenny was different.

Blake gingerly opened the cupboards. Registered where Jenny kept her mugs. Plates. Forks. Oatmeal. Peanut butter. Okay. She could work with that.

She tiptoed back into the bedroom. Jenny had rolled over. The sheet was down by her waist, her breasts exposed, perfect nipples hard from the slight early morning chill. Blake wanted to crawl in next to her. Just the sight of Jenny made her wet. Jenny opened her eyes halfway and looked at Blake standing in the doorway. Seeming to like what she saw, she smiled and closed her eyes again. "Found the coffee?" she said, the sleep making her voice a little croaky.

"I did," Blake said.

Jenny stretched her arms above her head and said, still with her eyes closed, "Lay down with me while you wait for it to beep."

Blake couldn't take one more step in the room, she knew, or she'd lose all control. "I want to make you breakfast, okay?"

Jenny opened her eyes and smiled. "I bought us fruit. All sorts of things. It's all in a bag in the fridge."

"Mind if I use your kitchen?"

Jenny smiled, wide. "What's mine is yours." Blake felt like there was a word missing at the end of that sentence, like Jenny wanted to say, "honey," or "sweetie."

And Blake wanted to say, "love." *What's mine is yours, my love.* But what did Blake have for Jenny? A dingy apartment. A sordid sexual past. Her art.

Blake went into the kitchen again and found the bag Jenny mentioned. She had bought pints of berries, a whole pineapple, pears. Blake smiled at the care Jenny had taken, the way she'd anticipated Blake's arrival so tenderly. She was struck again by the odd way they wanted to care for one another.

It felt like—no, Blake told herself, walking around the kitchen barefoot, feeling like she was floating—it *was*—love.

She put together breakfast as Jenny slept. Cinnamon oatmeal, a plate of fruit, popovers made with curdled soy milk, brown sugar, and canned pumpkin she found in the back of the cupboard, a little dusty. Almond milk smoothies. Steaming black coffee. She was about to carry it into the bedroom on a tray, when Jenny appeared in the doorway to the kitchen, wearing paisley blue pajamas—a matching set, shorts and a button-down shirt. She had combed her hair, and Blake could see from across the room that she'd put on a little lip gloss. She didn't need it, but the gesture touched Blake, both for what it said about her fastidiousness and what it said about how she wanted to impress her.

She put the tray on the table. "Sit. Breakfast. Piping hot."

Jenny sat obediently, curling her fingers around the warm mug, looking at Blake and the food with an expression of bewilderment.

"My gosh, how long have I been asleep?"

Blake sat across from her at the table. "I work fast."

They ate. Feasted, really. The acrobatics of the night before had left her ravenous. Jenny, too, was eating the way she made love to Blake, with a sense of urgency and a desire to take it slow and savor it, all at the same time. Jenny wanted to taste everything in quick succession, but she also seemed to want it to last.

"Where'd you learn to cook?" she asked, between bits of popover.

"It's just breakfast," Blake said. Jenny shook her head.

"I usually have a granola bar. Really. How?"

"Out of necessity, I guess. Living in New York, it was always takeout food, the bodega around the corner. Good stuff. Real Chinese food with lip-numbing Sichuan peppers, New York pizza, the Neapolitan kind. Then I went vegan. It's easy now, it takes basically no effort at all, but it wasn't always. We didn't have a real stove for a while, so I got one of those camp burners. Now in my studio that's how I cook, mostly. Your kitchen is really nice."

"This is nothing," Jenny said. "My mother is going through the cookbook canon. Her kitchen—it's one of those suburban ones with the huge stove and a fan and everything."

"Double door fridge?"

Jenny popped a strawberry into her mouth and looked at Blake. "Yes, and a fan over the stove, and a microwave that pops

out in a strange little drawer with a lot of very fancy settings."
Jenny paused, as if considering whether to continue. "She
retired and started channeling all her energy into it."

"Food?"

"Cooking, not even food. I'm not sure she likes eating all
that much. And…"

"What else?"

"Me. Wanting a grandchild. Blah blah blah."

Blake looked over at her. The tenderness she had for her
mother and her unease about talking about her expectations
were apparent on Jenny's face. Her eyes were cast away from
Blake all of a sudden, looking down, as if the corner of the
table had some secrets on it that she was trying to decipher.
Blake wondered if Jenny was pushing them into the "talk." The
"figuring out" that they were going to do.

Blake didn't want go there. Not now. Grandchildren? She
couldn't talk about grandchildren. She was afraid she'd say
Okay! I'll do anything! She felt reckless, and she clammed up,
looking at the corner of the table too.

As if reading her mind, Jenny said, "Forget I said that.
Grandchildren! What am I talking about? Fruit! Have some
more fruit!" She picked up the raspberries, which were still out
of season but somehow sweet, and handed them over to Blake.
Blake couldn't help touching her. If she was reading Jenny's
nervousness correctly, it was based on that feeling of sublime
falling. She was afraid she'd said too much, but she hadn't. Blake
wanted to say yes. She grabbed Jenny's hand and interlaced their
fingers. They locked their eyes on each other, and Blake's heart
was beating loudly and quickly. Jenny's fingers were warm,
sending pulses of heat all over Blake's body. She stood up at
the table and leaned toward Jenny. They had both grown quiet,
serious. She brought Jenny's hand to her lips and kissed each of
her knuckles, slowly. Jenny seemed entranced, her eyes trained
on Blake as she kissed.

There was more in each kiss than any words Blake could
have thought of to utter.

Finally, Jenny broke the silence. "What time are you meeting Amy?"

"I pushed it off," Blake said, "to be with you. I don't want to go at all if you're not coming with me. So come with me."

"Okay," said Jenny, staring at Blake, as if she was making a declaration. "I will."

CHAPTER THIRTY-NINE

If Amy was surprised to see Jenny tagging along on the meeting, she didn't let on. The three of them sat in the parlor room upstairs with the Derain, adding to the already crowded color palate of the room. Jenny was sitting next to Blake on one of the overstuffed chairs, but the arms were so big it was impossible to hold hands. Amy was talking about gallery space and square footage and the logistics of opening in a few months, but all Jenny could think about was wanting to crawl into Blake's lap. To sit on the big chair, enveloped by her arms, with Blake running her fingers through her hair. Yes, that would be nice.

"Jenny?" Blake's voice broke her from her daydream. Jenny sat up straight. "I need to ask you something."

Jenny nodded. The voice in her head, which was getting louder, more insistent, the more time she spent with Blake, spoke clearly. *Anything. Yes. The answer is yes.*

Blake said, "Do you mind if there are drawings of you in the show?"

Jenny looked over at Amy, who was looking back at her expectantly with her hands under her chin and big eyes.

Jenny breathed in. She didn't want to say no to Blake, but she knew what Blake's drawings of her looked like. Some were nudes. They were sensual. They were recognizable.

"I'll show you them. You have veto power. Okay? I won't put any up that you aren't comfortable with."

"I haven't even seen the nudes of you," Amy said, reassuringly.

"Except in her apartment," Jenny said, blushing at the memory, the terrible morning before the press conference, after Ned had sent all of them the emails.

"Well, except for those."

Blake took out the oversized portfolio, which had about a hundred clear plastic sleeves with drawings of different sizes in each. A few dark, chiaroscuro ones of the Boston nightscape with a few figures in front. People on the bus and crowded on the subway. And then, sure enough, Jenny. First, just her face, recognizably her. Clothed, in a suit. Next, with a hammer in the gallery before the rooms were complete. Had Blake run behind a wall to draw her surreptitiously? Or was that from memory? And then nudes. Her body, first as imagined by Blake, from before their first night together, when she'd met her in the museum. Blake had also drawn nudes from her firsthand knowledge of Jenny's body, reverently drawn lines and folds and the curled, delicate hairs. There were live drawings, too. Jenny's back, sitting in the chair, illuminated by her computer screen. And later that morning, her breasts flopping to the side, a light open-mouthed smile on her face.

Jenny expected herself to want to say no. To tell Blake gently that she couldn't. She couldn't possibly. But seeing the images themselves changed her answer. The drawings were beautiful. They made Jenny feel beautiful. And all she wanted to say was yes. So she did.

"Sure. Sure, no problem," she said, still marveling at the rendering of her flesh. *So that's what I look like*, she thought. *Not half bad.*

"You mean 'sure' just to the clothed ones, right? Or the ones from behind. It's you, but no one will know—" Blake seemed nervous. She was thrown off and Jenny realized she had expected a rejection.

"All of them," Jenny said quietly. She turned the pages, seeing Blake's self-portraits. She had captured herself in the mirror, first clothed, and then not, rendering her flesh defiantly, like Manet's Olympia. They were strong drawings, technically masterful just at first glance, but all Blake's at the same time. All her freedom, all her bold irreverence. They were exquisite. Jenny could not look away.

Jenny ran her finger along the lines of Blake's leg in one of the reclining self-portraits, because it seemed to carry all the sensuality of the real thing.

"I can't believe you are going to erase these," she said. Blake had explained that by the end of the show, the lights would fade the drawings completely. People would see just blank, stiffened and thinned pieces of paper, with only the lightest trace of where the pencil had been.

"At least I'm not going to have to eat them this time," Blake said. Jenny laughed.

"It's graceful this way," Amy said. "Brilliant, really, the passing of time. The season fading into the next. Loss of love. The transience of intimacy."

Jenny opened her mouth. She had the immediate sense that Amy was wrong, that Amy didn't get it at all. But what did Jenny understand? A few months ago, she would have scoffed at the idea of destroying drawings for art. She would have thought all of this was absurd. Now, here she was, lending her image to it. Jenny closed the portfolio gently and handed it back to Blake. If Amy was right, and this new destruction project was about the transience intimacy, it meant that Jenny—and Blake's nude drawings of Jenny—the treasure of their time together, the gift of that—was meaningless and would disappear.

"It's not about the transience of intimacy, is it? Or seasons?" she asked Blake.

Blake scrunched up her face for a moment. "I'm not sure, I think, is the answer."

Amy turned to Jenny, her characteristic warmth seeming to reach toward her in the room. "Why, what do you think, Jennifer?"

Jenny looked between the two and took a deep breath. "Well, I think it's about control. We think that paper lives forever and that digital images are transient. Drawings of da Vinci behind glass or the Gutenberg Bible. We tend to think of paper as real and authentic. That's not quite right, though, and that's what you are saying with these." Neither of them said anything, and Jenny felt like she was rambling, but she took a deep breath and continued, "Ned accused you of taking his idea, calling into question your skill and your integrity. He made a cheap copy, but he sullied the idea of what was really yours. With these drawings, you're in charge and there's no ambiguity. You are in utter control. No one can pass them off as their own if you destroy them."

Blake and Amy were both silent for a moment, and Jenny started fearing that she had been wrong by making it about what Ned had done. Amy broke into a huge grin. "Why don't you just write the catalog essay for me?" she said.

Blake smiled too, and reached over the arm of the chair and squeezed Jenny's leg. The simple motion felt intimate, loving, and sent Jenny's body into a warm flush. "Yes. Thank you," Blake said, simply, but it meant everything. It meant "I know you understand."

Amy left the room to ask the cook to put lunch on the table, and Blake started rolling the few oversized drawings she'd brought in her backpack. Jenny sat in the chair, watching her treat the drawings with reverence, wishing she had a similar ability—she wanted to capture Blake. Show Blake how it felt to be seen.

Blake turned around and knelt in front of Jenny. "It's not about the transience of intimacy," she said, adopting Amy's accent when she said the phrase.

Jenny nodded. Blake took her hands. "I don't want our intimacy to be transient. Got it?"

Jenny nodded again and then croaked, "Me neither." Blake smiled and returned to rolling the drawings. Jenny sunk back into the chair, gobsmacked. If their intimacy wasn't transient, was it permanent? Was that what Blake meant?

Jenny ate lunch quietly. She could feel her life changing at the dining room table, sitting near Amy as she and Blake made chit-chat about the latest shows, the new Whitney opening, the Venice Biennial. "Soon it will be your year," Amy said to Blake, and Jenny thought then about the possibility of them walking along the swampy city streets. She had never been but had seen pictures and the Sergeant paintings of the pigeon-populated squares. She imagined standing with Blake there, hobnobbing with international collectors wearing sculptural dresses and strange shoes. Could she do it? Would Blake be happy to have her on her arm? Could Jenny function in Blake's world?

It didn't matter if she could. She understood that she needed to. She didn't want to have a life that didn't have Blake in it.

She was in love.

"Hey, you okay?" Blake asked.

"Yeah, fine," Jenny said, choking down her food. Maybe if they were alone she would have said it. Maybe. She felt so scared, and so alive, she wasn't sure what she was capable of. She had just agreed to have naked drawings of her strewn along the walls of a Boston gallery. She was ready to do anything, be anyone, and go anywhere, if Blake asked.

CHAPTER FORTY

Blake could tell something was wrong. It was Sunday afternoon. Her Amtrak back to New York was in an hour. She and Jenny had spent the morning in bed and the afternoon walking around the city, down by the seaport where spring was showing in the green grass around the condo buildings, of which there was a new one every week, just as Jenny had said. *The new buildings, popping up like pimples.* The wind was still a winter kind of cold. They had walked arm in arm there along the water, Jenny pointing out things in Boston history. Blake trying to figure out a way to share the hood from her sweatshirt with Jenny.

Jenny leaned into her, and Blake eased into the feeling. Her body was fed by Jenny's touch. But now Jenny wasn't saying much and was leaning less. A distance was creeping in. They were walking to South Station. Blake's backpack was too heavy. So, apparently, was Jenny's mood.

"Come visit me next weekend," Blake said. Jenny nodded. No ecstatic, "Yes!" Blake noticed. Maybe she had misread everything. She went through the weekend. Everything had been perfect, right? Maybe Jenny was upset about the drawings? Regretted saying yes? That was fine. Blake could pull them from the show. She didn't want to do anything to make Jenny unhappy.

The squat but stately coffee-colored brick of South Station came into view. "We're here. When's your train?" Jenny asked.

As if she didn't know. As if Jenny hadn't been draped over her shoulder, naked, as she booked it this morning, saying, "Okay, that should give us enough time for lunch, too."

"3:15," Blake said.

"Here's the problem," Jenny said, stopping by a park bench on the Greenway. Blake sat, next to her, bracing herself. *Here it comes.* The breakup. But their legs were touching, and Jenny wasn't pulling her leg away.

Jenny turned to Blake. "I will come and see you in New York next weekend. Yes. But the problem is that there are five days between then and now."

Blake nodded, watching Jenny's lips. My God, had lips ever been so inviting? "That is a problem," she said, her heart beating loudly in her chest, the "I love you" sitting in her throat, ready to jump out.

"I don't know what to do about that," Jenny said.

"Me neither," Blake said, her voice catching.

They sat next to each other, both staring straight ahead. Blake wanted to kiss Jenny, but it didn't feel right, the moment felt too heavy. She knew she needed to get back to her studio. She needed to meet with more technical experts, the lighting designers who could figure out how fast and how completely the pencil drawings would disintegrate. Her need to work on the show had not diminished at all. She was craving time to create. But now there was something else she was craving just as much, if not more. *Jenny.* It was a simple, enormous truth. The five days did feel long. What then? This perpetual back and forth? Trains and planes? Blake closed her eyes, imagined their life in Boston, and couldn't.

"It's just five days," Blake croaked, but as she said it, it felt hollow. It was more than that. It was that they didn't know what to do next or what anything meant.

Jenny leaned toward Blake and their lips touched briefly. They looked at one another, and kissed again. It was tender, searching, gentler than she was used to. Loving. The quintessential park bench kiss. Blake noted that Jenny wasn't pulling away, wasn't looking around her at all, wasn't worried about who saw or who knew. Blake shrugged off her backpack and leaned into Jenny more, tasting the sweetness of her mouth, feeling her nose, which was a little cold, dig into her cheek a bit.

Jenny pulled back, breathing heavier, but sitting up straight on the bench, like she was trying to gird herself against something. "Your train is leaving soon."

"They're always delayed," Blake said, leaning into her again. Jenny pulled away.

"Really. It's time."

Blake's whole body went cold again. The whole day had been like this. A yoyo of hope and faith and rejection. Jenny's eyes looked steely, like the first day Blake had met her. They hugged goodbye in the middle of the train station, hearing the click clack of the board above, announcing Blake's track. Jenny gripped Blake's back in what felt like tender desperation, but her expression was unreadable when she said, "See you soon."

Blake nodded. She couldn't speak. Because the only words she wanted to say—the only words that felt true—were too risky. Too crazy. She had to get on that train.

She slung her pack on the top rack and sunk into a window seat, trying to think of the good things ahead. The ride through Connecticut, the water view. The way that New York would hit her with its thick air and smells when she stepped out of the subway. A Gray's papaya juice on the walk to her studio.

None of those things was Jenny. Blake looked down at her own hand, stained a little with graphite, and it looked as empty as it felt. Jenny's hand was supposed to be there, too. Gripping hers, tracking the line of her palm, squeezing it in assurance. Blake thought about the months ahead, the travel she had scheduled, the trip to Paris that Amy had booked for her. Steve's insistence that she follow the room show to Minneapolis and Los Angeles. She thought of the hotels she'd be staying in, the little Airbnb rentals. She wanted Jenny with her. Needed Jenny with her. And she wanted to be with Jenny too. Sitting at her kitchen table, helping her proofread her grad school applications, giving her a cup of chamomile tea when she was working too late. Walking around Boston with her, seeing her childhood home, meeting her parents, and trying one of her mother's cooking experiments. Somehow. Somehow if they were together, Blake felt like she could be several places at once.

She looked around the train. People were still getting on, settling in. They hadn't pulled out of the station yet. She pulled her backpack from the rack and put it back on, saying, "Excuse me, excuse me," loudly as she walked the length of the car, trying to scoot by people rolling too-big bags down the aisle. When she stepped across the threshold of the train door, back onto the platform, she felt rollicking, overwhelming relief.

Home. Back, safe, home again. Because Jenny was here. She walked quickly back into the station and looked at the food stalls. She couldn't have gone too far, could she have? Blake bounded out the front door of South Station, looking around outside.

And there she was, right across the street, waiting at the crosswalk to land back on the Greenway. Blake darted out into traffic, and the ensuing honks made Jenny turn. She looked startled and then smiled, moving toward Blake at a clip.

"Hi," they both said in unison. Blake touched Jenny's forearms, holding her in front of her, to make sure she was real, not a vision. She knew her own heart. She knew her own mind. There was only one thing to say. She grabbed Jenny's hands and held them. She had the absurd desire to get down on one knee, because it felt that real, that complete. As crazy as it was, Blake had never been so sure of anything.

"Jenny, I love you," she said, her voice coming out louder than she thought it would, bold, sure. Jenny started to cry. The tears came lightly at first, just one or two cascading down her cheek, and then sobs in earnest, and finally laughter. Blake hugged her, letting the cries roll into her shoulder, not needing to hear it back, knowing that the cries were of relief that Blake understood. She had been as unsure, but now that it was said by one of them, it was as good as said by both.

Jenny sniffled, and looked up at Blake smiling, her chestnut hair a little ruffled around the edges, the bun windblown.

They sat together on the curb, letting the wind whip around them. There was nowhere to go that was better, more important, than being with Jenny. They would figure out where to live, how to be together, and they would not be apart.

They walked slowly back to Jenny's condo, through Chinatown and up through the rail park by Back Bay, marveling at the plants that had all just come alive, the bursts of color on the trees and bushes. Even the houseplants sitting inside windows of the townhouses looked especially hungry and alive. When they made it back to Jenny's they felt like the pulsing, verdant houseplants themselves. Thirsty for sun and water. Needing each other to breathe.

They removed one another's clothes wordlessly. Blake pulled off Jenny's jacket and blouse with reverence, and Jenny unzipped Blake's sweatshirt with slow, deliberate tenderness. Blake felt like she was seeing and feeling Jenny for the first time, appreciating her skin, the angles of her body, the curve of her breasts. They lay on the bed, kissing, stroking one another's hair and face, tongues intertwined, bodies pressed together, moving their hips together. Blake dipped her hand between Jenny's legs, and Jenny did the same to Blake. They fit together perfectly, moving in time, locking their lips and eyes together, breathing in the same rhythm.

"I want you," Blake said.

"You have me," responded Jenny.

They continued kissing, their bodies together feeling nothing short of perfect. Blake breathed heavily, feeling not just close to orgasm, but like she was floating through space. She opened her eyes to look at Jenny. Their sweat mingled, and Blake felt delirious. She could feel her body tightening around

Jenny's hand, and Jenny hugged herself into Blake, tightly, and whispered into her ear, as Blake shook with pleasure, "I love you."

Those three words took Blake over the edge; the orgasm ripped through her and she pushed her whole hand inside Jenny, who shook herself, crying out, "Oh God." Blake felt waves and waves of the orgasm wash over her as she panted into Jenny's ear, "I love you too."

They collapsed together, still shaking a little, like lightbulbs flickering out. It was Blake's turn to cry with joy, release, relief, and love. Jenny enveloped her in her arms and pulled the quilt over both of them, ushering them into a luxurious, tangled sleep.

CHAPTER FORTY-ONE

Jenny looked at herself in the mirror. The black tuxedo gown looked as wonderful as it had six months ago at Blake's opening gala. But Jenny herself could see that she looked even better than she had that night. It was love and happiness, and she wore it well.

The event wasn't even black tie. She had figured what the hell. Might as go out with a bang.

Blake appeared beside her, snaking her arm around Jenny's waist and kissing her cheek. They looked at themselves and at one another in the mirror. They fit together perfectly, Jenny thought. Their magnetic pull was evident and made their coupling seem balanced, like an Archimedean solid.

Still, Blake's touch could tip her over in a minute. Blake started unzipping the side of Jenny's dress and slipped her fingers underneath the fabric. Jenny got goose bumps and stepped away. "I'm not going to show up smelling of sex," she said to Blake, who laughed.

"Probably prudent, especially since your parents will be there."

They walked to Petit Robert, the hot summer night carrying with it a bit of the chill of fall. Blake had promised they'd be out of Boston by November, in Europe for the winter, missing the snow this year, missing the T shutdowns and snow farms and frozen, gray, chunky-iced streets.

Lydia had rented out the whole place and forced the firm to pay. "It's just a few of your billable hours, for Christ's sake, so we are having escargot and champagne." When Jenny and Blake arrived, the place was already nearly full. Lawyers and staff from the firm, Amy, Davis, and her parents, standing in a corner by the back, looking uncomfortable, but willing—eager, even, with glasses of wine, the bar area of the restaurant covered in balloons, and the long railway dining room just crowded enough to feel perfectly festive. On the chalkboard, instead of an announcement about the usual leek soup special, there was a note: *Future Dr. O'Toole!* Above that was a huge banner, which looked professionally printed by their in-house trial graphics department, said *Goodbye and Good Luck, Jenny!* Her official firm portrait had been reproduced almost to life-size. Decorations around the banner, apropos of nothing, floated a few formulas, $e=mc^2$—*A physics formula?* Jenny thought, laughing—and such. Yes, this had Lydia written all over it.

Blake seemed to see the sweetness of it, too, and squeezed Jenny's hand in tender acknowledgment. Jenny pulled her to where her parents stood by the windows of the dining room. "Blenny!" Jenny's mother yelled, combining their names like a celebrity couple. She hugged them both, and Blake broke into one of her enormous, room-enveloping smiles. Jenny couldn't help but bask in it with pride.

"Not Blakeniffer? Or Jake?" Jenny said to her mother, raising her eyebrows at Blake, who laughed.

"We're coming to your show!" Jenny's mother squealed. Blake's eyes went wide for a moment. Jenny squeezed her arm. "They're going the week of closing."

"Jenny told us to wait and see the final product when there's nothing left on the walls. So we're doing as she says."

"So you have some modesty left?" Blake whispered in Jenny's ear. Her warm breath tingled her spine.

"Just a little," she replied, surreptitiously squeezing Blake's ass.

Jenny's father, not noticing—or pretending not to notice— their sidebar, cleared his throat and turned to Blake. He was a little red from the wine already, but jolly, looking like his arthritis was in a good spell. "It's like Buddhist monks, what you're doing? I saw something about a mandala on WGBH. Very interesting. The monks just got rid of the whole thing when they were done."

"Yes, very much like that, I suppose, but the difference is that the drawings I made were not initially made to be destroyed. The mandalas are an act of devotion; the art is in the process of making the mandala. It was never meant to be permanent. My show makes the decomposition, rather than the composition, the focus."

"Ah, okay, I see," Blake's father said, a little too loudly, and then went silent. Jenny got the sense he had been saving up the mandala tidbit for days, relieved to have something to say, and now it was gone. Nonetheless, the four of them stood smiling at one another companionably. Blake and her father had some kind of strange chemistry. When she and Jenny went over there for dinner, Blake and her father often disappeared into the sitting room together, quietly drinking whiskey, unbothered by the silence.

The sound of clinking glass turned their heads toward the front of the restaurant, where Michael was standing, teetering on a chair. "Hear ye, hear ye," he was saying. Her stomach clenched. Michael had barely spoken to her since she told him she was quitting. He sent junior associates to her office so she could train them but never showed up to make the introductions himself.

The crowd settled down. Jenny held Blake's hand tight, willing some of her nervousness to flow into her.

"As many of you know, I've worked with Jenny for five years now. I know her to be a supremely intelligent, nearly unflappable, strong, and gracious coworker. She is unafraid. She has integrity. Honesty. Qualities which make her a lousy lawyer."

The room laughed, and Jenny did too, feeling both elation and surprise. *He's being nice, right when I'm leaving,* she thought. *Figures.* Michael continued, "No, of course, she is an excellent lawyer. She just wants to be something different. Jenny, I look forward to hiring you as a trial expert someday, no matter what your rates are. And if you turn me down, I'll know I have a rotten case. Thank you. Here's to your future."

Everyone raised their glasses, and Jenny felt like she was floating or like her insides were floating out of her body. She wanted to pin it all down, stop time, hold the feeling of happiness and possibility in her palm. She looked at Blake. Blake was the closest thing to a physical manifestation of her happiness.

Jenny's hand instinctively went to her chest, where she had tucked the ring in her bra. She was going to give it to Blake sometime in the next few days. She was looking for the right moment. They were leaving for Prague in a week, and she wanted it on Blake's finger when they boarded the plane. She wanted her "yes" before they began their next adventure.

It was a simple ring, just a recycled gold band, but Jenny knew that's all it needed to be. Jenny was taking a few months off, then starting her economics program and working as a freelancer with one of the economic consulting firms she'd worked with as a lawyer. Blake had said, "Whatever city you end up in, I'll come with you. There are people to draw there. There's always art to be made."

Blake's MacArthur buzz was growing. A new profile in *ArtForum* referred to her as starting a movement: *Pacifist Destructivism.* Blake had laughed at that and flopped down on Jenny's bed. "Whatever pays the bills, my sweet," she said, kissing Jenny's stomach playfully. They had been splitting their time between New York and Boston, spending only a few nights apart at a time. And for the next several months, they'd be traveling together. Blake had gotten a travel grant and Jenny renewed her passport.

The night flowed well. She could see the envy on her colleagues' faces, except, of course, for Lydia, who still loved her job, and whose only emotion was sadness at missing Jenny. "Who am I going to make fun of Michael with?" she said.

"There's always someone willing to do that," Jenny answered and pulled her in for a close hug. "Thanks for everything. For the party. For being my friend."

Lydia had a tear in her eye. "Anytime. I'm happy for you." Taking Blake's hand, Lydia said, "So, you guys getting hitched?"

Jenny almost jumped back. She hadn't told anyone about the ring! She composed herself enough to answer, "Not yet."

Leaving, her mother had invited Blake to dinner for that weekend ("I'll make lentils," she said), and her father, again with the proprietary, hard handshake, looked Blake square in the eye and said, "See you soon. She makes a hell of a stew." Jenny almost laughed, but kept her composure, waving to her parents as they slowly got into the cab the restaurant had called for them, one rickety limb after rickety limb.

By the end, when most everyone had left, Jenny was dying to take off her stockings, her bra, and sit with Blake on the couch debriefing everything. She patted her chest again, felt the cool round ring there. She would wait for the morning and maybe put it on a saucer with her coffee mug.

Michael went to hug Jenny goodbye, but she thrust out her hand to shake instead. He seemed almost relieved and gave her a real smile. "Well done, staying through July, you'll get half your bonus," he said, and took a moment to squeeze her shoulder. "Thanks for everything," were his final, quiet words, and she watched him go.

Lydia handed Blake and Jenny each a small vase with short roses, packed tight. The centerpieces. "Take them, they are yours," she said with a flourish.

"We're not going to be home for more than a day," Jenny protested.

"Just take." Lydia almost glared. Stepping off the curb, she pointed at Blake, who was carrying an armful of Jenny's goodbye gifts. "You're good together," she said, and blew them both a kiss.

Blake and Jenny would have held hands on the walk home, but they had too much to carry. Flowers, coats, and the pair of heels that it took Jenny two blisters to realize were too tight, so she'd spent the rest of the night barefoot. The hem of her dress carried not only the old rip from the Albie gala but was now also dirty.

"Gorgeous night."

"It is." The moon was almost full, and the air was the perfect temperature. It felt quiet, too, but not in a deserted way. It just felt calm. Jenny looked over at Blake, who seemed to be concentrating on something on the sidewalk. Blake stopped, suddenly, looking down.

"Hon, what's wrong?" Jenny asked.

Blake shook her head. "Nothing, I just…"

Blake placed the vase down on the sidewalk, as if that finished her thought. She dumped out the water and gathered a few of the roses in her fist. She put her other hand in her pocket, and then, keeping it there, knelt in front of Jenny on the sidewalk.

Jenny knew what was happening, or at least her heart knew. Her head hadn't caught up yet. She felt like her whole body was going to float up into the sky like a balloon.

Blake pulled her hand out of her pocket and held a sparkling ring up to Jenny. It looked like it was a collage of smooth shards of gold and crystal. Even in the dark of night, the ring was picking up the lights all around them and reflecting them back. The glowing moon seemed to be inside of it.

"Jenny, will you marry me?"

Jenny didn't answer, but knelt down on the sidewalk too, and her dress, with its gorgeous black silken fabric, scarred by the small rip in its hem, pooled around her as she did. She fished her hand into her bra, making Blake laugh, and handed Blake the simple band.

"Yes," Jenny said, "if you'll marry me."

Blake nodded, the dimple on her cheek showing deep, her eyes sparkling like they were filled with a city of tiny LEDs. She took the ring from Jenny. "I will," she said, putting the gold band on her finger. The gold shone, too, grabbing the light of the moon and the surrounding buildings. "Yes, I will."

Bella Books, Inc.

Women. Books. Even Better Together.

P.O. Box 10543
Tallahassee, FL 32302

Phone: 800-729-4992
www.bellabooks.com

Lightning Source UK Ltd.
Milton Keynes UK
UKHW041224060522
402558UK00002B/627